THE FRANCO SISTERS

Loretta Phelps de Córdova

For my family

NIGHT SONG
— P R E S S —

CHAPTER ONE

A gallant nature. The soul has its elegance, its nobility of spirit, whose gallant acts transform the heart. All do not possess this, since it presupposes magnanimity...
Number 131. Baltasar Gracián, **The Pocket Oracle and the Art of Prudence** (Spain, 1647)

US Federal District Court, Alexandria, Virginia

The tall-ceilinged, oak-paneled courtroom was almost empty. Sitting at the front table next to her lawyer in private silence, Cristina heard hushed murmurings in the background. Her mind was elsewhere, stimulated by the scent of lemon oil polish from the judge's gleaming hardwood dais. Her memory was roving high in the Spanish Pyrenees, the wee village of Roncesvalles. Climbing that great wooden staircase in the century- old chalet hostel on Calle Unica, breathing deeply of the refreshing aroma. It evoked cleanliness, order, tradition, well-being. Now in Virginia, she took another deep breath and almost smiled at the memory. That had been the first day trekking the Camino de Santiago de Compostela, an event she'd once thought seminal in her life.

Another time, another place.

In the midst of the world's blood-streaked acts of one World

3

Trade Center building tumbling after another and a crashing missile-jet glaring on global television, Cristina Franco's low-key arrest and trial had rushed forward unnoticed by the media. The United States had learned that great oceans protecting its vast landmass no longer sufficed against attack. Conflict and media outrage were the norm here and everywhere. Adding to the hyped confusion, the country was girding itself to face increasing domestic terrorism and political chaos. One more spy story wasn't newsworthy unless it was exceptionally laced with blood and gore. Few cared about past sins. Only up to date horrifics mattered.

The murmuring stopped as the judge entered. The court was in session, the drama had begun.

Cristina appeared stone-faced. Her unlined but mature high-cheeked face, an aging Vogue cover lookalike, reflected no expression. Though her attorney John Whittaker briefly spoke in her defense, he had little doubt of the end. He'd convinced her to plea bargain to avoid the possible death penalty. That was the reality.

Finally, it came time for her to speak. She stood and said clearly in measured fashion though her heart beat wildly, "I plead guilty as charged. Even so, in my own conscience…I am innocent." Her large brown eyes fixed the judge and shut out the rest of the world. She doubted her testimony would carry weight, but character demanded she speak her mind.

The judge, a heavy-set, austere-looking black woman with cropped steel-grey hair and mien to go with it, gazed unblinkingly at the accused. She ruled. "Treason is treason. You used your high position in government to betray the United States for Cuba. Thirty years with no possibility of parole in the maximum-security federal prison for women."

Peering over her wire-rimmed spectacles that threatened to slip off her nose, the judge added severely, "That's in Texas. The only one in the country." As though the Lone Star State executed the coup de grace.

She paused a moment, adjusted her black silk robe to avoid creases, and banged the gavel. "The court is adjourned."
The bailiff ordered, "All rise."

Prosecutor, defense attorney and the five specially-vetted spectators dutifully arose. The judge observed them sternly, gathered her robe and left the sealed courtroom. As at all federal facilities, the frigid air cast its own cold shroud over the hearings. At the prisoner's request and prosecutors' acceptance, there were no reporters. And no outside observers. The US government wasn't eager to share the mismanagement of its vaunted intelligence system with the world, exposing its constant promotion of a spy within its highest ranks. This woman had received a medal for exceptional service from the CIA director and been destined for even higher position.

The deputy chief investigator from the Department of Defense counterintelligence for the Latin American division clasped the arm of his boss, smiled, and whispered, "It's done." His glistening eyes beamed with satisfaction and his mouth kept working as he tried to control a big grin, inappropriate for this somber setting. Billy Bottoms had been pursuing Cristina for years, and she'd become the *cause célèbre* of his division. This was the high point of his career in the shadows. Now his superiors and peers in the office would show him some respect and stop teasing him about his obsession with this woman. Bottoms willed her to look at him, her prime accuser, a modern day Javert in his quest to catch the criminal. But he would not end in the Seine's murky waters like Jean Valjean's pursuer in **Les Miserables**. And she would go to prison. Cristina's nemesis would be rewarded somehow, then return to his office and fixate on another case.

5

But the prisoner didn't glance his way. Her whole being resolved in strict self-control. It was a quality `that had defined her to this moment and would always, with effort, permeate her nature. She could quake inside yet keep a stoic demeanor. She'd pledged it as a child, even though passion might speed through her so fiercely. For just a second, she closed her eyes. *Calm yourself,* she thought. *Life goes on. I did what was right.*

She looked over at her sister. Elena, the only person she'd asked to come today, stood transfixed at the first bench. Having had just a glimmer of what had been going on throughout the past years, Elena was trying to understand her beloved older sister, once her protector against their bullying father. The girls had been close, and greatly relieved when their mother finally left her husband, abandoning the airbase in Germany to flee to the girls' tropical birthplace of Puerto Rico. They all had yearned for a new beginning, that the balmy days and tropical skies and Caribbean Spanish there would heal their wounds.

Now Elena grasped the arm of her *amante* Paul Fitzgerald and held back tears. Her mother's brilliant Bavarian blue eyes had dominated the Latin dark brown genes of the father while her honey blonde hair also reflected German genes over the Spanish ones. She straightened up and lifted her chin, inadvertently mimicking her sister's proud movement in reaction to the judge's words. The women's affection was as deep as their political philosophy, personality, and life path were so distant. Cristina was as cool as Elena was warm. Elena questioned herself, *How did Cristina ever get into this? And why did I never notice? Could I have helped?* She grimaced at the thought while staring with love and puzzlement at her dear sister.

Fitzgerald moved yet closer to Elena. He'd earlier caught just a hint of Cristina's role when he'd done a job in Central America and realized her importance as director of the US Department of Defense counter intelligence for the region. But he, too, was amazed at her profound deception and its huge impact on the intelligence world, extending even to the presidency. Her information had proved invaluable to Cuba: what Castro couldn't use directly, he'd sold to his benefactors and puppet masters, the Russians. And that had surely led to deaths and bungles in the US intelligence world. Strategies depended on secrecy as well as public diplomacy, and murder as well as blandishments.

Fitzgerald and Elena watched the scene unfolding before them as both reflected on the irony of Elena's own job at the FBI. She'd first worked with poor Latin migrants streaming up to the United States from the battered southern countries before doing research for the federal government, where she still held her position. Might she have inadvertently helped ferret out her sister's secrets?

The court drama was about to end. Cristina managed a slight smile for her sister and raised her hand to her lips, sending a kiss. Her eyes were grave. *My dear Elena. I hope Fitzgerald is good to you. Men are so unreliable. I know. So many paramours have failed me. Betrayal. Does it matter?* Cristina gazed around the stately courtroom. *My last experience in the free world until I'm an old lady. If I last that long. Asthma. A moldy prison. Human cruelty. Grime. Así es la vida.*

Dressed in a simple, elegant black linen sheath dress and Italian soft leather high heels, Cristina realized with a jolt that she appreciated nice clothing and the trappings of fashion, the good life. Her plain gold earrings were a staple she wouldn't be allowed in prison. And she would feel naked without them. She touched her lustrous chestnut brown hair wrapped for today in an elegant French twist, then stopped. *What foolish things to think of, of all times,* she mused....*I must hold fast.*

She walked slowly, calmly, to the side door, a marshal at either side. Each step was measured.

7

Cristina didn't bother to thank the lawyer. He'd done his work, earned his pay. Glancing at his client without expression, he shook his head. He'd never figured out her character. He stuffed papers into his boxy legal briefcase, eager to get going and gulp down a nice dry martini. The accomplished criminal defense attorney had to hurry to meet his partners for lunch at the Jockey Club. Whittaker had become wealthy in the process of exercising his profession, representing important people accused of high crime. Usually, it was political corruption and money laundering, a burgeoning field for both criminals and their lawyers. And the city of Washington was exceptionally rich in well-off thieving clients. But this had been tops in importance, if not in fees. Cristina Franco was the highest-level spy he'd ever defended. Cleared for highest security as a senior analyst and operations director in the Department of Defense Intelligence Agency, privy to sitting at the table of the president of the United States, confidant to the director of the agency, she was a brilliant star in the opaque world of espionage.

Fidel Castro had seen her as a jewel in his crown though he'd perhaps led to her downfall. He'd boast to his inner circle about having a precious mole high within the US government. Had he bragged to the wrong person? The US had almost as many spies in Havana as Cuba had in Miami. And who ever knew what inspired the bearded caudillo's restless brain, his loquacious, narcissistic and eloquent tongue? It appeared that no one knew the whole story. Surely not Cristina.

Cristina stared ahead. *I'll be fully aware of my surroundings, show no emotion, be self-controlled - a constant goal for the next decades in my cell. I'll build on that. Remember my dear guru Baltasar Gracián. I'll write. Think. Read. Study. Re-read* **The Brothers Karamazov.** *And consider others' turmoil. Surely Seneca.* **La vida es breve.**

She sighed, for a moment blotting out her surroundings...*life's mystery. Catch a falling star. Maybe I can find some modern-day spy stories by Le Carré. I like his subtlety and cynicism. Elena can bring me Unamuno and Cervantes. And I'll remain the same. Strong, not victim nor aggressor. Stoic. As a child I lived through books. I'll reread* **Kristin Lavransdatter***. I can do it again.*

The door opened and she exited, the marshals delivering her into the hands of the prison matron. The razor-thin, white-haired woman had a lined, pink, drawn face and small bright brown eyes exuding authority. But they did not emanate meanness. *Gracias a Dios.*

"Come along then, miss," she said brusquely. Not cruelly. She radiated no-nonsense but no delight in hurting another. At least that, thought Cristina. She always noticed small acts. Her habit, so valuable in the world of spies, would be much needed in the frightening new world she was entering. Awareness of surroundings, attention to detail, suspicion, acute boredom, gross food, slovenly and dangerous guards and nasty fellow prisoners: she knew this awaited. Purgatory had begun. Or perhaps Inferno?

Paul Fitzgerald

Paul Fitzgerald mulled over this scene. *How had it begun? This web of intrigue weaving together the netherworlds of US government bureaucracy, El Salvador death-squads, plots of Fidel, Puerto Rico unstable politics, American massive power...Idealism and evil, counterplotting, diplomacy and violence mashing together. Only one thing certain: nothing is as it seems.*

He felt Elena quiver next to him as they watched her sister enter her new reality.

Elena and Cristina will rise to the occasion, he thought. *They both have a will of iron.*

Paul knew something of Cristina's importance in El Salvador

9

since distant cousin Congressman O'Neill - Tío Tip, he still called him - had requested he go to that beautiful, ravaged country and bring back some answers about the rape and killing of four American nuns there. The women were from Massachusetts, O'Neill's home state.

Paul had said, "Why me?"
O'Neill had grinned. "You know why. You're family. You'll tell me the truth."

Paul was a former JAG attorney who tried to avoid politics and the inevitable Washington power-lust while practicing law in the nation's capital. And he spoke Spanish. Mostly he researched and wrote estate work, now and then appearing in court, keeping up his part of a moderately successful two-man firm, with the help of two aides. The tasks appealed to his wish for order, making sense of things. At times an interesting case provided a challenge. He shied away from anything that stank of partisan politics, though he knew O'Neill was master of that smelly pool and could have thrown him a lot of work. As in all capital cities, Washington offered dreams and ambition and treachery to spur a man and woman. But it wasn't Paul's place. In non-political cases that were clearly above the usual murkiness, Paul enjoyed working for O'Neill. It paid the bills and allayed the humdrum of his daily job dealing with wills and wealthy families' corporate dross and play-making.

Making enough to support the small office allowed him to camp out in the West Virginia mountains, read dozens of books, play jazz on the piano, bicycle miles on the north Virginia paths, watch sports on television, make culinary inventions with his Cuban cousins who had left their native island when children. He chose friends who also liked the wilderness of the next-door state and weren't scared of turning over a kayak in a fast-moving icy river. And after a brief, unhappy marriage with the wrong woman, he'd found solace with an occasional woman before re-encountering Elena. At last. The right woman.

Today in the courtroom, Paul considered how his and Cristina's paths had crossed in the last few years. How he'd first met the sisters many moons ago on the beach. He shook his head at the memory, that time he'd visited Puerto Rico after graduating from college. His tennis partner in college James Whalen had called his Franco cousins to go to the beach with them. Puerto Ricans, as did the Irish, kept family in a special place. It was primal at source, tribal in strength, sometimes fierce. Even distant cousins held common blood.

The four had met at a long wide swath of golden sand right in the middle of the Condado tourist area of metropolitan San Juan. Paul would never forget that day, an arc in the golden years of his youth. At this moment in court, he replayed that great scene.

CHAPTER TWO

Earlier
Condado Beach, San Juan, Puerto Rico

He'd plunged leaping, then swimming with great gusto in the bracing cool water. The salt water freshened his body and sparked the electric sensation of a passion for life. *I am alive!* It transformed corpus and spirit. So much more welcoming than the infernally cold swells at Virginia Beach! Or even worse, the Cape! These waves roared eternally, fresh from the deep Puerto Rico Trench, a gift for the pure exhilaration of bodysurfing through the water, that deep primitive joy of being at one with nature. Oneself alone. The ocean's constancy and strength never failed. Looking north, he saw on the rich blue horizon the deep waters surging from distant Nova Scotia to this eastern Caribbean island. It was closer to Caracas than to Miami, another world altogether. Under US law and skin, it throbbed with Latin heart. He could bask in the here and now, the center of the known earth. Or so all islanders considered their special piece of earth in the great sea.

Golden sand was dotted with tourists and locals, all of them worshiping the sun. And the ocean. The mother of life. Glorious!

Flecking off the saltwater, Paul flopped on the sand, took a deep breath of the warm, heavy tropical air. Beyond, further west on the same coast, he could almost see the outlines of

San Cristobal, the partner of San Felipe del Morro Fort that loomed over the entrance to San Juan Bay. For four centuries El Morro had overlooked convoys from the mother country of Spain besides enemies from England and Holland; then from 1898 the US flag and fleets of cruise ships and fishing vessels from all over, as they sailed past the giant walls to safety in the big, natural harbor. *I'm part of history here,* he thought. Puerto Rico exuded a cultural richness and tropical climate matched only by Cuba in the Caribbean. What a great idea this post-college trip had been!

His gaze rested on the two beautiful young women sharing space with James and himself. Their glowing tanned skin gleamed in the unremitting sun, as did their aura. So different one from the other. Both so smart and attractive. Fully enticing to the male of the species. Cristina, tall, brunette, intense. Elena, compact, blonde, vivacious. Totally aware of their world. Both exuding the good and the passion for life. Bodies well-curved, beautiful, filled with spirit, joy. *Simpáticas.* Someday he'd return to this blessed island and marry one of them, he thought. *Ojalá.* Perhaps. If God wills it.

All four stretched out on the towels and put their heads together, talking and listening at the same time with that special effervescence and abandon God gives that age, and the special charge that male and female make together. Their illusions. All of them would see and change the world. In that, they were sure. The girls, inspired in high school by volunteering in a public housing project, saw their futures outside the pursuit of money. Cristina wanted revolution a la Fidel, while Elena sought radical reform a la Dorothy Day. A product of Gonzaga High School in DC and then Holy Cross College in Massachusetts, James would stretch his mind with philosophy and save souls, and his quest would take him to the Society of Jesus, the Jesuits. That brotherhood still held the allure of intellectual, physical, and spiritual challenge, a rarity in a culture consumed by other

13

kinds of ambition. And Paul would become a beekeeper with the Peace Corps in Chiquimula, Guatemala, bringing peace and order to the world in a most unusual way before engaging in what his father deemed "serious work." He would set up a long line of hives to breed the calmer Guatemalan bees with the more aggressive Africanized bees on their way north, and voilá! More productive honey-makers, fewer dangerous stings. His boyhood time as a summer beekeeper in the Virginia countryside had been more important than his honors history degree at Holy Cross, he'd been told. And it hadn't hurt that his mother's old friend Morty was a priest in Washington, confessor to the director of the agency, highly competitive in those days. Paul remembered the priest's sardonic comment. "I'll tell her that for penance she has to take my friend's son, Paul Fitzgerald, to the Peace Corps in Latin America." Who knows? Maybe he really had done that. The upshot was that Paul would be doing what he wanted. It would be an experience to mark him for life, casting a spell over the everydayness of modern America. It would leave him always just a little out of place. And that would feel just fine, put a fine edge on everything.

Wonderful what a modern Mendelian application will do! Teach the villagers how to handle the enterprise and take over when he left. All in the midst of a fascinating if violent land that still held dozens of indigenous tongues and customs in the dense forested hills. And underfoot, everywhere, ruins of the ancestors, the ancient people of the Mayas.

Cristina in San Juan
Cristina's worldview had developed with the aid of powerful mentors. She'd seen children in the projects, hounded by those who would use them for drugs, sex, thievery, whatever. Through another lens Cristina had seen herself, a student from a middle-class family that prized education, moving within a system that offered opportunity and economic security within a poverty-pocked island. Her Catholic mother's devout faith had not

passed on to this daughter. Cristina, recalling a faithless father, always felt unsure of her own future in this confusing world.

Yet she'd always found her way in books. Led by a brilliant history teacher at the university high school, she'd immersed herself in Marx, Lenin, and the nationalist intellectual movement in Puerto Rico that had been primed by the leadership of the island's black Harvard-educated *independentista* lawyer, Pedro Albizu Campos, back in the 1920s and beyond.

Just a year later, in a profound moment in her young life, Cristina discovered Doctor Juan Carlos Terún at the University of Puerto Rico. The esteemed professor of political science at the island's banner academic site in Río Piedras, inspired her with his fervor. His own fierce spirit to seize the moment, the movement, the thought, the sex, the pleasure, the excitement… captured her too.

That first day of class she walked through the courtyard where the famous watchtower of the campus rose in its glory. Red *cruz de malta* flowers and white jasmine lined the dirt path that had been scuffed by almost a century of student feet. A bit of grass tufted here and there. Then up the worn stairs through the arched colonnade to the classroom. She stopped to make sure of the classroom number and then, just a bit nervous, inadvertently dropped her unzipped backpack right in front of the professor. Books, papers, pencils and pens scattered over the polished cement floor. Flushing pink, Cristina apologized for her clumsiness. Terún smiled at the flustered girl.

"Not to worry, *señorita*. We all have our days!" He bent down to help her pick up the mess. "It's hard to get organized at first. By next week, you'll have everything in order."

He looked into her eyes and smiled. With a pounding heart, she responded to this man's captivating manner, formal and

15

intense. He was looking through her, into her very being. Yes, she would get everything in order.

Room 101. The number so apt. It was a beginning. She and twenty other classmates found their desks in the crowded old salon. In its high ceilings circled three lazily moving fans. The tall, wood-shuttered windows, much needing a coat of green paint, let in a breath of tropical air. The walls had been light yellow a decade or so ago. Battered desks were just a mismatch of discarded furniture. But a sense of excitement hung in the limpid air. These students had been lucky in their assignment; many aspired to the few seats in the class of this renowned professor who had won PEN awards for his novel, a Pulitzer mention for his book of political essays and a Cervantes award in Spain for his poetry. These students were the crème de la crème, deemed worthy.

The professor's handsome sun-browned face turned to his new class, eyes shining with a dynamic spirit. The students were his. "We are here to learn, to discover, to explore the reality of Puerto Rico. Not to hear folk tales of famous people or glorify the Taínos, the inhabitants of Borinquen when the Spanish fell upon this island. Nor rave about the first governorship of that reprobate Ponce de León. But we *will* learn of their culture and read the first-hand accounts of our land going back five hundred years, up to the American invasion and the present. And we *will* discuss the underpinnings of our communal life. What makes us who we are. How we will grow and emerge as a just society…"

His eyes passed over the students, who sat tensely with pens poised over paper. He let a moment of silence grow. Then he said, "May I assume that no one here considers that we have a just society?"

A head here and there nodded in agreement, but no one said a word.

16

"Well. Let us begin. Let us dissect our reality."

His tales of the first days of the American colonial system in Puerto Rico on the heels of Spain's four centuries and the ongoing corruption of the island's political and social system deepened her commitment and seared her spirit. She was a patriot all right. A Puerto Rican patriot.

Cristina admired Terún's taut athletic build, tousled black hair shot through with grey, Italian movie star features, intelligent dark brown eyes and confident bearing. He'd won men and women throughout the university. Few could match his eloquent expression and demeanor, beautifully honed at Dartmouth and Oxford in English, at Madrid Complutense in Spanish, and practiced here at the University of Puerto Rico and occasional appearances at decolonization meetings of the United Nations and throughout Latin America, especially Cuba and Mexico. His charisma captured Cristina and all the class. She doubted she could ever win his interest other than the gracious attention he showed everyone. But she could hope. Soon, with his help, she found yet another hero in a neighboring island.

Never would she forget that first glimpse of Fidel on black and white television. Even through the wavering, blurry little picture, the leader's magnetism captured her. His personal force and speech leapt off the screen. A combat uniform draped his tall, mountain-honed strong body. Bushy beard covered an angular face. Brilliant black eyes captivated the onlooker. His voice, passionate and articulate, spoke to her heart. Castro seemed an extension of Juan Carlos Terún in Puerto Rico.

By the end of her first year at college, Cristina was a committed Marxist-Leninist *independentista*. Fidel enthralled her. The brotherhood of man, the need for equality, education and jobs for all, destroying the dominance of the wealthy. Of course! Besides, on another level, so *sexxxy*. He was magnetic, captivating, with that laconic smile that could change from humor to wrath in a moment. With him in mind the students marched down the streets of San Juan and chanted, "Yankee, go home!" The United States had long been, after all, the evil archangel representing the capitalistic system and a dominating imperialism in Latin America. Cuba was a twin to Puerto Rico in so many ways. She sought out kindred spirits.

In her second year of political science class, she met a young man who seemed a younger version of Terún, understandably just a little rougher around the edges. His glossy straight black hair covered a well-shaped head, and dark hazel eyes shone out at the world with unusual intensity. His cinnamon-colored skin appeared like that of an American Indian. Moderately tall with a body's sinewy strength, a half-smile, a polite nature. His way attracted her. Masculine, intelligent and gentlemanly: he shone in these troubled days. She'd heard he was a product of La Perla, that poor and dangerous settlement on the hillside in Old San Juan, sliding into the sea just beyond the fort San Cristóbal. That in itself interested her: a young man who could rise from that slum to the competitiveness of the University of Puerto Rico had to have great will. And a great brain. He even dressed well. The white shirt and jeans were clean and ironed. He exuded maleness.

He'd asked to borrow a pen in class.

She smiled. "Only if you return it. I'm running low on ballpoints."

He grinned in return. "Of course, Cristina. Appreciated. Mine just gave up the ghost. My name's Hector, by the way."

He extended his left arm, that seemed to be disabled in some way, in a sort of salute. "My nickname is Manco, in honor of Cervantes."

18

Cristina lifted an eyebrow at this unexpected comment. Curious fellow. His character, his will would be far beyond her wildest imagining.

Within days he'd joined the select group gathered around Terún: the future leaders of the movement and what they desperately hoped, of a to-be-liberated Puerto Rico. Manco would become one of Cristina's best friends. Briefly, a lover. But always a friend.

§

Cristina's friend Hector, El Manco
La Perla, San Juan

Hector had adopted "El Manco" as his sobriquet from his idol, author Manuel Cervantes Saavedra, who'd taken the nickname from his wound in fighting the Moors in the great sea battle of Lepanto. It meant the one-armed man. Left with a somewhat withered limb and a personal commendation for bravery from the admiral, Cervantes had then survived being a prisoner of war in an Algerian camp run by Muslim pirates. Time and again he'd tried to escape, been caught, and then bravely took the brunt of punishment for the group. Just before being sent as a slave to Istanbul, Cervantes had been finally rescued by a priest who'd brought ransom money from his mother in Spain. All those epic adventures and more to come, the hero-writer had included in his novel, **Don Quijote de la Mancha**. The book, still intensely studied wherever Spanish literature was read, would become Spain's epic.

In high school class Hector learned that Cervantes's other surname, "Saavedra", in a similar Arabic word meant both one-armed and a person who lived on the edge, on the fringe of normal life. The boy couldn't help but identify with the writer warrior. Time and again he read parts of **Quijote**. Cervantes's own incredible adventures and fame captivated the boy. And he

19

named himself Manco, his followers the Quijotes, though they surely didn't match the novel's illusions of saving the world nor the author's own strong moral code. But this modern-day Manco did live dangerously, on the edge, in common with the famous author. Just as Cervantes, Hector had received his own wound in combat.

§

The boy's scrawny father, drunk as usual, unwashed and mean, was beating his wife in their little shack in La Perla, down the hill of the Old San Juan City walls and close to the ocean. The most undesirable spot for centuries, the community had spread over the spot where once upon a time a heretic or two had been burned. Jumbled houses, some freshly painted, others displaying peeling cement, covered the hill down to the sea. The poor and the predators still perched here. Outsiders should beware. Young Hector had sharpened his machete to a fine edge, clear in his mind about what he would do. He kept it ready under his mattress on the floor of the one-room shack. When his father Ambrosio began his wife's nightly savage beating, the thirteen-year-old got out his well-honed weapon and pushed his father away from the fragile wreck of a woman.

"Leave her alone, you scum!" he yelled at his father.

Grabbing his own always-near machete hanging from a nail on the wall, the staggering father struck with it at Hector's left arm.

"Ai!" the youngster shouted, in great pain from the savage blow. But in fit shape, growing fast and strong and far more agile than Ambrosio, Hector with his right arm sliced his father's throat with one swing even more savage from his machete. He added another hefty swing just to make sure it worked.

The father grabbed his neck and fell, his miserable life flowing out on the rickety wooden floor. Copious blood from an open wound confirm the attack's severity.

Hector looked at the heaving older man who suddenly bucked up and gave his last breath. Dead. Hector's first kill. It was bloody. It was done.

He saw his mother throwing herself on the double dirty mattress she'd shared with her dissolute husband. Weeping and as always in a dope-addled state, she wouldn't remember a thing. In fact, based on his observance of other human wrecks in the neighborhood, he figured she had barely weeks left in her debauched life. Well, at least she wouldn't be beaten in these last days. He thought he remembered her far back in his early childhood, when she'd been a loving mother. Sober. He sighed. So long ago. Bloody and sweating, the boy reached down to pull out the plastic garbage bags from under his own dirty mattress that he'd covered with a white clean sheet. Bought with money he'd made selling drugs on the street, it covered his sleeping kit. Each week he bought a sheet from a New York Department Store in Old San Juan, together with a white shirt for the school uniform. The hut had no laundry facilities, and he wasn't about to enter that particular business, though he did hand-wash a pair of khaki pants and a week's set of underwear each Saturday. Now he ripped apart a t-shirt and bound his lower arm in a quick tourniquet. He looked at his upper arm. Still strong. He inhaled the air of the sea, now mingled with the stench of blood. He finished the task.

He cut his father's limbs off with the same machete and put the parts in trash bags to drag the mess to the sea. The cleanup act gave him no special pleasure, and he was glad to finish the grisly work. There was no front door, just a tattered grey rag. He pulled it aside and looked out. No one down here in the wee hours. The blackness of night covered the tropical sky.

21

This was the last shabby structure on the block, while next door sat an empty shack and beyond that, up the hill, a mud pile and a lone water faucet. The two huts were damp from spray of daily ocean surges. Immediately downhill in front, rocks stopped the tides. Only drug addicts from the neighborhood went there sometimes, to lie down alone, uncomfortable and remote from the world. But no one seemed to be around now. It must be about two in the morning. Nice and dark. From up at the hilltop came sounds of *salsa*, but here only the wind blew. Silent. Above in the vast sky, stars shone brightly, their light untouched by man's squalor.

Hector dragged the carnage out the door to the water, clambered over the rocks, and dumped the bloody trash into the dark sea. Before climbing back, Hector saw the shark fins move in. Everyone threw garbage here and the collectors of the deep were always ready. In less than an hour, it would all be gone. Totally recyclable he thought. He'd thought about saving the head, but the stink would have bothered him.

He picked up the hose in front of his shack, connected it to the communal faucet, and washed off his deep arm wound. Then he turned the water on the contaminated floor. It was so ruined already that spots of blood wouldn't be noticed anyway, he thought. He disconnected and replaced the hose. Returning to his hovel and pulling up his mattress, Hector pulled out his cache: a clean towel, a bottle of hydrogen peroxide, antibiotic and a clean t-shirt. He glanced at his mother, still out in her drug-induced sleep.

He managed to pour the peroxide on his arm and wrap up the t-shirt on his own mangled arm and knew to rush to the nearby emergency clinic on top of the hill, staffed all night by a nurse. They were used to this sort of thing and the questions would be desultory. He knew better than to ask for hospital care, despite the pain.

22

The medic took twenty stitches in the deep wound and wrapped layers of bandages around the arm, while plunging the boy's vein full of pain medication and strong antibiotics. No questions asked. The student would miss school for two weeks to rest and plan, carefully taking small amounts of morphine and pumping antibiotics for his lame arm.

He'd called the first lieutenant in his gang, using a gong next to his shack, that he'd bought in one of the many tourist shops in the old city.

"Rafa, I was wounded in a fight, so just keep everything going for me. Slow down until I'm back. Give me a week or so, but report to me every day. Go to my school and tell them I'm sick but I'll return soon. Bring me the homework."

His cohort knew better than to dispute his trusted, fierce leader. When it had healed enough to allow him to re-enter the world, the bandaging and antibiotics would continue after the stitches were cut out. He resisted overdosing the dope for he well knew the results.

Hector continued to give extra drugs for his mother so she would die in ecstasy. She was not long for this world, and he could at least help the poor woman exit as painlessly as possible. She'd loved him as best she could, he thought. In just three weeks she was dead, and he'd made sure she'd staggered up the path in the middle of the night as violent seizures began; he gave her the overdose to make sure it would end quickly. Neighbors would maintain silence. Her body was removed by the police from the scene. Yet another nameless victim to drugs was nothing to worry about, especially in this neighborhood.

He cleaned up the damp shack as best it allowed. Scrubbed and varnished the floor. Threw out all the ragtag articles. Put in a real door and painted it bright red. He painted the hut a dark brown, bought a real bed, a desk, and installed light and water, taken from a common source. He might not own the land, but he owned the wooden shack, a place to sleep and bathe with a jerry-built shower. Studies and work went on. He was making more than three thousand dollars a week by his junior year of high school and maintained high grades. Hector was respected and feared in the neighborhood: tall, handsome, brilliant, solitary and ruthless. No one bothered him. About anything.

§

Six years later Hector was a wealthy young man, owning an upscale small condominium apartment in front of Luis Munoz Rivera Park, overlooking the ocean at the entrance to Old San Juan. Walking distance from the upscale Caribe Hilton, La Puerta de Tierra area was a charming door of land. A world apart from La Perla. Even so, he kept his shack as an office of sorts. Also, roots were roots, he thought. Dirty those roots may be, but…

At nineteen he'd begun his studies at the University of Puerto Rico, a little older but far more knowledgeable than his classmates, more well-read than most, moving easily among the intellectual and revolutionary elite culled mostly from the island's professional middle class and the smartest of the poor. A new epoch of his life awaited. His friendship with Cristina and easy acceptance into her circle added yet another element to his existence. And, of course, a new clientele grew as well. His wealth increased, while his fiscal generosity to the movement assured his stature.

Elena in New York
A year behind Cristina in school, Elena struck out in a different path. Her success as both outstanding student and volleyball player, being able to spring up to snag the ball and pass it on in a game and to write masterful essays in English class and

monthly columns in the Spanish language university paper molded her path: her gifts had won her a graduate scholarship to New York University, preparing for a career in social work, and for a time to do some volunteer work at Dorothy Day's Catholic Worker house. It was then she learned her idol was a human being, not a plaster saint. And she learned something for herself.

Usually, Elena helped in assembling the **Catholic Worker** publication and selling it for a penny on a street corner, but now and then she'd put in a few hours at the friendship house, that offered soup and shower and kind treatment for the street-ravaged human refuse that no one else would even look at.

She was mopping up the vomit in a shower stall, barely able to stifle vomiting herself. She finally set the bucket and mop aside and stripped off her gloves. Looked at the stall. Clean enough through it still smelled. *That will never go away,* she thought.
An aging Dorothy suddenly appeared on the scene, as always, her grey hair pulled back in a makeshift bun, her clean dress taken from the donations pile, a pencil lodged above her ear in case she had to make a note of something. She smiled in that funny, sort of lopsided way she had, a blend of intensity, irony and good humor struggling for dominance. Her personality would never be buttonholed; her passion to serve the poor for Christ was all-demanding in her world.

"You're Elena, right? The new girl who's studying social work? Who helps out with the paper now and then?"
Startled that Dorothy would remember her from among the many come-and-go volunteers, Elena smiled back, thrilled to be recognized. "Yes, I am."

"Good. Welcome. Clean that shower again. It must be very good for the use of our guests. It has to smell good."

Elena was startled. "Yes, of course. But I think we've run out of the pine-smelling disinfectant."

Miss Day fixed her with those piercing brown eyes and spoke firmly but kindly. "Then find some."

Suddenly the icon remembered her manners. "And thank you." With that, Dorothy hurried off to her never-ceasing task to attend to the poorest of the poor.

Within half an hour, Elena found some pine scent cleaner and had mopped again. It at least no longer stank of vomit. Just a puzzling antiseptic scent, hinting oddly at lavender. *Well,* she thought. *That was certainly a different class in what social work is. The street people are guests, human beings, not clients. Remember that.* Then it was back to the university to learn what academia taught.

§

CHAPTER THREE

Yo soy un hombre sincero
De donde crece la palma
Y antes de morirme quiero
Echar mis versos del alma.

-José Martí (1853-1895) Cuban poet and revolutionary
(I am a sincere man from where the palm tree grows And before
dying I want to spill out my verses from my soul.)

Fidel Castro, Cuba

Fidel Castro, with his hodgepodge of dedicated, bedraggled but
fearless warriors hiding out in the Sierra Maestra mountains
of Cuba, had struck repeatedly against the Fulgencio Batista
regime before overthrowing the dictator. Always supported
by his brother Raúl since those early days in politics at law
school in Havana, Fidel built on his charismatic personality,
extraordinary eloquence, enormous ambition and well-honed
Jesuit-trained mind to lead. His will to power and tremendous
intensity were a given.

"I am in the mold of José Martí!" he would claim.

He allowed deposed dictator Batista to leave and the
revolutionaries assumed the country's leadership. At first Castro
was the young commander in chief of the new government – he

27

was only 32 years old. In three months, Fidel had fully wrested the government from his elders. The New Cuba truly began.

Son of a native maid and a Spanish-born prosperous landowner who didn't grant him legitimacy until his seventeenth year, Fidel seemed to understand the plaint of the powerless.

Cuba adored this messiah and at first applauded his commitment to right injustice and to take back the island from the homegrown predators and bullies and the Yankee fist. Almost immediately he expropriated the vast sugar mill plantations and mills owned by US corporations and their wealthy Cuban partners. He let it be known that he would eventually reimburse them, at the same rate as they'd been evaluated at years past to avoid paying taxes. The US government reacted angrily though people of all classes in Cuba seemed to acquiesce. After all, they thought, it was a necessary first step to readjust the system. Things would eventually level out. Surely.

One of the many followers was Arturo Martín, who'd studied with Fidel at law school in Havana. Arturo had convinced his father to let Fidel use their large house in El Vedado as a refuge. A perfect sanctuary, off the beaten track in an upper-class enclave. Meanwhile Arturo's father - don Gervasio - was wasting away with a stomach tumor, yet pleased that his home was being used to build a new Cuba. Knowing the end was near, he asked his son to request Fidel visit him at the sickbed. It was done.

The two young rebels entered the dimly lighted room, heavy combat boots scuffling on the tile floor. They wore olive-colored uniforms. While Arturos's was rather raggedy, Fidel's had been well-pressed by one of his mistresses. They both smelled just a little ripe with the sweat of the tropics.

Next to the bed stood a small porcelain statue of *La Virgen de Caridad de Cobre,* a constant in most Cuban homes. The image of the Virgin Mary held the Christ child and a gold cross, suspended over a little boat holding three fishermen – "*los tres Juanes*". Don Gervasio's hand inadvertently touched the statue, as though calling it to attention, as Arturo and Fidel walked in. Affectionately known as *Cachita*, the Virgin's lineage traced back to 1612 when a young black slave and his two Indian companions reported seeing a vision at sea. The story would capture the heart of Cuba and a basilica rose in her honor near the copper mines in Santiago de Cuba, where people filled it with symbols of pilgrimage. In modern days Ernest Hemingway left his Nobel Prize medal there. Now, in this darkened room, *Cachita* watched over them.

Arturo and Fidel deferentially approached don Gervasio and the son held his father's long, boney hand.

Fidel bowed slightly to the older man. "Sir, I am so sorry to see you like this. Arturo is my brother…Not everyone has to carry a gun to lead us to victory. It's thanks to you and others like you, we've been able to overthrow Batista and start a new life for Cuba. Please accept my gratitude. And my prayers."

The father smiled at the young leader, who radiated *carisma*. "It's been an honor to help our country go forward. And…I know you're taking over the Yankee properties. They've strangled our progress for years and aided the dictators and that's how it must be done. But I have a favor to ask, Generalissimo…"

Fidel waved aside the title. "Of course, whatever…and just Fidel, please."

"My family has a productive farm, you know. Not huge, but ample. Some 900 acres in cattle, everything in use. Beef and milk and goats and mangos and much else. Almost another hundred acres of lime-trees and oranges and plantains and coffee. The *campesinos* who work the land are well-treated…

29

For generations – since my great-great grandfather came from *la madrepatria*, my family has been known to be generous. We've always supported a couple of schools and made sure the workers have a decent living. You've been out there with Arturo, when he's gone out on horseback to check on everything. You know that's so. It's that..."

The ailing, aging man stopped a moment, blushing at himself for what he was about to say. He'd been a stern but fair *hacendado* - the owner of an *hacienda* - not the sort to ask favors of anyone. But he was now fearful of how these young revolutionaries would change his beloved island. He'd heard tales. Arturo's father must do his best for the family.

Fixing Fidel with the large green eyes that he'd inherited from ancestors who'd made their way from that dry, desolate area of Extremadura to the fecund colony of Cuba, don Gervasio continued. "I beg you not to take away our livelihood. We are part of the real backbone of our country... hard-working, honest landowners. We've never exploited the workers...we should be encouraged to continue and serve as models. We can build a vibrant, just country...a true patria."

He dared say more. "That's why we supported you. We know you want to help the poor country-folk to education and proper health care. We know our political system needs reform. We have faith in you, Fidel."

Fidel smiled at the octogenarian and gently replied in his fine diction. "Of course. I will reward your loyalty and your service to our country. I agree. Don't worry, don Gervasio. I know you've always been a good man, as have so many of our compatriots." He repeated, "You shouldn't worry."

Fidel turned and gripped Arturo's arm. "Your son is my comrade, my brother. We will build a strong, good Cuba. Thank you for your thoughts, don Gervasio."

Fidel's luminous, expressive eyes emanated his sincerity. His tall, large frame testified to his past ability as a champion athlete at the high school in Havana. The body had then been tempered in the Sierra Maestra mountains, where he'd tested his mental and physical strength, building up his guerilla warriors.

Facing this indomitable force from his bed, Don Gervasio emitted a small sigh of relief and closed his eyes. He could die in peace.

In fact, it took two weeks for don Gervasio to die, four months for Fidel to expropriate the family's land. And seven months for Arturo to flee Cuba with his newly-wedded wife Teresita and a very small cache of his grandmother's gold and diamond rings, first to Mexico, then to Florida, and finally to Puerto Rico where he put down new roots with thousands of his fleeing countrymen.

§

Fidel's followers grew in number, even years later, such as Cristina Santiago in Puerto Rico. Just seeing the old newscasts of Fidel's charismatic talking for hours enthralled Cristina and her cohorts.

True believers such as Cristina, strengthened in their faith. Who could argue with Fidel's words? He spoke for hours to a besotted crowd, exhorting them to courage. "…when the humble men and women of a country are without work, without land to cultivate, without education, they must revolt…to attain these things it is not enough to take up arms against tyranny; it is also necessary to make all those changes that are now being made in our country."

What reasonable person could not respond? she thought. *This shall be my life too.*

31

CHAPTER FOUR

The world is very different now. For man holds in his mortal hands the power to abolish all forms of human poverty and all forms of human life. And yet these same revolutionary beliefs for which our forebears fought are still at issue around the globe – the belief that the rights of man come not from the generosity of the state, but from the hand of God.
-John F. Kennedy's Inaugural Address, January 20, 1961

As Cristina was ending her studies at the University of Puerto Rico, she saw the world as a never-ending international whirlstorm. Handsome and articulate John Fitzgerald Kennedy won the presidency on the back of his magnetic presence and attuned intelligence, supported by his father's money and gifted aides. She heard his moving inaugural address. He spoke of idealism and serving one's country. He inspired the nation's youth.

Cristina thought, *yes, my country. That's Puerto Rico, not the United States. We are controlled by American finances, American laws, the English language, Hollywood babble. Our poor remain poor. Our revolution has yet to be.* Though her island's independence movement was small, it was passionate and so was Cristina.

Graduating in three years with highest honors, as Cristina mounted the stage to receive the medal in economics for best in class, the university president wryly said, "You may as well remain up here, *Señorita* Franco. I see you have first place in all the classes you took. Congratulations! A wonderful achievement." He raised his eyes to the heavens. "Why don't our young men do as well as the women!"

University President Jaime Benítez was a brilliant scholar in his own right. He was also a gifted showman who could recite poetry and the classics by heart. In his theatrical way, Don Jaime tossed back his famous lank of hair from his eyes.

"Always count on my recommendation, my dear, to advance the name of Puerto Rico." This man knew quality: he'd opened doors to those fleeing the Spanish Civil War, and enticed several Nobel prizewinners to serve as adjunct faculty. He'd built this university to become respected as *una casa de estudios,* a house of studies. Cristina was proud to study at UPR. She smiled broadly and glanced at the audience where her beaming mother, sister and brother sat, delighted in her fleeting moment of glory. "Thank you, don Jaime. I will always do my best."

The ceremony continued, with the young woman standing next to the president for the rest of the awards. She saw it as the first visible step up in her career and imagined future conversations with Fidel and other luminaries.

§

Cristina was avidly following the news regarding the CIA's targeting of Cuba. According to Castro's followers the island not even a hundred miles from the tip of Florida had been a virtual US colony since the Spanish American War. Acclaimed poet José Martí and his fellow patriots had fought Spain and bled for Cuban independence in the late nineteenth century. And now this.Following plans from Eisenhower's previous administration, President Kennedy approved of, then refused air cover of the CIA-backed Bay of Pigs invasion of Cuba with anti-Castro militants - or patriots, depending on your point of view.

The Cubans went forward anyway and Castro easily defeated the misbegotten invasion. Many died. Arturo Martín, once Fidel's fervent lieutenant and don Gervasio's favorite son, lay sprawled on the hot sand, felled by a barrage of machine gun bullets. As he felt his life's blood ebbing away, amazingly he felt no fear. Nor rage. Rather, at the last moment, Arturo felt his spirit surge to the light. *Aha!* He thought. *It's not over!*

Fidel filled the jails with dissidents and enemies of the regime, reminding his countrymen that true revolution must be strong to succeed.

Even so, the lure of the United States was strong, with its magic images of prosperity and freedom. Cubans of every social class kept fleeing to Florida by creaky rafts and fishing dinghies, transforming Miami into what would become the virtual capital of Cuba and of Latin America. Signs sprang up on storefronts with the words, "English Spoken Here."

Meanwhile the United States wrestled with another conundrum. Faced by the Berlin Wall in Germany and the drumbeat of world communism ever stronger in the increasingly icy but potentially fiery Cold War, the US stepped up the war in Southeast Asia. The USSR rattled its sabers and tightened its control of the so-called republics of eastern Europe.

Throughout the world, the have-nots competed with the haves, and monsters sought to rule. So it has ever been. The earth's population was forty-four percent illiterate. And Fidel and his soul brother Che Guevara became world-wide cult figures for their clarion calls for revolution.

While the US roiled with contradiction and strife, the illusion of a comfortable middle-class way of life for all America wavered. Racist reality festered. Terrorism flourished. The world teetered on the verge of dramatic, endless conflict. *Or perhaps it was always that way,* Cristina thought. *I just hadn't realized that it was so. It is an exciting time to be alive,* she thought. *To be young. And noble. And take risks.*

She began to teach high school Spanish, specializing in masterpieces from Spain's *siglo de oro* – the golden age - at University High School. There is nothing like great literature to mold the spirit and she inspired her students with dreams of bravery and glory. Hers was not the erotic mystical poetry, *la noche oscura* of San Juan de la Cruz nor the interior castle of Teresa de Avila, though she surely didn't deny their brilliance. But her idols were others, beginning with Cervantes' doomed hero Don Quijote who rode off on his nag to right wrongs throughout La Mancha. He and Shakespeare had died the same year, and just as Shakespeare still resounded in English classes around the globe, so did Cervantes in Spanish classes.

He wasn't the only one. A great moment in her class was when she questioned how they were going to change the world, and they chanted as one, "*Fuenteovejuna!*"

Seventeenth century classic writer Lope de Vega's spine-chilling play of villagers' courage against oppression was summed up in the people's claim, in the face of torture, that all of them were responsible for the death of the brutal *commandante*. Questioned repeatedly about who killed the tyrant, the villagers of Fuenteovejuna had chanted, "*Todo el pueblo, a una.*" All the people, as one. Cristina loved to compare the communal bravery of the old Spanish townspeople to Fidel's success in leading the masses to overthrow Batista. The class was a huge success. The English-speaking world, Cristina thought, marched to a different drum.

Later

Johns Hopkins University SAIS in Washington accepted her for graduate study in international relations and the University of Puerto Rico gave her a scholarship to study there. Jaime Benítez, true to his word, highly recommended the brilliant young scholar. It was time to move on.

On a sparkling June afternoon, the sun shining as always, Cristina was bayside in Old San Juan with her lover and former professor, Juan Carlos Terún. She'd managed to bed him, a not unremarkable act which she shared with many other comely students. *He understands me,* she thought.

They watched the ferry's trail in the calm waters as it chugged across the huge harbor to Cataño. Terún's longish hair flew in the constant warm breeze. His shaggy graying mane and trimmed beard were trademarks of the Puerto Rican intelligentsia, to which he solidly belonged as a renowned professor. Exceptionally focused in action and deep in thought, Terún served as a beacon for those seeking a reason for being in a special society. Cristina knew his background.

Underneath that hair, Terún had a lined, handsome face. Just under six feet, he was lean and muscular, evidence of his daily running and push-up regimen. As a young man just out of college and before entering law school, he'd joined the US Marines for a stint. He figured that as a dedicated revolutionary, he should have formal military training. It had also given him the chance to see the enemy - the Yankee - from the inside.

Within a virile and self-contained bearing, Terún exuded a masculinity that women found alluring and men found impressive. Cristina had early fallen into his spell. Sexually and mentally, her commitment flowered. She had become a true believer in all senses.

36

The artists, the musicians, the Spanish and history teachers and professors of Puerto Rico powered the independence movement. They were driven by cultural and nationalistic pride. And traditional hatred for all things Yankee. US actions in Latin America had been spurred by entrepreneurial greed far more than by idealism. That reality had cultivated an almost universal distrust of the wealthy giant to the North that prided itself on democracy. Within the anti-American movement existed a smaller and more virulent group: the island's Communist cadre, in which Terún played a starring role.

The charismatic professor and his former student held hands, strolling aside the massive old masonry walls of the city that dated back to Juan Ponce de León's century. They stopped to admire a white flowering jasmine crowding the bits of earth at the side of the narrow road and emitting a scent from heaven. It was a beautiful day.

On the bay, framed by mountains in the distance, the deep blue water slowly slushed. Four little wooden fishing boats, relics of times past, bobbed with the slight waves. High above, puffy white clouds dominated the blue sky as they prepared to turn to their dark red of sundown. The scene was magical.

Their cargo shorts with a dozen pockets were similar and Terún's t-shirt sported the face of Che. Cristina wouldn't go that far in her fashion statement: her plain yellow linen blouse was tied at the midriff. They both wore the comfortable water buffalo sandals from India that sold all over the island.

Flattered to be linked with such an eminence in the pantheon of local leaders, Cristina gazed at her older *novio,* her boyfriend. They were almost the same height, and he wasn't short. "Juan Carlos, look at me. It's time for you to take me more seriously."

He looked sideways at this vibrant young woman, marveling

anew at his good fortune to attract such lovely and sexually motivated females as Cristina. She was especially bright, not the usual groupie. He had not tired of her. Yet. And he could visualize her value to the movement once their dalliance ended, which would happen soon. He knew how to keep her in the fold intellectually.

Terún advised yet once again another course. "Please, *querida.* Just wait. Stay quiet. Be patient."

He gazed around him. Though no one was near he spoke quietly. "The FBI is watching us and we must be careful...very careful. We're secretly working in bomb-making and arms use. Those are basic skills. But you just continue to help us with pamphleteering and writing news releases. Quietly. Fidel is helping to fund us. And you...keep your head down and stay with the peaceful independence group...Keep on learning. Inspiring your students. You'll be much more helpful later. You're pursuing that job in the US government, which I'm confident you'll get. Your English is so good. Great academic honors. Lovely presence. You're going places."

He smiled at her trusting face. Her whole being radiated commitment. She listened to his counsel.

"Better stay under the radar and we'll see what happens next. For sure, your day will come. Okay with you?"

Reluctantly, she said, "For now. Don't make me wait too long."

At least she remained active, sub rosa. She told herself, *My day will come.*

At the same time
The CIA was convinced that if Fidel were not stopped, the Cubans would topple Latin American governments and re-

place them with Castro's allies. He was wily and aggressive. His Marxism, though a different brand from that of Moscow, was just as strong. He was as alert to danger as Stalin had been.

Castro said, "If avoiding assassination were an Olympic sport, I would have many gold medals!"

One of Cristina's inner circle had seen some of the inside machinations in DC. A Georgetown graduate and White House intern from San Juan, Pedro Berríos now worked at the Puerto Rico state department. She found him to be a fount of information. Smart. Low key. Dedicated. Reliable. His parents had taken him as a boy from Havana to San Juan but his heart belonged to Fidel. Puerto Rico was filled with Cubans who had fled and become wealthy and powerful in their new home. Pedro was related to some important people; his brains and connections assured him his own niche at mid-level civil service in the island's government. He had no ambition to go further at this moment. At any rate, his heart was in Cuba.

His manner was a bit arch, his humor droll, his knowledge encyclopedic. A little weight on him now, no longer the svelte youth of a few years ago. Always impeccably dressed. His thinning dark hair was cut short, stylish. His well-clipped moustache completed the dapper image of a Latin gentleman. Cristina found him scintillating company, enlivened by a vast collection of fascinating tales and an incredible memory about Puerto Rican history and Washington politics. He'd finished his internship a while back but kept contact with his DC connections.

They were having a drink after work at La Barrachina bar on Calle Fortaleza in Old San Juan. Just around the corner from his office. The afternoon sun was about ready to go down and the air was still. Above them, a ceiling fan whirred through the soft air. A small stray cat came through the tall arched open

39

door. The waiter shooed it out with a piece of ham as bait.

It was warm and comfortable and smelled slightly of mold, as did so many of the centuries-old buildings. Cristina considered it the odor of history. She didn't mind.

They were exchanging stories with the ease that friendship and a shared political philosophy made possible. Cristina knew she'd eventually end up in DC. She stored away Pedro's insights of his days there.

He said, "I was always quiet and accommodating and no one noticed me. I listened and observed. I went everywhere in the White House without being questioned. Besides, I'm a little dark skinned. They like to feel pious being nice to people of color. Especially to ones dressed in expensive suits. Like me! And an Hispanic at that! So there I was…"

Cristina laughed, amused at Pedro's keen sense of irony.

Pedro remembered lingering next to the half-open door in the White House. He'd take in a tray of water and ice and shortbread cookies in the middle of the meeting. Unobtrusively. Then self-confidently lean against a wall, reading through a sheaf of papers. Pedro's elegant, casual figure fit into the scenery so well no one would ever comment. He listened to the mayhem being plotted. Week after week, at least a half hour or so at a time. And in turn he'd pass the essence of what he'd heard to his friend in Miami, who thereupon shunted the information to Havana.

"You can't imagine the weird things the attorney general and his group came up with. Since he was the president's brother, he was always around, and he gathered his advisors for the CIA there. You should have heard their suggestions in dealing with Fidel… *Los Tres Chiflados*, The Three Stooges! Poisoned pens and capsules. Deadly fungus in scuba gear. One of the committee said, sure of his brilliance, that as he was shaving that morning, he had yet another stupendous idea: they'd insert bombs into the sea shells at the beach where Fidel likes to swim. As the *Líder* goes among the conch, Wham! The good guys explode the shells and make mincemeat of the bad guy! This brilliant thought came a few days after their idea to put exploding cigars in Fidel's box."

She sipped her rum punch before speaking. The guava and pineapple juices with the rum made for a cool and delicious drink. Then she spoke. "Are you serious?"

"Yes. I'm afraid so. Hard to believe these Ivy hotshots can be so very stupid, isn't it?"

On a different note Pedro continued, "You know the president admired the island's governor at the time. Muñoz Marín was a great leader, with great presence. Good English, too, so they could understand each other. Just as important for the US, he kept a tight rein on the independence group. On us. The governor's secretary of justice made secret lists of independence backers and shared them with the FBI. I hope you're not on it. It might affect your getting a job with the federal government."

He thought for a moment and added, "Or worse, maybe they'll give you a job just to keep an eye on you."

"You're right. I didn't know this list still existed."

He said, "Of course! I'm sure Terún is on it, so keep that relationship under wraps." Pedro grinned coyly. "Be discreet."

She frowned at his assuming superior knowledge. She knew he was right.

Pedro went on with his narrative. "Of course, the governor had been connected with President Roosevelt's New Dealers in the early days, so that paved the way for the new generation. Muñoz

41

was considered the harbinger of a new wave of democracy in Latin America. A real plus for Washington. He was honored with the presidential Medal of Freedom. And President Kennedy even hosted him at a state dinner at the White House. That's usually given only for the head of a sovereign state. A very big deal."

The former intern continued to regale her with his stories. "I was there, of course, in a very minor role. It was terrific! There was famous *catalán* cellist Pablo Casals, now living in our island, playing heavenly Bach. Lovely Jacqueline Kennedy and her magnetic husband bewitching the crowd. Not too many people. Even the governor's ugly wife looked good in subdued lighting." They laughed at the thought. Doña Inés's plain face didn't match her sharp brain
.

Cristina interrupted. "Champagne and roses and exalted music are rare in the world. Life is always a struggle, isn't it, Pedro?"

"Of course, Cristina."

"Speaking of struggle, have you been back to Cuba since the missile crisis?"

The USSR had secretly put up nuclear missiles aimed at nearby Florida after the disastrous Bay of Pigs battle. US Intelligence spotted more on the way on Russian cargo ships. There was a dangerous time between Khrushchev and Kennedy that seemed to promise world war. At the last moment Russia had turned back its ships and dismantled the rockets in Cuba. To Fidel's dismay. Then the US took out its own missiles in Turkey aimed at the Soviet Union.

Pedro thoughtfully said, "Yes. I'll tell you about it later. At leisure. Calmly."

He went on, "There is so much intrigue, you can't believe it! Some day these stories may come out...But when? Well informed reporters keep secrets since they get access to the top.

Of course we at the White House all knew JFK had a stable of women brought in while his wife rode horseback in Virginia. He even had a mistress referred by the Mafia and she served a don as well… a great source of amusement to those of us within the mansion. You already know the CIA played footsie with Mafia mobsters who resented losing their casinos in Havana. Also a great secret… Can you imagine the corruption all that entailed? It stinks. At least we Puerto Ricans get our own concubines! I don't know if we do anything else right!"

He used his hands in a flourish to express his disdain. "Anyway. Secrets!"

Cristina knew the media reported half truth half the time. The reader could never pinpoint which was the right half.

She said, "Speaking of secrets…Remember those two extraordinary photographs you showed me? The first of the president walking on the beach near his beachfront compound. Well-trimmed hair blows in the wind. Handsome face bravely faces the sun with aviator sunglasses shielding his eyes. He strides alone on the sand, carrying the world on sweater-clad shoulders. Behind him, a swelling sea matches the great leader's intensity. I think every paper in America carried it. The public heart swelled with emotion."

Pedro said, "Right! And I showed you the second photograph. The reality. The president was tailed by dozens of photographers in his wake. So much for the solitary and inspiring moment. It was laughable. Talk about a set up!!"

Cristina interjected, "Just as phony as Puerto Rico's status, playing that we're not a colony. I get so sick of it all, Pedro. The masquerade."

He smiled faintly. "Well, so do I, Cristina. And it's not laughable, is it? But we have to learn that lesson ourselves, how to use the media… Remember that. We'll change things. You'll see."

43

§

The world turned further askew.

President John F. Kennedy was assassinated. Then Martin Luther King. Then Bobby Kennedy.

The Vietnam War escalated and hundreds of thousands of Americans took to the streets in protest. Students rioted. Blood flowed. It was a time of national rage. Primal and savage. In Asia US soldiers had to face guerilla warfare for the first time since great-grandpa's cavalry had almost exterminated the Sioux.

New president Lyndon B. Johnson was, within months, accosted by cries of, "Hey! Hey! LBJ! How many boys did you kill today?"

Even that most prideful of men couldn't take it anymore. He decided not to run for re-election. Rather, he retired to his large ranch in Texas and let his hair grow long. Tricky Dick Nixon became president.

Cristina's own rage grew as she realized the impossibility of seeing the Island's independence granted by the US Congress. Money and power controlled the fate of the island, just as they did the destiny of the United States. As did all American readers, she'd learned of Senator Edward Kennedy drunkenly causing the drowning death of his woman passenger while crossing the bridge at Chappaquiddick Island. He left the scene, court records were sealed and the woman's parents settled a lawsuit. Yet he would continue his trajectory to become the most powerful man in the US Senate.

Neil Armstrong walked on the moon in the Sea of Tranquility. It was 1969.

Así es la vida.

CHAPTER FIVE

As for us, we are like plants that have the one choice of being in or out of the light.
-Simone Weil. (1909-1943) **Waiting for God**

Around the same time
Elena and Josh Revard
New York City and Puerto Rico

Elena saw the same thing but chose a radically different path from that of her sister. She'd announced, "I'm going to be a social worker. I'm going to save the world, a bit at a time."

And she'd added, "And I'm going to have a great time doing it! Carpe diem!"

Filled with altruism and brains, fun and laughter, she studied for her MA in Social Work at Columbia University. In the City, as in San Juan, men and women were drawn to Elena's special exuberance that spilled over into everything she did. In her presence people felt vital. Young males flocked to her radiance, as well as to her beautiful body.

She chose Josh Revard out of the queue, seized by his intense sexuality and intelligence, his joie de vivre, focusing on her. She saw him as exotic, strong, handsome, and in tune with the honesty of her own character. He even read her favorite thinkers, Simone Weil and Pierre Teilhard de Chardin. His French-Osage Indian heritage underlined the young jet pilot's warrior ethos, so different from Elena's passion to help others. But they were so alike in an unusual centeredness of being. His commitment to living life to the fullest matched hers.

On the wooden deck of a weekend shack in Punta Aloe in the offshore island of Puerto Rico called Culebra, Elena and Josh lay in each other's arms and gazed up at the vast Caribbean sky. She asked, "Could anywhere on earth ever match this sensation, this limitless, black space that consumes us?"

"Hmm." He was delighting in her and this vast universe was all part of it.

The brilliant heavens in that enormous dark universe reached through and touched one's being. "Look! Another shooting star!"

The light shot through space. A moment only. Gone. Breathtaking.

"Yes," he murmured. He, too, arched through the heavens.

Over coffee the next morning at the tiny airport, he told her, "This island is a Shangri-la, Elena. We'll always come back here. As soon as I get back from Vietnam we'll return to this very spot. It will be our special place."

"Yes," Elena murmured. "It's meant for us. Forever."

They climbed aboard the old Piper Super Cub Josh had borrowed from a pilot friend in San Juan. It took off like a butterfly. One moment touching earth. The next second airborne, lightly fluttering in the wind. The little island of Culebra, its long beautiful Flamingo Beach reaching out through the bluest of Caribbean seas shone in the sun. National Geographic had listed it among the ten most beautiful beaches in the world. Though she disliked the magazine's assuming the role of taste arbiter, she had to agree with it according to what she'd seen in the Caribbean. She'd never seen the Pacific.

"Look!" Cristina said, pointing at rusted old tank caught in the wild vines, its cannon a disintegrating brown that aimed at the limpid empty air. Wild almond trees and seagrapes had taken over all the surroundings. "Thank heavens the Navy is no longer using the island for target practice, and we can use that lovely beach."

"Sure," Josh replied. "But I'm glad the US still has Vieques. At least that was able to prepare me for Viet Nam. Maybe I'll survive. There are always at least two sides to each story, remember, dear."

"Yes, Josh. I know," she replied, just a little abashed. She surely wanted him to live through this stupid war, after all. Would men ever stop fighting? she wondered.

She changed the subject. "This is flying!" Elena said. "I feel like a bird...a *pitirre*! That's the little Puerto Rican bird that attacks the red-tailed hawk. The saying is that *cada guaraguao tiene su pitirre* ...Every big bird has its pursuer... Maybe you're the *guaraguao* and I'm your *pitirre*."

Suddenly she blushed as she thought about the possible application to Josh's career. He slid over her subtle reference. "You should take lessons," Josh replied. "Truly. Nothing like it in the world. Give me this or a jet! Nothing in between."

The Cub, one of the simplest and most manageable small planes ever manufactured, flew in its glory in an unregimented world. Bush pilots in Alaska and Amazonian jungles kept them going with a bit of duct tape and a lot of knowledge.

47

First it skimmed low over the waves. Then soared up to admire the vibrant green of Puerto Rico's plains and mountains, the surf on the golden sand. Josh had grown up with a Cub on his grandfather's ranch back in the Oklahoma hills. Nothing beat the little plane, as far as he was concerned. He'd been happy to accept a pilot friend's offer to use the Piper while in Puerto Rico to meet Elena's family and attend a wedding. His. Hers. Theirs.

Within an hour they were in San Juan. Josh flew over the entrance to the Bay, just to appreciate El Morro Castle looming over the water.

"This view takes my breath away, Josh. Let's do it again sometime," Elena said.

"Right! Now!" he answered, turning the butterfly around to circle and soar once more above the monumental stone fort that rose from the sea. San Felipe del Morro had started up in the 16th century and still commanded the portal to Old San Juan. Once a Spanish citadel guarding against the many enemies attacking from the sea, the mammoth structure now watched over huge cruise ships from Florida. Rusty freighters from down island. Pleasure fishing boats returning from the marlin search. Sail boats with wide jibs. A kayak or two. They all had to enter the mouth of this lovely bay. Century after century. Impressive.

The small plane flew next to the huge stone walls guarding La Fortaleza, the governor's palace built right on top. Elena saw a big Spanish flag waving from up on the ramparts, appearing to emerge from the governor's residence.

She pointed it out to Josh and laughed. "Look! They're at it again! The Spanish nuns there run an elder hostel that's cheek by jowl with La Fortaleza, the governor's mansion. When they

48

spot a Spanish vessel entering the harbor, they unfurl the flag of Spain and wave it in welcome."

Josh saw the sight, the flag slowly waving from a stone building above the massive walls. "That must confuse the tourists on cruise ships…wondering if they've come to the right island, after all. Or if politics here is all that volatile! Maybe Spain took it back, after all!"

He grinned at the nun's bravura and flew a little closer. "She must be all of five feet tall and that flag is enormous. Even with her fellow sister holding on to her, she'll be lucky if the flag doesn't catch a gust of wind and sail them both over the side. Now THAT would be a sight! Nuns and flag flying through the air, drifting from the castle!"

He wiggled the wings in salute. Together, the five nuns standing there smiled greatly at their admirer from the skies and waved to him.

He said, "Life is filled with the unexpected, isn't it, Elena?"

"It is. It is. What a delight! A wonderful way to finish our trip to Culebra!"

"It's not over, yet, my dear. Just wait!"

In minutes they were taxiing at Isla Grande airport, the landing strip jutting out in San Juan Bay. The big jets touched down at the big newer airport in Isla Verde, but smaller planes could still land here. The breeze blew up from the ocean, barely rocking the Cub as Josh tied it down on the tarmac.

That afternoon they changed at their room in the hallmark Caribe Hilton, donning semi-formal wear for the small wedding, and taking a cab for the short ride to the Old San Juan cathe-

49

dral. A bit of traffic clogged the blue cobblestoned Calle Cristo, but they finally pulled up to the venerable church. Holding hands, the couple quickly scaled the steps. At the narthex their families clustered together, making conversation.

Elena's mother arched her eyebrow as Elena and Josh entered the church. She drily commented, "I was beginning to wonder if you'd make it, my dear."

She smiled then. "I'm glad you did," and whispered to her daughter, "His parents are a pleasure." She'd made all the arrangements for this quickly planned Catholic Mass, since her daughter and Josh already had had a simple civil ceremony in New York.

Elena's sister Cristina, maid of honor, was speaking quietly to Josh's father and mother. His parents had barely made it on time, arriving from Tulsa in the wee hours. Both smiling, they came up to hug their son's wife. His mother exuded vivacity, his father quiet self-confidence.

"Welcome to our family," his mother said. She was tall and slender, an attractive blend of French and Indian with high cheekbones, pale skin and huge black eyes. Josh said that in her youth she'd been an accomplished dancer with the Ballet Russe de Monte Carlo under the mentorship of Maria Tall-chief, the renowned prima ballerina from the Osage Tribe. A severely torn ligament in her tibia had cut short his mother's own professional career and she now helped her husband run his family's cattle and bison ranch near Pawhuska.

Josh had told Elena the story of his tribe, now in the state of Oklahoma which was once meant to be Indian Territory forever. The Osages owned their own land and dispersed the mineral rights to the tribe through headrights, becoming rich through the huge petroleum deposits. Josh's paternal grandparents had kept their couple thousand acres from the original allotment to run cattle. After studying agronomy and with his own parents' blessing, Josh's young father took half the land to begin burning back the scrub oak, as the Indians did in the old days, and started raising bison. Now their bison and cattle fed on tall prairie grass, bluestem and wild rye, a partial restoration of the tallgrass prairie.

Josh was proud of them and gloried in the beauty of the restored land. "But my grandfather's Piper Cub is what really inspired me. That's why I fly jets today."

Still riding horseback and flying his small plane on a daily basis, Josh's father was dark in skin, tall in height, white-haired, distinguished in carriage. He was as quiet spoken as his wife was vivacious.

Meeting his parents for the first time, Elena felt their kinship. She'd looked forward to this. Someday she would visit Josh's Osage homeland.

An attractive couple, thought Cristina. She'd wondered what her sister was getting into, marrying an Indian. She'd never met one before. Puerto Ricans were a mix of black and white, with drops of the old Taíno blood, all inextricably combined. She was impressed with this Osage.

Josh's parents looked about the old church. They too were impressed, with this ancient structure.

Elena's cousin James, newly-ordained as a priest, sat at the altar patiently reading through the prayers for the wedding. Brides on this island were never on time. Cousins sat in the pews. Waiting was almost an art form on this island, cultivated through centuries of waiting for government officials.

51

The cathedral was an aging grand dame, visited through years by hurricanes, privateers, fire, attack. Still she went on, enduring facelifts and rebuilding. At the back hid the little gothic chapel from the 1500s. Side altars revered this and that one man from its history: here Bishop Alonso Manso, the first bishop of the Americas, there the island's first governor Ponce de León. There was a special chapel for la *Virgen de la Providencia,* the patron of Puerto Rico. The cathedral's grand sense of history, its dust, its filtered sunlight from the open doors moved the bride. Elena felt at home as she walked down the aisle on her uncle's arm to the strains of Lutheran Bach at the organ.

Her father had not been invited. They assumed he was still at an US Air Force Base somewhere in Alabama.

James said the Mass. Short and reverent, it was soon over.

Pausing for a moment before taking Josh's arm to walk up the aisle, Elena lay her simple bouquet of fragrant long-stemmed *azucenas* at the foot of the Virgin, *Nuestra Señora de la Providencia.* In the adjoining altar lay the bones of Juan Ponce de León. The bride glanced at his tomb, thinking, *Look where the search for eternal youth brought you! ...a marble symbol for the fleeting quality of life. We must take all that is with us at the moment. No. Suck out the marrow! Today!* She smiled at herself, her sense of connecting her own life with art and history.

Chattering and happy, the small party crossed the street to the iconic El Convento Hotel, that had been erected on the site of a centuries-old Carmelite convent. Elena's mother had requested a small supper for the body and a trio from the conservatory for the spirit. A champagne toast. It was over.

Josh left the next day to report for duty and be on his way to war, while Elena returned to her work in New York City. The South Bronx would be her home.

Elena's delight in their marriage lasted almost a year. She was able to see her husband once in Hawaii. And then his jet crashed and burned over Da Nang in far off Asia.

She'd been visiting a hungry but hospitable Dominican family in the projects that day, sitting at their kitchen table drinking coffee when a messenger came up from the project office, to report back to NYC Family Services. *Please God, no.*

Last night she'd watched, once again, the violent encounters in Vietnam. The children running in the streets, horror-stricken faces. The bombs, the fires, the explosions, the machinegun chatters, the refugees, the soldiers. Battle, bars, camps, jungles, muddy rivers. Jets screeching through the sky. White, black and Asian faces appearing and reappearing throughout the smoke of the burning inferno. All this was juxtaposed to demonstrators throughout American campuses, yelling and waving signs, running in the streets and protesting the war.

Now Josh Revard was gone. The news of his death brought with it the most acute pain she'd ever known.

Falling to depression, she quit her job and returned to Puerto Rico.

One morning she was drinking coffee with her ageing grandfather, the two of them rocking in the cane chairs on the back of his terrace in La Rambla in Ponce. This rugged, vibrant man had lived a long, turbulent life, even marching in Ponce's infamous massacre back in his youth. His dark eyes, still bright and intelligent, measured his favorite grandchild. "I would so much appreciate it if you could restore the little cottage your grandmother and I first lived in when I sold produce at the local market, the *plaza mercado.* That's how I started, you know. I had no education to speak of. My skin's a little dark and my access to wealth was limited, too many brothers and sisters. That

53

bit of land was lent to me by a distant cousin. I finally bought it, after five years of working it and selling and bartering and winning a good wife."

"Yes, Abu, I know," Elena said. "I've always admired your determination. I think your character now runs in the family."

He smiled at the compliment. This granddaughter of his could overcome her tragedy. "It's apart from my big coffee plantation, only has about twenty *cuerdas* or so. That was the beginning of my fortune. It was when I realized I could prosper in this harsh world. If you'd do that for me, I could come by and visit now and then, and remember the days. If you would do that for me, it's yours."

The young widow accepted, and nurtured her spirit back to health, slowly working to reignite her joy in life.

Did any of it make sense?

Elena was uncertain.

CHAPTER SIX

Know how to sell your wares.
-Number 150. Baltasar Gracián, **The Pocket Oracle**

Later
Cristina
Fort Buchanan, Puerto Rico

At the US Army Base of Fort Buchanan in San Juan, Cristina sat for the interview. She'd applied for a job at the Department of Defense Intelligence in Washington, DC and thought her credentials made up an impressive package, considering her age. A semester abroad in Madrid, a summer at London School of Economics, *magna cum laude* in three years at university, five years teaching high school Spanish literature at a premier school in San Juan. Community service in the public housing projects. Of course her significant skills which had been honed in Marxist analysis and organizational work went unmentioned.

Her interviewer asked, "What about your loyalty to the United States? Your citizenship? Can you assure me about that? I see you were born in Spain."

She answered, "I am a loyal American, who believes strongly in all those freedoms in the Bill of Rights...freedom of speech, of religion, of assembly...And, as you know, I was born at an Air Force Base in Spain, so technically US territory, where my father was an officer."

"Of course, of course," he replied.

Cristina's luminous brown eyes glowed with radiance as she looked at her interviewer. She'd prepared for this moment. "You can be sure of my commitments. I would not dare apply for a job with the US government, otherwise."

Her apparent sincerity and vibrancy impressed him. "Yes, yes. Well, we'll let you know. I must comment that your academics are outstanding. And you received high ratings from your superiors at your teaching job and personal references. I see an officer at the Pentagon wrote a fulsome letter of recommendation. But are you sure you want to move to Washington, where this job is?"

"Yes, yes! I look forward to a change of pace, of being in the capital of the United States, the powerhouse of the world. It will be a wonderful challenge. And I look forward to going on with my studies at Johns Hopkins on a partial scholarship. I want to work my way up the ladder at the Department of Defense."

While her mind raced with the possibilities, her interviewer responded to her enthusiasm and looks. He smiled.

"Well, again, congratulations on your endeavors. We'll be in touch with you about a week or so, to let you know our decision." He paused. "We're moving fast on this."

The middle aged gentleman stood up to escort her to the door, signaling the interview's end. She observed the twinkling in his eyes and thought, *My lord, they are all the same*! She walked in front of him, demonstrating the faint but persistent undulation of all Latin women's bodies in movement. Especially hips. Whether fat or thin, tall or short, old or young, they all seemed to move with the same rhythm.

Amazing, he thought. *How lovely.*

She exited the simple aluminum hut that housed the DoD offices. In front she looked out at the well-tended nine-hole golf course where *flamboyán* trees and vibrant greens invited the player. She and Elena had been here a few times with Uncle Frank, a convivial sort who played almost as badly as they did. None of them bothered counting the strokes. Even so, they all enjoyed walking through the lush scenery that sat in the midst of urban rushabout. Now an aging but well-placed Army lieutenant colonel, he'd happily recommended his niece to this entry position in the Department of Defense. Cristina knew to use all stops in pursuit of her goal. Nothing, as she was well aware, was certain in life. But this looked fairly good. She thought to herself, *and I'll be able to play golf here when I come back to visit. Good. I love to hit the ball and walk among the greenery. Even if the capitalists do it. They can do some things right and this is one of them.*

A week later, she'd received the invite and three weeks further on departed to her new entry-level career in Washington.

Once established, her intelligence and absolute concentration to the task at hand, her ability to placate and flatter her superiors, her superior bilingual education, her serious and attractive manner, would propel the young woman steadily and quickly upwards in the ranks of the federal government. The fact that she was at prestigious Johns Hopkins surely helped as well. Cristina was on her way. The only drawback was that she had no love life to speak of with her intense schedule of work and study. She quietly kept abreast of deep-set political loyalties with Juan Carlos Terún and other old friends from Puerto Rico. In turn, they referred her to new people in the District. She awaited the moment. She regretted the bloodletting she knew was going on in the new Cuba. *But what else can He do? You must ferret out the weasels to solidify the system. Fidel knows.*

What do the Americans say? You have to break eggs to make a good omelette?

She and her sister Elena had learned not to discuss politics since they occupied different sides of the equation with equal firmness.

Within three months in Washington Cristina had been invited by a young lobbyist for Puerto Rico to a party at the Argentine embassy. Amidst clinking glasses and laughter and an undertone of Carlos Gardel singing from the speakers, she and her friend drifted around the crowd. Until…

"Cristina, meet Jorge Parrachini. Jorge and I studied law together in San Juan. I went into criminal defense practice and Jorge worked as a state prosecutor before joining the governor's office in Washington. But we've stayed friends out of court! He's going places. And so are you, from what I hear. As far as my practice is concerned…many clients…"

Jorge laughed a little uncomfortably. With his blonde hair and blue eyes and tall stature, he surely didn't look the stereotype Puerto Rican. But as Cristina well knew, Puerto Ricans came in all colors and sizes. Many bloodlines, mostly Spanish. In the 1800s a surge in European Catholic immigrants arrived in Puerto Rico, and the Corsicans went to the mountains and grew coffee. Some were Jorge's ancestors. The grandmother's side, that had been in the island for a couple of centuries, had been Portuguese Jews. Another significant bloodline. Typically Caribbean.

Briefly, they talked politics while their mutual friend wandered off to chat in the crowd. Then Jorge said, "Do you like to dance? Salsa? Merengue? Tango?"

"I love to," she replied. "All."

"Do you like to swim in the ocean?" he went on.

"Love to."

"Live music…blues and symphonies?"

She laughed at the inquisition. "Both. Why all the questions?"

"I'd like to invite you to go out with me and wonder what to suggest we do. How about blues in Alexandria? Would that interest you?"

"Yes, it would. I've never heard live blues. Years ago I used to listen to Ma Rainey and Leadbelly and Muddy Waters."

"Good enough! Next week, Friday night?"

"I think so." Pause. "Yes, I'd enjoy that."

And so it began. Their relationship caught on and endured. Their affection was real, though Cristina's dedication to the cause remained paramount and secret. She compartmentalized her affections. There was no doubt which was the more important. Personal affection and sex were one thing, her overriding dedication to the cause another. Her spirit, totally committed to her beliefs, simply grew stronger. She surely enjoyed Jorge's company. His happy spirit. And his lissome body. Her work was demanding, night classes were interesting and yoga helped keep her toned. It was a busy life.

CHAPTER SEVEN

-Think with the few and speak with the many. To want to go against the current is as impossible for the wise as it is easy for the reckless. Only a Socrates could undertake this...truth is for the few; deception is as common as it is vulgar.
Number 43. Baltasar Gracián, **The Pocket Oracle**

Twenty years before the judgment
San Salvador, El Salvador
Cristina's first visit
Cristina arrived in the beleaguered country late at night from the Dallas direct flight. Returning migrants had packed the plane, their suitcases filled to the brim with gifts for their families. They could happily demonstrate their success and share their wealth even in their homeland's poverty. Clean and simply dressed, carrying big bundles and boxes, they were a far cry from how they'd left their country.

Next to Cristina on the plane sat a stocky short woman with one tooth missing in the front, grey hair pulled back in a bun. Hard-worked women age early. Still, her vivacious dark brown eyes danced in anticipation of seeing her parents and her 12-year old son.

"The gangs are after him," she said. "It is now either join them or be killed. So I must take him to the safety of the US." Emotion swept over her brown broad face. Fear for her child. And delight at the thought of rescuing him. She spoke in uneducated Spanish, since she'd never had the chance to go to school.

She couldn't keep from smiling as she told her story to Cristina, who was eager to listen

"Five years ago I went to Fairfax in Virginia, to join my sister who has a job cleaning hotel rooms. My husband left to California the year before but I've never heard from him again. Once he got on the bus that was it. No word, no money to help support us. Even so, the grapevine tells me he's alive and in Los Angeles. So I left my son, crossed the vast country of Mexico, and finally crawled through a hole in the fence to get to the United States."

Cristina said, "Don't tell me all this! What if I were to report you? Be careful who you talk too, Julia. Please!"

"I can tell you are a good person. And I'll always find the way. I'll never give up!"

"So…" Julia insisted on going on with her story. "I had a little money from my sister and uncle, who paid my way. Once in the United States I bought a visitor's visa in the underground and immediately started cleaning rooms at a hotel at night, cleaning homes in the daytime. I stay with my sister so we both save money. We've been able to send money home and I've paid her back."

"And now?" Cristina had asked this determined woman. "Won't you stay to buy a home in El Salvador? Take care of your boy here?"

An incredulous look came over Julia's face and she laughed. "Stay? When I am almost ready to get a green card in the United States? And I can get my son away from the gangs?"

61

The woman recalled her exodus. Getting to Mexico from El Salvador was easy. A bus to Guatemala, then to Monterrey. Then with a group to the western desert country. Once there, she lingered behind the coyote who preyed on all the young women who'd paid him to guide them north. One of the two gangster-guides was merely mean. The other was truly evil. He kept selecting a young female from the herd of ten, to rape at night. He even took a young boy. All were fearful and no one dared fight against him. The fourth night, Julia had quietly slunk away, aware that she was on the list of prey. Somehow she'd found the way to hide and then, far in the rear, followed yet another group as they trudged through the suffocating heat. Two days later, at the border, she waited for hours until this new group inched through the hole cut into the fence at dusk. Then, at night, alone, she crawled through and kept on going. After a mere night's plodding, she'd come to an isolated farm whose owner gave her water and three oranges. And directed her to a refugee camp that took her in. She wrote down her reasons for leaving her country, and they sped her on with a smile and a new pair of shoes.

Since then, late at night she'd wake up suddenly in the midst of that fateful walk. That miracle. She could still taste the grit. Feel the pitiless sun on her grimy head. See the faces of her fellow pilgrims. How had she survived when so many had fallen?

Julia answered her own question. "No, no, no! Maybe when I am a very old lady and want eternal sunshine and no more dreams for the future. If ever there is peace in my country. But no! I bring money to help my parents put a real floor on their little house. Give them a water line. And take my son César with me so he can go to school in the States. Both the gangs and the guerillas are already trying to take him. But he'll go with me, learn to read and write. Maybe become a doctor. He'll join the choir in my church in Fairfax. Learn the guitar. Play soccer in the park. Have a future. My homeland offers nothing but misery and death."

Julia's ebullience captivated Cristina. She clasped the woman's strong, work-worn hands in her own, ruminating over her tale and her vision of the United States as the land of milk and honey. So different from her own.

"Good, Julia! So very good. Never give up your dreams for your son! He's fortunate to have a mother who cares for him so very much. Who works so hard. Who is so brave."

The two women leaned over the seats of the plane to hug awkwardly, both of them a little teary. Then Cristina closed her eyes and thought over this valiant woman's story as she drifted to sleep.

The plane landed on a bumpy tarmac, ground to a stop. Cristina halted a moment as she left the plane, breathing in the warm humid tropical air. It relaxed her. The other passengers didn't seem to mind her blocking the line as they excitedly chatted and picked up their own belongings. They'd pick up their big boxes of clothes and linen and kitchenware and toys at customs.

Cristina slung her two small brown leather bags over her shoulders and walked easily through the stamping officials at cracked linoleum customs and immigration booths, under the eye of machinegun-toting guards, through the noisy crowd who managed to ignore the armed soldiers.

On the other side of the obstacle course, she spotted her cousin waving.

"James! James! I finally made it to El Salvador!" She waved to him.

He was easy to see among the short Salvadorans. James towered over the people around him with his sinewy six foot six frame. A rather tattered black cassock draped his lean body and his black Irish good looks attracted admiring glances. His genuine bonhomie captured the heart of the good, disarmed momen-

63

tarily the heart of the cruel.

They mounted his little Suzuki jeep and barreled along the pitted roads to the simple guest house near his residence. She'd decided to stay there rather than the government-sanctioned hotel. Cristina sat in the bouncy passenger seat, inhaling with all her senses the feel of this troubled country. Not much traffic in the dark and dangerous night, other than a rumbling army truck or two. The insistent sounds of the night creatures, a hundred thousand insects and frogs, filled the air.

James turned from peering through the unlit streets to smile at his cousin. "You'll find bottled water and *pupusas* and orange juice in your room. In your honor we turned on the hot water for your shower. Sleep late and tomorrow we walk and talk."

"Thanks, dear. How good to see you!"

She yawned at the thought of sleep. Within half an hour, she'd bathed and fallen in bed. Tomorrow was another day.

§

The next day
Daybreak
That bloody day had begun so beautifully.

Cristina was awakened by a rooster crowing. *That's it,* she thought cheerfully. *So much for sleeping late! That hailing of the new day. The vigor. What's not to like?*

She fastened back the mosquito netting and opened the shutters to let in light. Almost entering the window were the fronds of a tamarind tree, its huge pods just now beginning to bloom. Cristina deeply breathed in the warm tropical air. She was happy to be alive.

Then she heard some squawks and peered out the window, to see the fast cock pursuing a ponderous fat hen. *Así es la vida!* Such is life.

As usual in the tropics there'd been a slight morning shower, just a drizzle, to cool the ground before a persistent sun would begin to bake the earth. Cristina looked out the window to gaze up at the cloudless rich blue sky. *Passion and verve, rather than the pleasant middling blue of Washington that reflected the controlled culture of the north.* She laughed at herself for making such a theatrical comparison.

She looked around the room, appreciated the space. Maybe fourteen by fourteen. She opened the unlocked door to pad down the hall to the bathroom. No keys, no locks. White-washed walls. Everything clean and old and orderly.

She returned to her room and made the double bed with a thick Portuguese-style cotton quilt. Simple. Neat. A little Mexican-style rug on the red-tiled floor. A small desk and wooden chair. A big old-fashioned wooden armoire to hold the clothes. A tiny sink. Double-shuttered window, no screens. A carved wooden crucifix on the wall. The building had once been the private home of a Spaniard from Navarra, a widower with no children, who replicated one of his homeland's country chalets for his last years in this country, deeding it to the church upon his death. It now served as a guest house for visitors to the Jesuits, and Cristina had chosen it over a hotel.

It reminded Cristina of a charming *hospedaje* in the village of Roncesvalles in northern Spain, when she'd joined a group from college walking the *Camino de Santiago,* the Way of Saint James, a dozen years back. Just taking out the old leather travel bags to unpack had reminded her of those gypsy days and the aromatic pine trees of the Pyrenees.

She'd already hung out her tried and true Chanel knockoff

65

linen black pants-suit, three silk blouses and three scarves of turquoise, magenta, and white, all very proper for office and embassy. Two pairs of flats stood in the armoire as well. At five foot eight, she didn't need to add height to look elegant.

She pulled off the comfortable white kaftan, perfect for home-wear, and put on a pair of good-looking cream-colored jeans, a bright yellow cotton sweater, and scuffed espadrilles. That would do for the market. She arranged her always-present books on the desk: the Gracián *pensamientos* and a tattered, much-read compendium of poetry by Antonio Machado. She knew many of the verses by heart, but still enjoyed seeing the words on paper. They'd become a mantra of sorts.

She repeated them again, singing happily,

Todo pasa y todo queda,
pero lo nuestro es pasar,
pasar haciendo caminos,
caminos sobre la mar.

(All passes and all remains, but our fate is to pass, making our way, a way upon the sea.)

Later, over hot, lip-smacking *café con leche* and a chunk of de-licious *pan criollo* - fresh locally-baked bread - delivered daily throughout the neighborhood, James sat across from her at the kitchen table. He played a tape of Bishop Romero's most recent radio program on the little boom-box. The bishop's well-spun voice with a clear educated Salvadoran accent, said, "We must stop this senseless killing! We must seek justice and peace! How many more must be murdered? Landowners, do not oppress the peasants, but seek fairness for your brothers in Christ! Sol-diers and National Guard: put down your arms. Refuse to mur-der! Rebels, Marxists, seek reform peacefully...no more armed resistance that creates more killing!"

James turned off the tape and they both sat in silence a moment.

Taking a deep breath, the young priest said, "*El Monseñor* is a voice crying in the wilderness. When the bloodlust is high, people are terrified and don't know where to turn. The country bleeds while left and right seek control."

He tore off a chunk of bread and spread on it a dollop of the homemade guava jam made by the housekeeper. The combination of fresh bread and the fruit's sweet tartness was delicious. A simple and exquisite pleasure in the midst of chaos. *Así es la vida.*

"Cristina, both sides hate the bishop. Both are bloodthirsty. The government spies within the villages, member of *Orden* pinpoint rural leaders to the government. Then the military drags the villagers from their homes, beats them, kills them and throws the lifeless bodies on the roadside a few days later."

He swallowed a sip of water and continued. "With my own eyes I've seen stacks of bodies along the roads. Communists from Nicaragua and Castro's Cuba meanwhile bring arms to the villagers, who in turn join the guerillas. And if they don't join or at least feed the guerillas, they're killed...Then the villagers learn to fight well and kill, on whichever side, just as the US-trained soldiers at the School of the Americas do. The US covertly gives arms to the military. One of their graduates, the rightist leader Roberto d'Aubuisson, leads the death squads and the Atacatl battalion to terrorize the peasants into submission. Meanwhile gang members are starting to filter in in from Los Angeles and start another whole subculture. The poor really have nowhere to turn."

James gloomily considered the dregs of his coffee mug. "And I'll only tell you this because you're my beloved cousin...Some of my fellow Jesuits – the ones from Spain, especially – can be a little extreme sometimes, seeming a little more inspired by Marx. Social justice is a constant, of course. We follow Christ. Christianity is revolutionary in a very real sense. It must be. That's good enough. Even so, we know that the Church hierarchy in Latin America traditionally acted with the elites. Thank God that's changing! But I'm very much afraid my brothers in the Company may alienate some of those we're trying to convert. The bishop's on the right track. We have to be strong. But leave the door open to both sides to seek peace…"

He shook his head in disgust and murmured to himself, "There's no simple way."

The cousins looked at each other in silence. What more could be said?

James heaved a sigh. "And this bishop? He also started an Alcoholics Anonymous group. Good thing for me. I was falling by the wayside. He's been following Escrivá's Opus Dei to deepen priestly spirituality. Another good example for me. It has much in common with Ignatian tradition, you know. We Jesuits need order to temper our brilliance." He laughed at himself.

Quiet.

"Good, James. I'm happy for you."

That conversation was over. Confidence shared.

Just before noon they'd walked down the dusty street of the capital city, potholes taking over the cracked asphalt pavement and sprouting wild grass. James was taking her to the *plaza del mercado* to buy fresh fruit for lunch.

The simple market held the sort of food she loved to eat in

Puerto Rico. The tubers she recognized: *ñame* and *yuca* and *batata*. The big *calabaza*s or local pumpkin to flavor the ubiquitous beans. *Garbanzos* or chickpeas awaiting a delicious stew. Green cucumbers and bright red tomatoes in pyramids next to the yellow and red peppers and garlic hanging in clusters. Some kind of *chorizo* or sausage dangling at the side. And of course stacks and stacks of corn, the staple of Mexico and Central America. A few scrawny live chickens squawking in wooden cages. A couple of guinea hens making their ungodly racket. And the fruits! Oranges, limes, papayas, mangos, little bananas from the ravaged countryside…

Cristina hadn't a taste for the *atole,* a morning drink made of corn, but liked the local *horchata*, a shake made of ground rice, cinnamon and almond milk. The omnipresent *pupusas,* a kind of *tortilla,* sat in a row at different vendors, waiting to be stuffed and devoured. This was the most common food, cheap and relatively filling. In this hungry country, few could afford to buy much else.

She watched raggedly-clothed barefoot children, mostly bare-chested little boys, wandering from one stall to another. Longingly feasting their eyes at the displays, later they'd go to garbage cans to scavenge for edibles. Somehow, she thought, they always seemed to smile. Buyers at the market were often maids dressed in their uniforms and muddied gardeners in their jeans sent by their masters and mistresses to buy something for the household. An occasional white-collar worker meandered about to check out the wares.

"Hey, Cristina, there's the archbishop."

Called *El Monseñor* by his flock, the bishop was greeting a vendor at his stall and counting out a few coins from a little black leather purse to pay for a papaya. He was of average height, slender but strong-looking, his light olive skin declaring him a *mestizo*, a mix of white and Indian. A few strands of white ran in the coal black hair. Manly and just short of goodlooking, he had a simple, quiet grace about him.

Going up to him and waiting his turn before speaking, James said, "*Monseñor,* I'd like you to meet my cousin from Puerto Rico, Cristina Franco. She works with the US government in Washington. She's here just for a short time."

The Salvadoran turned around in surprise. His black cassock, as worn as James' garb, a little dusty along the hem, swept the earth. He smiled and greeted him. "Good to see you, James." Giving him a big Latin hug, he added, "Keep up the good work at the university."

Then he looked at Cristina, giving her his full attention. He radiated kindness. And intelligence.

El Monseñor looked at her quietly for a moment. "Good to meet you," he said with a small smile. "Welcome to our country, Cristina. I trust you will help us. We live in troubled times and need the United States to stop providing arms to the military and aid to a repressive regime."

He really calls it! she thought.

She murmured hello and then the bishop returned to his conversation with the papaya vendor.
Cristina and James moved to the next stall, where beautiful huge pineapples, bright brown and dark golden colors with prickly surface and green spiky topknot, were artistically displayed.

Admiring the succulent fruit's bold dress, she looked a moment, then leaned over to whisper to her cousin, "Well! I never expected to meet the archbishop at the public market. He has the common touch, doesn't he?"

James answered, "*Carisma*, actually. And it's only a couple of years ago he became so vocal. At first he seemed like most priests. Just talking down from the pulpit about Christ's message but not doing much about it. But when his friend Rutilio Grande was shot down on the road with an old peasant and a teenager, the bishop found his way. Rutilio was my friend too. A fellow Jesuit, a good man."

He paused before going on. "*El Monseñor* has become a different man. He was simply a good man before. Now he is a living saint. He's become passionate about the need to serve the poor. But the rightists, the military, most of the elite – they all hate him now."

Nodding, Cristina said, "Of course they do. Before I came, I read his open letter to the president of the United States, pleading with him to stop military aid to the Salvadoran regime. And of course, that radio program you played for me. Impressive! Brave! He must fear for his life."

She looked forward to seeing the bishop on the altar and listening to his sermon, although going to Mass was a habit she'd dropped in childhood. Even so she'd keep her cousin company in the afternoon to observe the ritual here. She hadn't been to church since last Christmas, to celebrate with her mother and sister. This one would be for James.
They returned to her residence for some cheese, bread and fruit. And, of course, more rich Salvadoran coffee.

James left and they agreed to meet in two hours.

She rested in bed, thinking of James, of the bishop, of herself. The paths that converged, then forged out, each person ultimately alone. And my part? *Mi camino...*

CHAPTER EIGHT

Caminante, son tus huellas el camino, y nada más,
Caminante, no hay camino, se hace camino al andar.
Al andar se hace camino, y a volver la vista atrás se ve la senda
Que nunca se ha de volver a pisar.
Caminante, no hay camino, sino estelas en la mar.
-Antonio Machado (1875-1939) **Campos de Castilla** (Wanderer, your imprint is the path, nothing more, Wanderer, there is no path, your walking makes the path. In making it, one looks behind to see the path that never will be trod again, Wanderer, there is no path, only wakes upon the sea.)

When James returned, they walked from where she was staying at the residence. Again, they trod the broken asphalt road where she noticed the straggling yellow wildflowers, the *morivivi* – that little razor-sharp plant that cut, closed and sprang open again. The word stemmed from death/life, a wonderful metaphor, she thought. Mildew was everywhere, a constant in the tropics, a trade-off for no dry cold. She coughed a bit and began to perspire, but it no longer bothered her. The humidity was growth, life, abundance. No air conditioning would be found in the church. That was for a developed, energy-guzzling country. Not here. Here was sweat.

James and Cristina entered the chapel. They walked down the rough cement floor and slid into the bench towards the front.

People were jostling about. Cristina closed her eyes and briefly, in some sort of way, prayed for family. That is, except for her father. She would never forgive him. Actually, this was one of the reasons she disliked the practice of prayer. It prompted her to recall her early youth. And think profoundly of the present. *Oh, how I hated him,* she thought. *I still do. Please, God, keep my mother and sister safe. And my brother, cousins and grandparents. And damn my father and all like him to hell. I will show no pity to the cruel ones.... Christ? Never. The bullies of the world shall suffer in this world. To pray is to...*

Opening her eyes then, she gazed around the mix of nurses, doctors and *campesinos,* the country folk, filling the limited space of *La Divina Providencia.* From very brown to very white faces. *A nice mix, this mestizaje of El Salvador,* she thought. *Everybody whispering and squirming about. It's a good feeling to be part of this.*

They all stood as the bishop entered the altar with two young very dark altar boys in their white tunics. He said, "Let us begin, as always, with the Sign of the Cross." People abruptly quieted. The ancient ritual began.

Cristina Franco sat in the rough wooden pew, uncomfortable and a bit anxious at being in church again, even accompanied by James, her favorite cousin. How ironic. This blood-streaked country was named The Savior, El Salvador, by the Conquistadors in the early 1500s. It still awaited The Savior.

It felt a bit odd to fit into this assignment as analyst in the Department of Defense Intelligence Agency, the DIA. This new mission was a challenge. She'd skyrocketed in her work and she remembered her conversations with Terún back in Puerto Rico. That had been years ago. "Your day will come." Soon.

Kneeling next to her, James had his eyes closed, praying intensely. His black soutane just a little ragged, she noted. He'd

73

always been rather disheveled. Cristina glanced at him and her thoughts wandered...

Even at this moment, in this situation, Cristina enjoyed her cousin's company. She'd always appreciated his ready smile, at this time understandably rare. As children, they'd climbed giant trees to pluck the magenta-tinted mangoes, laughing in the sun. A little older, they'd plunged into the rolling waves as he taught her to surf the daunting waters at Tortuguero Beach. Sharks liked those waters too, adding an extra frisson of excitement. Then, late in high school years, the cousins had ventured together to San Juan with the crowd scene of the city's youth who hung out every weekend in the Old City, going from plaza to plaza, bar to bar, swizzling beer and rum in paper cups as they meandered over the blue cobble-stoned streets... It had been like *La Movida* in Madrid, young people yearning to be together, roaming around until dawn, chattering all the while. He wouldn't go with her on the political marches at the university though. James had a much different agenda from hers.

And now they were both here in El Salvador, each on a mission.

The soft tropical air wafted through the open doors of the church, bringing sounds of the street and the marketplace. It did not disturb the smell of sweat. A mangy black and white dog sat in front of the altar, its ribs announcing hunger, its scratching announcing fleas. A lost sparrow fluttered at the high ceiling, seeking an exit.

On the altar the bishop's vibrant baritone reflected both Salvadoran country folk upbringing and Roman seminary graduate studies. Though his father had been teaching him to be a carpenter, his brain and heart had led him to the priesthood. His Spanish was clear, educated, unaffected. His doctorate in theology had not introduced a pedantic undertone in his speech. Cristina liked that.

She relished the heaven-bound music, the voices exuberantly singing, "*Santo, Santo, Santo! Santo es el Señor! Dios del universo, Santo es el Señor!*" (Holy is the Lord! God of the universe.) Strains of a flute and guitar lingered in the background. Lovely. She might have lost her faith, but not her love of ritual.

Three brightly-colored hangings from neighboring Guatemala dotted the mildewed white plastered walls. She wondered how the Indian culture of El Salvador had perished, for just next door, as it were, people still spoke many different Indian languages and continued the old way. This country was solidly *mestizo,* the blend of white and Indian, all hues, but lacking the vibrant indigenous cultures of Guatemala. This chapel offered solace to those within, even, perhaps, to Cristina. The shuttered windows and big wooden doors were wide open, letting in a welcome breeze. A few women clicked their fans open and closed, waving them back and forth with a flick of the wrist.

That click-click of the fans…Again Cristina's mind wandered. It returned to her childhood in Puerto Rico, where her mother had taken the children from the US Air Force base in Spain to escape their abusive father. The scene replayed in her head.

§

After an all-night Atlantic crossing, they'd arrived in San Juan where a cousin met them at the airport. That day, they'd piled into the cousin's spare bedroom and started to put their lives back together. A highly different culture from that of the military base, but not all that different from Spain itself. She'd discover Puerto Rico to be a rare mixture of *la madrepatria (* the mother land), the United States, the Caribbean and the Americas.

They'd all been taken to Mass on Sunday in San José church in Villa Caparra. They hadn't gone to church at the base in

75

Spain. In Puerto Rico young Cristina had been fascinated by the lovely silk mantillas draping ladies' heads. Rose and black and silver and white. The rhythmic snap-snap as the women's sandalwood fans moved tropical air. Candles, chanting. Lovely theatre. Even one who had no faith could appreciate it.

Across the street from the church lay the sixteenth century ruins of Juan Ponce de León's first village, called Villa Caparra. That was exciting. The *conquistador* had married the daughter of a Taíno chief – a *cacique* – become Puerto Rico's first governor, and then gone off, driven by his own demons, to seek the fountain of youth in what is now called Florida. He found death instead.

She felt that history that permeated Caparra. The aroma of San José was the scent of fresh and inexpensive Evangeline cologne, blending with the fresh gardenias on the altar. It wafted in the air, struggling to overpower the smell of ripe human bodies. No air conditioning chilled the warm church air. She looked at her sister Elena. As always, she was focused on her prayers, attentively looking at the priest on the altar. The child was so intent on the moment. Each girl so very much different one from the other.

Cristina was always thinking about the rest of the world. Her newly-discovered island was stumbling eagerly to become a second-world territory (going beyond its third world state) or tiny republic or maybe a state of the United States, puzzling and agitating Cristina as she tried to understand the economic and social realities of a people. Her own life had felt so conflictive since the first days of childhood. She could identify with a highly conflictive society.

I love it here, she said exuberantly to herself. *It's where I belong!*

She fell in love with Puerto Rico, its culture, its dichotomies, its history. And she fell in love shortly after with Marxism, drawn to its commitment, its cold passion to right wrongs no matter what. She had no religious faith. This secular faith became her *norte,* her north on the compass of life.

§

Now, El Salvador. Cristina watched *El Monseñor* kneel at the Eucharist and continue the rite of the consecration. Then he lifted the chalice. Just as the monsignor raised the wine-filled gold chalice and said, *"Esta es mi sangre,"* (This is my blood), a far-off sharp retort barely echoed in the small space. Bishop Romero staggered and bright red blood splotched his white chasuble

The assassin had found his mark.

El Monseñor fell, cup still in hand, spilling the wine. Grape and blood truly mixed.. The young altar boys valiantly tried to staunch the blood, to massage his heart. To no end. The small church erupted with a full-throated moan. Then screams and yells. Pandemonium. Another had fallen in the bloodbath.

CHAPTER NINE

Choose your friends. You must examine them with discretion, test them by fortune, and understand them. Although friendship is one of the most important things in life, it's usually the one over which least care is taken: some are forced upon us. Most are the result of chance. A person is defined by the friends he has. The wise never make friends with fools. Some friends are mere amusement, not true friends with true intimacy – it can simply mean enjoying their humor rather than having any confidence in their actual abilities…Remember then: choose friends carefully, do not depend on mere luck.
-Number 156. Baltasar Gracián, **The Pocket Oracle**

Days later
Palm Sunday
San Salvador, El Salvador

Once again Cristina and James were at Mass. This time it was the funeral for *El Monseñor.* at the *Catedral Metropolitana de San Salvador,* the grand cathedral built where the centuries-old church had earlier stood. She wondered what effect the bishop's killing would have on the political situation. In such an unstable world, people and leaders and happenstance mixed in a most unreal way. No matter what the experts and pundits might predict, unpredictable fate won out in the long run.

She looked at James now, smiling rather grimly as they made their way to the front of the cathedral. The funeral Mass for

78

Bishop Romero would be celebrated with all the pomp and ceremony his church could muster in this bloody country.

Here were robes, cassocks, habits, elegant and simple dress, country-folk and aristocrats, everyone neat and clean for the occasion. Cristina recognized two derelicts, spruced up for the occasion, standing at the back. They were the same beggars who'd cried on the steps where the body of *El Monseñor* was being loaded into the ambulance.

Outside, the crowd grew and grew in the huge plaza. Peasants from all over the countryside had streamed into the capital. Sounds of crying and keening and prayers filled the air, causing a sort of electric feel to the whole that penetrated the very essence of the church. This time havoc would occur outside rather than within.

The churchmen and acolytes began to process down the aisle, their cassocks and white robes swaying almost in unison. Some priests stopped to talk to those in the pews as the procession continued.

The casket would remain on the altar for half a day longer, with honor guards kneeling next to it. Incense hung heavily in the air.

Pop! Pop! Pop! She heard the abrupt loud sounds. Strange.

They do like their fireworks, thought Cristina at first. *I suppose they consider this a celebration of sorts…Heaven-bound, or something…You never know…Surely it's not…*

Then the screams and acrid smells.

Shouts and laments reverberated in the plaza and into the church. Repeatedly then. The unmistakable barking of gunfire.

What hell have I come to? she thought.

People rushed to the doors. A vast moan reverberated through the church. The worshipers had heard the stories of flocks burned inside their temples throughout the centuries. And in this country of violence anything could happen.

The cousins trailed the group and pushed out through the huge wooden doors opening to the plaza. Thousands of men, women and children ran wildly about, seeking refuge. People hid behind little benches. Others were lying down, wounded, dead or feigning death. Bodies seemed to be flung about, arms and legs akimbo.

Cristina stared at the horrifying scene.

She nudged James, saying, "Look. Up there."

She pointed to the tops of buildings, where rifles peeked out and sharpshooters brought death to the crowd.

Cristina pulled back into the church foyer, heart pounding. But James ran out into the melée to minister to the wounded and dying.

I can't believe I'm actually here. San Juan and Madrid were never this bad. Never these random killings. Just men cracking each other's heads. Water hoses brought out. Yelling. Drum beats. Cars overturned. Shop windows broken. Sure. But not this.

There are other ways to fight…this is the beginning.. I must act…I will act.

That evening, shaken to her very bones, she called her Cuban friend in Washington. "Let's meet next week, Marta. How about noon at that nice grill in Arlington, say, Friday? I'll be returning shortly. I'll tell you about it when we see each other. I can't talk now. I can't. "

§

The following day
Ambassador Richard Warrens's office
The US Embassy, San Salvador

The US Marine Corps aide greeted her and led her down a long hallway to the ambassador's office, unlocking and locking a couple of doors as they went. A fortress of sorts. Cristina had heard much about Richard Warren, whose reputation among the liberals in Congress was as honored as it was denigrated among the conservatives. Intelligent and pragmatic, she'd heard. He was supposed to be a real professional who'd had his ups and downs in Washington. She respected what she'd read about Warren. A young veteran in World War II who later studied on the GI Bill, he'd made his mark as a man of perception and integrity in the Foreign Service. As ambassador to Paraguay, where the tyrant Stroessner was still in power, it was said he'd been able to achieve some progress. Just recently Warren had recently been named ambassador to El Salvador.

Cristina considered the president, in spite of his often-declared high ground and as a supporter of a human rights agenda, to be a waffler more than a leader on the world stage. He seemed to hover between the advice of his dove-ish secretary of state and his hawk-ish national security advisor. Some called it the "fudge factory." It would be interesting to meet Mister Warren, the president's official emissary. She'd learned to keep her own counsel. Now, in her more elevated position, it was imperative.

In a moment the Marine smartly opened a large door and she was greeted by the ambassador himself.

"Come in, Miss Franco. Good to meet you. Sit here, please.

81

Coffee? Tea?" His manners were nice. Old school.

"No, thank you. And thank you for personally receiving me, in the midst of all this…havoc. I was there yesterday at the bloodbath."

Warren nodded, his saturnine face not betraying any emotion."And so was I," he said.

The ambassador looked in his sixties, body still fit, his manner correct but on edge. Focused totally in the moment.

Without further preamble, he began.

"It's important that you know where you're going in this troubled country. I've been hoping that the money promised by the US could be used exclusively for aid, not military purposes. I tried to convince the archbishop to accept that, to seek a more centrist way. But the week before, he'd said in a sermon that Salvadoran soldiers should lay down their arms. I understand his analysis. But it seemed unlikely to me that it would have much positive effect. That strikes at the heart of the Salvadoran social order where the military, in effect, garrisons an unjust society. The army takes out either through intimidation or death anyone who is a serious dissenter."

He shook his head.

"We've seen the bloody result."

"Surely," she replied.

He continued. "I've kept on meeting with members of the junta, the church, the oligarchy, the politicians on all sides, the journalists and the guerillas and give them all the same message. We must seek land reform and we must stem the human-rights abuses. The way will only be through political and economic reform. I thought we should be open to talking to all. But now..."

Cristina said, "I understand."

His grey eyes sized her up, and he added abruptly, "Their military...D'Aubuisson and his crew... they'll kill anybody. He's a psychopathic killer. You haven't had the misfortune to meet him, have you?

"No."

"Unfortunately, he's won elections and we've had to deal with his gang. Up to now. I don't know what our government is going to do. I have ideas about how we should handle it. But..."

She maintained her quiet, calmly showing her deference to the ambassador.

Hmm, she thought. *He won't do anything. Can't. Has to obey the president anyway.*

"There's no clear way to handle this, is there?" he said, obviously not expecting an answer.

"No, sir."

"We have to keep putting the pressure on him. But...And... I will tell Washington clearly that that mob is a bunch of thugs."

More fudge, it sounds to me. He can't do anything but complain. The intelligence world will go its own way. And nothing will be achieved. Revolution is the only way. People deserve justice. Fidel is the only fearless one. Only he can fix this mess. And my life only has meaning if I work for justice. Not all this diplomatic dancing about.

CHAPTER TEN

"Cuba y Puerto Rico
Son de un pájaro las dos alas
Reciben flores y balas
Sobre el mismo corazón…
Con ferviente fantasía
De esta tierra y de la mía,
Hacer una patria sola".

-Lola Rodríguez de Tió,
first recited c. 1880 in San Juan, Puerto Rico

(Cuba and Puerto Rico are one bird with two wings, They receive flowers and bullets On the same heart, with fervor about this land and mine, to make one homeland.)

Later
Arlington, Virginia
The French Bistro served delicious food. Cristina ordered a Maryland tomato crab chowder, a wine glass of *cava brut* from Cataluña and a Virginia fresh flounder sautéed in scallions for lunch. She felt almost guilty as she awaited the fresh fish from the Chesapeake and coastal waters, knowing the waters of El Salvador's Pacific to provide seafood just as tasty. And sitting at an elegant dining spot instead of a common *friquitín* on the beach. Everything she did now reminded her of that poor

84

country. When she'd first returned, even looking into her closet shocked her with the number of fine clothes. She'd cull them soon.

Her own life was in the midst of dramatic change. But she could still take pleasure in small ways. Cristina ate simply at home, but this was a special moment. Her mother had taught her to enjoy good food. Now and then she liked to go to a fine restaurant, and this particular act today served to remind her of the other new life, juxtaposed in the present. This was a celebration of sorts.

Marta had earlier been referred to her by Juan Carlos Terún as a powerful connection to the cause. As Terún had said, "only to be used when absolutely necessary."

The time had arrived.

"Salud!"

They clinked wine glasses to toast their company in the quiet grill, white tablecloths and discreet waiters providing an elegant, subdued atmosphere. The food here was excellent and she'd never seen anyone of her acquaintance in the federal government here. It was a bit off the beaten track, a good place for private conversation and a special event. Stockbrokers, lawyers and bankers tended to be the more common patrons. But lobbyists, too, with a congressman in tow. They were everywhere.

Marxists can enjoy a good meal, too. And I don't have to wear a military uniform like Fidel. I don't have to announce my faith to the public.

"I want to share some things with you, Marta. I've had it. You know I've always admired Fidel. That's nothing new. Since high school days I've been furious with the US for fueling rightists'

85

power worldwide. I marched in Spain and England when I was in college. And of course in San Juan I belonged to our Marxist Puerto Rico Independence group, the FUPI. We owned the streets and the campus."

Marta laughed and said, "Haven't we all marched? A rite of passage!"

"True."

Marta said, "But we do grow older, right?"

"Of course. However, I've never forgotten what drove me then. That passion still burns. And now one has to make a living. That means quieting down and using my brain instead of marching my legs in demonstrations. I've concentrated on rising in the ranks. But it's time. I see it so clearly."

She picked up her glass of water and held it up, to observe. "As clear as this water."

She took a sip and put the glass on the table. "As long as dictators are friendly with the United States business interests, they're okay with the establishment. People starve. And the country keeps aiding the wealthy, the corrupt. I just saw it anew in El Salvador, where the US is training people like that criminal Roberto D'Aubuisson and his cohorts. Their politicians are just like ours, all centered on lining their own pockets and stamping out communism. Nothing changes. It's all the same bunch of thugs running everything there. And here in Washington too. *La misma mierda.*"

She paused, remembering the bloody scene in the plaza. "The death squads get worse and worse. The leftists, though divided into different claques, have been pretty much united by Villalobos and his Marxists. The rightist government is split too, but it has enforced the US economic austerity plan. The violence is escalating and, as usual, the US, the World Bank, all the same crowd wring their hands and stuff dollars and francs and pounds into the hands of the villains, train the military, provide weapons…"

She stopped to sip the wine and gather her wits. "My country is Puerto Rico. The United States is part and parcel of what's happening in El Salvador. As usual. Just as in Nicaragua and Honduras. Buy and sell, whether bananas for the United Fruit Company in Guatemala or the great sugar *centrales* in Cuba. The business of the United States is…"

Marta held up her hand and interrupted, "Business, of course. With willing aid from the elites. Cristina, Cristina! Stop! You're preaching to the choir, you know." She couldn't help but marvel at her friend's naiveté. All these Americans were the same. These Puerto Ricans were Americans, after all…

Cristina plunged on. "No, hear me out, Marta. In my youth in Puerto Rico I was well aware of the arrogance of the American empire. That dominating colonial mindset stifles my island. It has for a century, ever since the US seized it from Spain, which was another corrupt regime, that ruled it for four centuries. But the independence movement has never died. Never. You know my many friends from the old days. They'll be helpful in my new enterprise."

Marta said, "No doubt. No harm in rekindling those valuable old friendships. Your island has always felt a kinship for Cuba, for my island, hasn't it? Beyond our Marxist creed, I mean." She paused. "Interesting. That same kinship didn't develop with the Dominican Republic, even though it's right in the middle."

Cristina smiled. "Many historical reasons, including Haiti being half of Hispañola. That's another tangent…You know that poets carry the truth of a culture. And our most famous woman poet, Lola Rodríguez de Tió was a revolutionary against Spain. She was a real fighter. And how she loved Cuba! Just as I do. Her verse could be mine."

She launched into the recital of that acclaimed poem,

"Cuba y Puerto Rico
Son de un pájaro las dos alas
Reciben flores y balas
Sobre el mismo corazón..."

She continued, "Lola and her husband finally ended up making their home there, you know... Lola was a visionary, a model for me...And Fidel...Well, Fidel is one of a kind. I've always been entranced by him, you know. He has always been my hero."

This keen feeling bursting from Cristina was rare. Almost embarrassed, she closed her eyes a moment and recovered her calm.

She added, controlled, "But of course, you know my story, Marta. And you think me naive. I know that too."

Marta answered, "You see through me, do you?"

The two women burst out laughing at the exchange. The waiter appeared at their table. "Another bottle of wine, *damas?*"

In unison they shook their head no and the waiter discreetly retired.

Then Marta called him back. "*Mozo*, another glass, please. This is a celebration!"

Cristina plunged on. "Only Fidel can turn things around in Central America. I can wait no longer. El Salvador's guerillas have formed something they call Farabundo Martí National Liberation group, the FMLN. But they're in disarray and need leadership. Cuba is already providing it through the Sandinistas in Nicaragua. With all Cuba's problems, still…the big corporations and the oligarchs and the Mafia no longer run things …not perfect, but the poor can go to school now and see a doctor. Fidel is the answer."

Marta nodded in agreement.

Cristina swirled the wine in the goblet and studied it a moment before continuing. "Nothing happens overnight. We've discussed my working with you before. Now I'm ready. Just tell me. I just have to be very, very careful - there's always someone watching me at the DIA. Always. Memos proliferate on how to observe and report suspicious behavior in co-workers. I know they check my personal e-mails. I have to go through random polygraph checks. That's the way of life in my field. *Así es la vida.*"

The two women looked at each other silently for a moment.

Marta said, "*Vale, chica.* … just keep your eyes and ears open. And I have to be very careful, too, though I no longer work with the State Department. Being Cuban in exile is a double-edged sword in the States. They like me but are never sure if they can trust me. Having a husband with the Argentine government is great cover for me."

She took a sip of her *cava*, the Spanish-style champagne and hesitantly said, "You might look for a boyfriend in the right circles, too. Drop that political Puerto Rican lawyer. Jorge Parrachini, is it? He's a loose cannon, as the Yankees say."

Cristina grimaced. "Thanks for that unasked advice, Marta. Please." She paused, then added severely, "Do stay out of my love life! I can handle it! I know exactly what I'm doing."

Marta smiled. "Sure, sure. But I'll say more. I know you have an outstanding reputation, Cristina. Intense, brilliant, austere. But everyone who's been around you for more than a few minutes knows you have a real disdain for the role of the CIA in atrocities around the world. You have to tone down your rhetoric, *amiga!*"

Marta soberly looked at Cristina's large brown eyes radiating passion. The Puerto Rican's abundant black mane framed her well-molded face. Spanish and Austrian ancestors, maybe a touch of Taíno Indian and black, had left their stamp on this child of the Caribbean. Marta studied her, thinking of all those she'd mentored into the shadow world. It was time to be just a little brutal. She went on. "I don't know how you've had such a meteoric rise with the DIA, considering all your comments. The Americans astonish me with their ignorance! Anyway…"

"You know what I say! That the United States is a democratic nation claiming to prize freedom of speech. That does the trick, though I've tuned down my rhetoric in the last few months. I must admit I'm becoming more prudent. Probably Baltasar Gracián's influence." Cristina smiled as she considered how that answer had always disarmed her inquisitors. And how she treasured the thought of Gracián.

"Hmm. Well." Marta flicked her well-manicured fingers, dispensing with the subject. "Your thesis advisor at Johns Hopkins, Mateo Sanpietri, the Spaniard, will be your contact from now on. I'll get back to you. We'll still see each other in diplomatic circles, but for your sake it's probably better we don't get together so often. So I must tell you now: I admire and love you for what you're doing. You have a brave heart. A good brain. A disciplined attitude. You'll do well."

They toasted again.

The deal was sealed in wine. Again the waiter appeared.

"Yes, please, cheese and fruit, and then an espresso," said Marta.

The waiter smiled slightly, shrugged almost imperceptibly and went about his business. These women were the last in his shift. If they left fairly soon, he'd still have time to get to his yoga class.

§

Late that afternoon, towards dusk, Cristina jogged down the path at Rock Creek Park, not far from the Metro stop at the zoo. Aah! This air! Just a hint of drizzle. Refreshing! Even after the unaccustomed wine in her system, she could enjoy it. Late in the day was the best time to let go of stress, to breathe the rich air of the newly-greening woods, to feel her slender body become loose-limbed, her ever active mind be able to drift. Each day she spent almost two hours on the run, no matter sun nor snow nor rain. It kept her whole. And Rock Creek was a marvel, trees and rocks and hills snaking through much of Washington. It was worth the trip from her office at Clarendon. Otherwise she jogged from her apartment in Alexandria, following the path next to the Potomac. Life.

Next week she'd see Professor Sanpietri in his new role. Her new life would take shape.

Sanpietri wasn't one of her favorite professors, even though she'd chosen him for her thesis advisor. His connections were legendary. He was highly intelligent, pompous, handsome and vain, one of those people who smirked at his own wit. His long lank hair would fall in his eyes, and with an histrionic

91

air, he would flip it back in place, reminding her of the president of the University of Puerto Rico. His sparkling black eyes charmed many. Especially women. A long, thin nose adorned a long, thin face. He could have stepped out of one of El Greco's paintings of Christ's disciples in Toledo, even to the point of a sort of mystic air cloaking personal charism. He did challenge the students, intellectually and personally. Sanpietri would become her point man. She would force herself to find their common ground. The common good.

Pushed and pulled by her own conflicting loyalties, stoked with anger at the United States, Cristina considered the words issued by the US congressional delegation in its fact-finding trip to El Salvador after Congressman Tip O'Neill's intervention. They spoke against the oligarchy in power, but yet wanted to provide economic support to them.

She knew of Mao Zedong's directive to revolutionaries: "Drain the sea." It meant to eliminate insurgency by wiping out communities that might aid the opposition. In a war, especially a civil war, such brutality could be expected from both sides.

The congressional delegates, as usual, held both serious people and nitwits. Both sides had learned of Mao's edicts. Echoing him, they'd found that "the Salvadoran method of drying up the sea is to eliminate entire villages from the map to isolate guerillas and deny them any rural base from which they can feed." She knew, too, this was a directive the US Special Forces taught their pupils, as though their pupils needed coaching. Dictators and oligarchs knew the drill worldwide. It wasn't only Mao. She thought of the horrible bloody history of nearby Colombia in the late 1940s in the time of "La Violencia", while the World Bank and the United States aided the government in power. There was a long legacy of American support of the South American dictators and oligarchies.

Paul Fitzgerald had called her, but their conversation was sterile, a polite exchange. She told him Elena would be arriving and he could give her a ring later at her apartment. Their youthful encounter more than a decade or so ago had been agreeable. That was then. This was now. No other information given, none taken. Cristina surely didn't want to get involved with any of James's friends. But maybe Elena would. It might be good for her.

Cristina was learning to be circumspect about her beliefs. No longer she had to boom out Fidel's name. As much as she had volubly marveled at how Cuba's poor had surged forward, she was now beginning to keep her counsel. She'd fight her own war, for Puerto Rico's independence. And for social justice in Latin America, under the Marxist rubric, Latin-style, not Russian-style. With Fidel's leadership. Clandestinely....

CHAPTER ELEVEN

La tierra de Boriquen
Donde he nacido yo.
Es un jardín florido
Del mágico, primor
-La Borinqueña, National Anthem of Puerto Rico, F. Astol y
L. Quiñones
(The land of Boriquen, where I was born, is a flowered garden
of magic, care)

Elena
Sor Isolina Community Project
La Playa de Ponce, Puerto Rico
The office where Danny and Elena were to meet Sor Isolina lay
in a shabby old cement building. The paint was peeling off and
the black letters reading "Puerto Rico Iron Works" could barely
be seen. Earlier the building had held one of her brother's en-
terprises. Known as Don Luis, the wealthy industrialist pianist
philanthropist statehood politican supported and admired his
younger sister who had become a nun. It helped. Strong and
good characters both, brother and sister loved each other without reserve. But there was no doubt. This, the Centro, was Sor
Isolina's life work. Simple playing fields, classrooms for clubs,
tutoring, vocational workshops, a chapel, all strung through a
stretch of low-lying sand along the mangrove-fronted ocean.
The barrio was called La Playa de Ponce. Long a source of

hopelessness and violence until Isolina began her work, it was now often a place of hope. People-driven. The nun had put to good use her years fighting gangs and starting up community centers in the South Bronx and Fordham University.

Danny and Elena sauntered along the dusty path to the office. The two friends, so unalike in social class and educational formation, were so alike in their high octane approach to life. Both were creative souls, each with an intense longing to enjoy and live in the fullest sense. They gave everything they had with a generous and intense spirit. With joy. And their friendship with Sor Isolina, a woman dedicated to God and man, was special on many levels. She was fun! The three of them shared that bond, that kindred spirit.

Danny Rivera was famous in Puerto Rico and throughout the Latin world. He had a captivating lyrical voice to match his captivating personality. Probably the most beloved singer of his generation, he'd seen his records and concerts sold out worldwide. His songs captured the island's heartbeat, its beauty. Danny renewed many of the old traditional ballads and created new ones, with lush romantic modern arrangements, hard to resist by any age.

"Well, Danny, I don't think I've ever heard such a beautiful rendition of La Borinqueña you sang last night. It was the most lyrical, moving song…"

He smiled broadly, "Glad you liked it, Elena. It can be hard to sing anthems…some people turn them into showtunes, jazz tunes…I don't. I like to sing the song with a certain respect, I guess. Recalling why they were composed in the first place."

Thought Elena, *he is so simple. So rich in character. His success hasn't sullied his knowledge that he'd come from extreme poverty to the peak of fame. No one who knows this man and hears him sing can remain unmoved. She realized how valuable his talent was to the Centro, and that fortunately he was as much of a fan of the aging nun as she was of him. He treated them all like extended family.*

"Well, Danny, the only thing that worries me about your next concert here is…" she began. "Just say it, Elena. What?" he asked worriedly. Serious artists don't easily accept joking about their work. Especially from friends. And he also knew Elena knew music. Her years at piano and choral work had made her a fine musician.

She quickly repented her lightness. "I'm sorry to be silly," she said immediately. "It's that your show is always so …well…not just beautiful and inspiring, but over the top. How could anything match it? And yet, you've come back time and again, and each time it's…exquisite. Even more perfect, if such a thing is possible. I love it, Danny! I love you for bringing us this most extraordinary gift, that just transforms the people of La Playa. Truly!"

They were now standing in the road in front of the office, and "Sister" was at the entrance listening to their conversation. Her crystalline blue eyes set in a wrinkled, expressive face pierced the recipient as always, charming and truthful. So much tenderness, tempered with realism.

A wide grin cut across Danny's tanned rugged face that might be called plain on any one else. Sor Isolina and Elena saw his beauty. His dark eyes sparkled with the pure joy of life.

Isolina smiled broadly and opened her arms for a hug. "Danny, Elena's right. Fights stop, kids study, moms and dads take parenting workshops…It's amazing! All to hear your song. Unfortunately it only lasts for about two months. But believe me, each moment you give to us is a treasure!

"For you, Sister, anything. But…"

"It's fine, dear. People have to learn to accept the dullness and plodding times too…then the magical moments are even more dear. Right, Elena?"

"Right, sister. This is earth, not heaven. There's time for joy and for sorrow," she said. Josh's death had given her that experience of sorrow. And she'd learned again that the present moment could be joy.

CHAPTER TWELVE

Doblar los requisitos de la vida. Es doblar el vivir. No ha de ser única la dependencia,
ni se ha de estrechar a una cosa sola, aunque singular.
Num.134 Baltasar Gracián, **Los Oráculos**
(Double the requisites of life. That doubles life. Dependence must not be only one thing, singular though it may be.)

Cristina
The following week
Washington, DC
Going into Professor Sanpietri's office now had a dual role.

He greeted her effusively, the first time she'd seen such emotion in him.

"Hello, Cristina. How good to see you! I understand *el Jefe* Fidel was most impressed with your commitment...Congratulations! That's not a common occurrence."

She stammered a bit, surprised. "Please, Professor. Not so!"

"Yes. I heard it the following day. It makes me proud of you."

Cristina said nothing. His patronizing demeanor was legendary. Though she was accustomed to it, he did not entertain her.

"What else, Professor?"

Sanpietri pursed his lips, unhappy with her coolness. "We'd like you to go to the Dominican Republic for a short vacation. You have many days accumulated, so you can insist on a least a week. Soon. You need a decent rest, you'll say. You'll receive good training in basic tradecraft. Very important…You must be able to communicate with me and directly with Cuba without alerting your agency. Your agency may not like your absence, but they'll understand since you work so very hard and you produce. You'll stay at La Romana, a popular resort… big, laid out next to a sandy beach, golf courses and riding trails…"

Cristina said, "I've been there…a good place to be incognito."

Sanpietri continued. He didn't like to be interrupted. "You'll have a small house to yourself. A vettted maid to clean and cook. And one of those little Vespa scooters to get around. You'll take many books. The experience will be helpful for you in many ways. You'll learn a lot. You may even relax a little!"

Cristina nodded her head.

Sanpietri fixed his large grey eyes on her. "Cristina, I really want to congratulate you again!"

He couldn't help a very big smile, most unlike his usual pedantic and self-serving manner. He must have seen some reward in it for him.

"I've seen you as a brilliant student in international studies. Focused. Perceptive. Even inspiring."

"Thank you." She was surprised to hear him speak so fulsomely.

"I know your semester in Madrid when you were an undergraduate in Puerto Rico helped you learn about the larger world. Your studies in London and travels to Argentina and Central America…you came out of the University of Puerto Rico with some very good basic knowledge. But you've just taken off here at Johns Hopkins. You could teach some of the professors about world politics," he said lightly.

The professor stopped for a moment to light his pipe again, amusing Cristina with this so-academic-world stock in trade. At least he wasn't wearing leather patches on his tweed jacket!

He went on, eyes glowing, face serious. They were speaking in Spanish and his low baritone voice, his accent from Castilla la Vieja, his passion and intelligence shining in spite of his cultivated superiority.

"I feel honored to be chosen as your mentor in this new, challenging life you've chosen. You're offering great talents to a society that needs you so much."

"Please, Professor," Cristina tried to interject.

He ignored her. "As you've often well said, the United States has wielded the big stick so long and so effectively that smaller countries seeking their own destiny – especially Cuba in this instance – are simply not allowed to grow and flourish. The capitalist world lives and dies by exploiting the poor. We'll change that. You'll help transform society."

Cristina squirmed. When had she last heard such verbal bouquets? Her mother when she'd graduated from UPR with honors probably. She had to admit to herself: she liked it.

She returned to the subject at hand. "I hope I won't have any problem getting the time off, but you're right, I'm well overdue for a holiday. And of course I have many questions about what you call tradecraft. Maybe in three weeks? I should be able to manage that."

Her last vacation was three years ago. She'd gone to Segovia in Spain with Jorge, gloried in the remarkable Roman aqueduct, in walking along the town's walls, on eating the famous suckling lamb at Candido's. It had been something of an unmarried second honeymoon. The first had been to Quebec. But "something" was a key word there. In spite of the bond they shared, Cristina had made clear she was uninterested in marriage. Now...even less. There was no way she could share this new double life with him. Painful but realistic. Nor with Elena. Not with anyone she cared about.

Alone.

§

Cristina
Several days later
La Romana, the Dominican Republic
The American Airlines jet flew low over Haiti and Cristina peered out the window at the scorched brown earth below. Soon enough the view changed violently, as though a machete had slashed through the center of the island of Hispañola. The demarcation line separated the ravaged land of Haiti to the west, burned to the nub for firewood, grubbed to the raw earth. On the eastern part of the island luxuriated the vivid rich green of the Dominican Republic. The world knew of Haiti's desperate poverty, but this dramatic proof of its ravaged soil took Cristina's breath away. El Salvador might be purgatory but Haiti was hell.

She'd had no problem taking a week's vacation and Jorge, as always, understood her need to get away. He appreciated her penchant for being alone. He also knew La Romana had a reputation as a good place to relax, if you didn't care too much about eating out. She'd told him that she'd heard the hotel food was poor, but she liked fruit and salad and rice and beans – and

101

the famous Dominican special of *mangú*, the mashed green plantain with garlic. Perhaps a *chillo* or *mero* from the sea or *camarones* from the river. And maybe a little rum punch in the evening to finish the day. And the geography! Who could possibly complain about the glorious Caribbean Sea? Balm for the spirit. She told him she was taking a bag full of books and a notebook, not her laptop as a statement that she wasn't taking work with her. He and her office could always call the hotel proper if they needed to interrupt her retreat.

At the airport she spotted the sign saying "La Romana guests" so she made her way with a big group of Canadians to the bright yellow shuttle bus after going through immigration and customs. She noted that guards bearing machine guns stood at the exit, stern faces declaring their importance.

After speeding down a perfectly maintained road to the resort, she checked in at the open pavilion that greeted the hotel visitors.

A well-groomed young woman in a stylish red tunic and white pants and white sandals, the employees' uniform, greeted her with a broad smile. "Welcome to La Romana, Miss Franco. We hope you enjoy your stay. Your paper work is done, please just sign here and you'll be ready. Anything that you need, just call us." She handed her a lengthy brochure about the place. "And please be sure to go up to Altos de Chavón, a charming stone town built on the hills for our guests. Boutique shops, art galleries, restaurants, even an outdoor theatre for performances. Shuttles or taxis can take you there, or just ride up on your motor scooter."

Cristina noticed many guests were waiting impatiently in line at other desks. For some reason she'd gotten VIP treatment... Someone had paid extra money or a special word, since power and lucre are the commercial exchange.

The receptionist beckoned the bell boy to the desk. *"Jaime! Puedes llevar la señorita a su casita. Está en La Orquidea."* (You may take the lady to her cottage. She's in Orchid.)

A thin, dark, smiling boy buoyantly approached her, took the bag, and led her to the golf cart. Then they seemed to be on a racetrack, as he expertly tore around curves and crunched down the gravel path. Foliage lined the way, lush and abundant on the ground as it had appeared by air. Within minutes, he pulled up at the little wooden house that would be hers for the next week. It looked like an idealized cottage for Hansel and Gretel, a bit of gingerbread on the large porch, yellow window shutters and a steep roof with red tile. *My own fairytale begins*, she thought.

Jaime gestured royally as he leaped out of the cart with her bag. "The cart is yours until you leave, *dama*. I'll be delivering your scooter soon, just leave it in front of your porch. Everything you might need is here," said her gallant escort, guiding her through the bedroom, kitchen and living room, all decorated with bright colors that glowed in the sunny light. The bathroom had a huge tiled shower, one wall opening to the elements and a small interior garden with a chaise longue for private sunbathing. Colorful wall hangings depicting fruits and flowers adorned the rooms. He showed her the basic provisions in the refrigerator. Cheese, bread, milk, nuts, bananas, mangoes and orange juice. And of course, a bottle of red wine, another of white. On the counter sat a bottle of Brugal, a local rum.

"Should you need anything, please call the main desk. I'll be here in a minute. And whatever food you wish, simply tell Angelica. She'll clean the casita and look in on you at breakfast, lunch and dinner. Or you can order from the desk, or of course go to the main restaurant. Here's a map of the property. It's huge! And you should take the scooter up to the town on the hill. Very nice. We wish to please you, so you return to our beautiful island." His Spanish had that lilting cadence that distinguished Dominican poor folk.

He gave an especially big smile and almost bowed as he left after pocketing the ten dollar bill.

What a joyous child! she thought. *And he surely supports his family with this job. I'll try to remember his spirit when I become depressed…*

After showering and changing into a white pajama-like outfit that was as comfortable as it was practical, she wandered barefoot about the garden, detecting sweet-smelling *café de la india* among the hibiscus. An oasis!

As she wandered about the vegetation, a small tan bald man with thick lens perched on his prominent nose appeared on the path, struggling with his load of two computer satchels and a duffel bag. He paused to wipe the sweat from his head and face.

"Señorita Franco. Are you ready to begin your classes?"

Cristina laughed in surprise at the apparition. The brief time for enjoying the elements had ended. Work had begun.

She shook the man's wet palm and said, "What is your name, please?"

He raised his eyebrows, as though surprised that anyone should wish to know. "You can call me Juan. Juan Valiente," he replied seriously. His voice was low and a little gravelly in tone, but precisely enunciated.

"And yes, yes, that is really my name," he added with a little smile. "And from now on, in our communications, you will be called '*PALOMA*'. Do you like your new name?"

104

"Perfect, Juan." She assumed he was lying about his own name anyway.

"It is perfect, isn't it? And you? You will become a dove, *la paloma* bringing us information that will allow Cuba to grow and flourish. You will fly in your new freedom, soar, and help bring peace. From your vantage in the air, you will see the earth below as a fragmented place that must seek unity and brotherhood. Yes?"

"Well, Juan, you're a surprise. I expected a techie, not a poet!"

Juan began to lay out notebooks and two computers on the large wooden table. Again he smiled. He had been chosen well for this mission, his gentle manner as real as his intelligence, expertise and ferocious dedication to *fidelismo*. "We must all keep our souls intact, must we not? You, too, must be aware of this. As you study and synthesize information, you must be conscientious about your job for the United States government so you may continue to rise in responsibilities. You must be extraordinarily cautious, organized and alert in sending me material. This is a dangerous and rewarding challenge you are assuming. We admire you so much. Fidel told me personally that I was to be very, very attentive in working with you and to express to you that he truly appreciates your dedication. You are already one of our unsung heroes."

Cristina's face reddened with unexpected embarrassment at the praise. But how could she not be pleased?

Juan sat down on one chair and settled in front of a Smith Corona word processor, and indicated that she do the same at the other. "From now on, I will call you simply '*PALOMA*'. Is this acceptable to you?"

"Whatever, Juan, whatever."

105

"This is how we begin. I know from reports that you have a prodigious memory. Even so, you must work on it, as you may not bring home any documents from your office. You must summarize and memorize everything you think might be important. Each evening at home you will type your notes from memory on your new word processor, encrypt them and put the material on diskettes. Every two to three weeks you will turn over the disks to the Professor. He will officially be your handler, but I am your technological support and your contact in Cuba. You will also have a phone number to call me or the Professor, but he is your first point of reference. You will use public phones in DC, and punch in number codes. Then the Professor and I will pick up the pager and decode the information. We'll know when to listen to the shortwave radio. Things may change as we go along. In fact, things will change, in order to avoid patterns."

He stopped a moment to see her reaction so far. She was calm and quiet, expressionless.

"Please," he went on. "This week you will learn the numeric codes and also how to use the shortwave radio which I'll provide. I'll show you how to access it and understand its use while we're here. But back home in Virginia you'll buy a word processor of this series for home use. Your special instruction will be delivered to you in a handoff at the zoo, your first time doing that. They'll tell you when to expect a package with your shortwave radio to be delivered as a present from your mother in San Juan."

He stopped a moment to make sure she was following everything. "Amazing, isn't it. We are persistent and smart. Just as are you and I." He smiled modestly before going on.

"You don't go through customs with anything. I, on the other hand, travel by private plane and have diplomatic cover so have

106

no worry about customs or immigration. The Professor we will now give the name of *AVE*, for a bird. And my trade name is *DIVO*, since I love Verdi. Of course, if you wish to send a message that for some reason, all is not well, then I am Juan Valiente."

Cristina queried. "Do we really have to do this? These names and handoffs and all? Isn't it rather…dated and melodramatic? It sounds like a very old World War I spy novel. Really!"

He looked at her silently before he answered. "Yes. We really do have to do this. And no, it's not mere melodrama."

He pursed his lips disapprovingly at her language. "We have one of the top intelligence agencies in the world, though our principal preoccupation is obviously the United States. The Russian KBG trained us. Very well. Even the Israelis admire us. And their Mossad is the very best. We are successful because we are careful. And simple. And dedicated. And intelligent. It works." His tone was patient but firm.

There was another silence before he continued. "Agreed?"

"All right. You're the expert, *DIVO*," she replied. She enjoyed his mild but real sense of superiority. Baltasar Gracián would have liked him, she thought.

"Good. Thank you, *PALOMA*. But any questions you may have, please speak up. Most necessary. Now about our friend *AVE*. He's always in contact with me and you have free access to me as well. I move around a lot, but *AVE* is more stable. He lives close by Washington, right there in Chevy Chase, besides being in his office at Johns Hopkins SAIS three days a week. That's where you'll often see him. Other times at lunch or a park or a movie or a concert. He'll tell you each time. Between the two of us, you should have seamless communication."

He asked, "All understood?"

"Yes." It was so simple she was almost miffed at the question.

DIVO leaned back in his chair and scrutinized her as he continued. "As you know, the threat of what's called global terrorism as well as the so-called global economy has all countries taking special precautions and planning different strategies. When you have access to Russia, Asia, the Middle East, Europe - take it. We need it all, besides Latin America. There are many ways we can use this information for the good of Cuba and of course, in another sense, in alliance with other communist governments. Because of people like you we have one of the world's best intelligence services. We depend on people with a cause, not motivated by money."

Cristina nodded and smiled at his intensity. She said, "I understand."

"And *AVE* will, of course, be there for you to talk to as need be. Your reports will come directly to him, when you hand off disks to him. I repeat: he's your principal handler. If for some reason he's not available, you can call me and I'll get back to you immediately, or one of my very close assistants will communicate with you. Now and then you'll travel to New York City or Madrid or the Dominican Republic. Sometimes secretly to Cuba. Is that acceptable? Can you work with that?"

"Yes."

"Good. Then let us proceed with the details. Today I'm going to show you how to use the code and we'll practice it. When you get back to Washington, you will begin. AVE will give you a disk with all the codes on it to boot up."

All afternoon they worked and she collapsed in bed exhausted at the end of the evening. The next day and the next.

She learned how to become aware of others' observation, how to handle a lie detector test, how to keep thoughts even more inside than she had in the past. How to make passes, and use the old chalk-mark symbol to confirm meetings.

The fourth day they finished at noon so she could take a break and scooter up to Altos de Chavón. She wandered through the expensive boutiques, bought a colorful bowtie for Jorge and scarves for her mother and sister. Ate a fresh vegetable stew and fresh bread at a little bistro. Looked around the Disney-type sandstone and granite buildings that were built to emulate medieval Italy. Expensive but entertaining kitsch.

Then she hopped on the Vespa scooter to return to the cottage. She shot out at high speed on the solitary asphalt road back to the cottage, reveling in the fresh breeze and no traffic. A short swim in the ocean. The water was perfect. Crash early to bed. Lovely.

The fifth day they began with the shortwave radio.

Her tutor said, "All right, you turn it on like this. You'll receive encrypted messages at certain high frequencies, which you'll memorize now. The messages will be a series of numbers that you'll key into your machine, then use a diskette containing a decryption program to convert the apparently random series of numbers into a Spanish-language text. We'll practice this today."

As usual, Cristina learned quickly. Her very good memory was well exercised by her job. By late afternoon they stopped so she could take a dip in the sea. Floating and then doing cartwheels in the water were the best way in the world to break free of everyday life.

109

That evening and the next morning she did a rehash of all she'd learned this week. In the late afternoon she packed her bag for the flight home, with the understanding she'd return later in the year to La Romana for a refresher. And problem-solving if need be. She felt oddly unsettled with the idea of living parallel lives as she departed La Romana and bid farewell to her teacher. The double life would demand a reset in her mind.

As the plane landed at Dulles International Airport, her head and emotions cleared. Actually she felt a little frisson at the potential danger. She would have to be more careful than ever in her relations with Jorge and her sister Elena. Be even more cautious at work. All part of the game. Rather than fear, she felt an incredible sense of mission and excitement that she had never experienced before. This will give meaning to my life, she thought. At last, meaning!

CHAPTER THIRTEEN

-Knowledge and courage lead to greatness. Since they are immortal, they immortalize. You are as much as you know; a wise person can do anything. Man without knowledge, a world in darkness. Judgment and strength, eyes and hands; without courage, wisdom is sterile.
Number 4, Baltasar Gracián, **The Pocket Oracle**

Elena Franco
Eight months later, 1980
The hills outside Ponce, Puerto Rico
Elena was chopping fresh green onions and Italian parsley for an omelet, taking it easy this Saturday morning after a very rough week at the Centro. Trying to bring rival gangs together would test the talents of a Talleyrand.

Drinking another cup of the just-brewed Puerto Rican coffee, Elena sighed with pleasure and looked out her kitchen window at the stand of plantains. *Almost ready to pick*, she thought. *Tostones.* Squished *plátanos* fried in olive oil made the world's best appetizer. Yumm! The banana-like fruit peeked out from the large green leaves that waved slightly in the breeze.

This tiny cottage, once a *mayordomo*'s (manager's) house back in the day when it had been her grandfather's cattle farm, was an idyllic getaway. Now a very old crotchety man with a soft spot

111

for his granddaughter, *Abuelo* Antonio was letting his lands go to seed, sure that only he could care for them. On one of his good days, he'd agreed to let Elena, his favorite, renovate and stay on this property, giving her the money to fix it up. He simply abandoned the vast coffee plantation in Lares. No grandchild wanted to live way up there in the mountains anyway.

On the foothills looking over the town of Ponce and the blue Caribbean Sea beyond, this was a world apart. Close enough to commute, far enough to be isolated. Only one large room, with old-fashioned shuttered windows, it perfectly met her needs. She'd painted the sturdy thick cement walls a light grey, replaced the leaky zinc roof with modern-day blue aluminum and re-enforced wooden beams, polished the old black and white tile floors, installed electric lights, a gas stove, refrigerator, washer/dryer. And two nice wooden-bladed ceiling fans. Updated the primitive bathroom and the decaying wooden shutters called *persianas*. The simple accoutrements gave her pleasure. Good lighting. A mock-Persian rug and mission style mahogany furniture and bookshelves, with a sleeping alcove at the side. Two large water colors of Quixote by Irizarry. An ancient beautifully-carved crucifix she'd picked up in Bolivia two years ago. Elena called her well-feathered nest Villa Pou after her grandfather's last name.

After finishing her Masters degree in social work at Columbia University in New York City's hurly-burly, soon widowed, she'd come home to her island several years ago. Yet another new life. She'd signed up with Centro Sor Isolina in Ponce. A case study in many universities, the Centro had won the Presidential Medal for the nun and created a place of hope in the oceanside slum. And now Elena was an integral part of it, with Isolina a dear friend and valued mentor.

She turned up the sound on her stereo to revel in Bach while working in the kitchen. She was certain that the afterlife had to include J. Reilly Lewis at the organ playing the **Prelude and**

112

Fugue in F-Flat Major. After Bach, she'd put on Sanromá's piano to hear him bound through Gershwin's **American in Paris**. She'd heard that Gershwin told Chu-Chu Sanromá that he played Gershwin better than Gershwin himself did! She'd met the aging and charming Sanromá since he was married to a cousin of a cousin at another cousin's party in Vega Baja. So Puerto Rican…everyone was connected somehow with everyone on this beautiful and benighted island. Or maybe she'd put on the incredible heaven-soaring music of Arvo Part. Or…she mentally started running through strains of her other favorites.

Barely heard through Bach's vibrant, majestic music, her dogs were barking fiercely. She had two Alsatians, beautiful and territorial, who guarded her solitary existence with the gracious majesty of the breed. At the sound of barking she put down her chopping knife and looked for the loaded .38 caliber Smith and Wesson which always rested in her table desk drawer. Rural Puerto Rico could be a dangerous place. She checked it was loaded and went to open the front door.

Two men were approaching, a sawed-off shotgun in the hands of one, a revolver in the hands of the other. Her dogs snarled and crouched at the men's sides, threatening attack.

Half hiding behind the thick door, Elena called, "*Alto!*" (Halt!)

Only ten feet or so away, the men continued to advance as the shotgun bearer shouted, *"Abre la puerta, puta!"* (Open the door, bitch!)

He was the taller of the two thugs, pasty white, skinny and unkempt, with a straggly pony tail hanging down his neck. He turned towards the nearer dog and unloaded his shotgun. "*Cállate, perro!*" (Shut up, dog!)

The shot boomed. Her dog Max fell to the ground, his belly torn to shreds by the pellets.

113

The man turned back to her and re-cocked the shotgun, while the other grinned and let his revolver sag a bit.

Steadily aiming at the closer man's chest, the one with the shotgun, Elena fired twice quickly, just as she'd done at the shooting range. He fell with a ragged cry and dropped the shotgun, writhing on the ground.

His companion, the smaller one, brown and compact, snarled as though an animal himself. He lifted his revolver to point at Elena. But in the same instant, the other dog, Mocha, leapt at him, pulling the man's arm down as he shot the bullet into the dirt.

Elena got off another shot, hitting the man's shoulder. He staggered backwards in pain and surprise.

Slamming and locking the door, Elena sped around the cottage to shut all the open windows. In an instant she was calling 911 and jerkily explaining what was happening.

Then she hung up the phone and peered out the barred window inset of the big wooden door, to see the one man on the ground, the other lurching away but holding his pistol. Her dying Alsatian, Max, whimpered and crept up to the fallen man, licking his face. The other dog, Mocha, whimpered and ministered to her own dying mate.

"Dios mío," Elena muttered. "The nobililty of a dog!"

Much later the same day
La Playa de Ponce
Sor Isolina's office
At nightfall, Elena, after meeting with the police and the dis-

trict attorney, was sitting with Sor Rosalía and Sor Isolina at the little office at the Centro. The two nuns had spent years visiting shanties on stilts in the muddy mangrove swamp as Isolina put to use what she'd learned at her mother's side as a girl, and then in the convent, and the mean streets. The aging woman was as at home in the White House as she was in the most derelict shack. Somehow, wrinkles and old bones notwithstanding, Isolina had kept intact her lively sense of humor and a deep-set respect for others.

"Well, my dear. What do you have to say? I hear the *Avispas* gang is out to get you. You were too successful in luring some of their members into our rehab program. Your attack is surely related. And I'm afraid they won't give up easily. What do you think?"

Elena nodded in agreement. "Actually, I might have seen the one I killed in the neighborhood, always kind of lurking in the background. You should have seen the look in his eyes…"

"May he rest in peace…Or hell, wherever God sends him… And now?" Isolina took Elena's hand into her own old soft, spotted, bony ones and waited. Silently.

Taking a deep breath and closing her eyes, Elena, too, was quiet.

Then she said, "I'll have to leave. I'm sorry, Isolina. Just too shaken by all this. I know the gang will put another hit on me. I'll move to Washington, DC, where my sister lives. She works with the federal government there and can put me up while I look for something. I'll call her tonight."

She thought of Cristina. Always preoccupied with something or another, a little nervous these days about her own work, but her older sister was always supportive.

"I'll get a job somewhere. I've heard they have a good social services system and lots of Latins to be helped in Virginia. I have to be here for a trial, even though this was self defense… the district attorney said there's no problem about my going back and forth. I'll start making arrangements tonight. Have you any suggestions?"

Sor Isolina nodded her head in agreement and pursed her lips. "Let me think about it, Elena. You've been wonderful with the community. They love you. I do too. Besides your warm heart, we'll miss your gifts of planning and organization. Wherever you may be, you'll be a positive force. Someday you'll return to us, I think…"

She smiled, the wrinkles coming together and framing her brilliant blue eyes. "Go with God and know you're in our prayers. You did what you had to do. Don't carry guilt with you."

CHAPTER FOURTEEN

-Real depths make a true person. The interior should be that much better than the exterior in everything. Some people are all façade, like houses left unfinished because the money ran out, the entrance a palace, the rooms behind a shack. There seems no center because, after the first words, conversation dribbles out. They trot through the initial courtesies like Sicilian horses, then take a vow of silence. Words are quickly exhausted when there is no thought. Such people easily deceive other superficial people. But the astute look beneath the surface and see the hollowness.
Number 48. Baltasar Gracián, **The Pocket Oracle**

Several months later
Washington, DC

Paul Fitzgerald hopped off the Metro at Capitol South Station. His office at Court House on the orange line provided a direct ride and at this moment of the day, not too many people crowded about. His heavy black wool coat warded off the cold, and his old-fashioned homburg, picked up years ago at a haberdasher's in Madrid, kept his head warm. That, with a traditional tan scarf and leather gloves made up his downtown gear. He didn't care if he looked like the 'fifties. He was warm and could walk anywhere in the city without freezing.

Paul's tanned face was weathered from weekly tennis, white-water kayaking and hiking in West Virginia. His green eyes

117

were used to searching his surroundings. Whenever he could escape the city, he was on the water or mountain paths. The best of all worlds, he thought. Living and working in this busy park-studded city on the Potomac, but just a few hours from wild water and hills.

Just short of six feet and fit, he seldom took the car. Washington traffic was only good if you had a driver. And Paul worked as a lawyer for himself and his partner, not a mogul for the government. His quick pace dated back to his time as an ROTC Navy cadet in college.

At the bottom of the station stairs, Fitzgerald glanced at his watch. Time to spare. Good. His military days had made him appreciate the value of time. Besides, Tip was a stickler about promptness. Paul had seen his strong-willed temper flare at an aide for just a minute's tardiness. As he'd grown in political power as Speaker of the House in 1977, he tended to lose patience with others. A common trait with most power brokers. But O'Neill never forgot his base, nor his friendship with Fitzgerald's father. Loyalty was all to Tip. Success was just as important.

Fitzgerald had just finished drafting a brief to present to the US Court of Appeals for the Federal Circuit Court in the District of Columbia next week, when Congressman O'Neill, nicknamed by everyone as "Tip", had called to ask him to a quick lunch at the congressional dining room.

"It's urgent," the congressman had said, in that deep Boston voice of his. "You know I normally wouldn't bother you for a quick turnaround, but I need to talk to someone I trust deeply. You're the man, Paul."

"Of course," Fitzgerald answered, touched by the Speaker's comment. "I can carve out a couple of hours and work later tonight. No problem, sir. One o'clock sharp."

O'Neill had immediate access to dozens of attorneys of the highest rank. But Paul was not one of the pack. Rather than doing regular law work for the congressman, Fitzgerald now and then followed up on confidential matters for the Speaker. O'Neill knew better than to approach him for one of those quasi-shady deals that all politicians must indulge in, so obviously this matter would fall in the permissible category.

Paul briskly mounted the stairs of the tortoise-paced escalator and just as briskly walked the few blocks to the Capitol. Once there, he went up another set of stairs, passing a couple of young interns on their way to their jobs at the House of Representatives and a group of visitors from Oregon who were chatting about their congressman. This was the beating heart of American politics. Entering the Capitol, as always Fitzgerald felt a slight frisson. No matter how many times he'd trodden these steps, he couldn't help but consider how fortunate he was to be living in a country that elected its leaders and that in most ways used its institutions to honor the tenets of the Bill of Rights.

After the Peace Corps and law school, Paul had worked as a Judge Advocate at the gargantuan Navy base in San Diego before entering civilian life. He'd seen the dark sides of life as well as the occasional inspiring incident. He'd dealt with torture and murders as well as embezzlement and desertions. He'd seen the ambitious, the lazy, the staid, the wild. He'd seen the underside close-up. Somehow, though, Fitzgerald still sought the good.

As a native of Fairfax, Virginia, Paul naturally gravitated from California back to the east coast and began his legal career with an older man, Robert Arone, a retired Navy commander. Now partners, they shared a military background and strong work ethic. They intentionally kept their practice of international intellectual property and estates, fairly small, having seen how the big law firms often went spinning out of control. Money and power so easily became the meaning of professional life,

119

while personal life became sucked into that maelstrom and became an add-on.

Paul always scrambled to stay above that malaise. He'd grown up with an alcoholic father, charming and brilliant and unstable, and a mostly absent mother. He considered marriage a flawed arrangement between the sexes, principally existing as a device to satisfy concupiscence and contribute to the survival of the species. But repopulation of the globe was not one of his goals. As a single forty-ish male, he appreciated the female of the species without pledging eternal love and loyalty. Even so, he thought someday he'd encounter a woman who would become his mate.

Deep in his intellectual and spiritual gut, he harbored that sense of justice and idealism which had led him as a young man to the Peace Corps. He still referred to Victor Frankl's **Man Search for Meaning.** Paul's own search was as real as it was inconstant.

O'Neill and Fitzgerald had just finished the famous – and tasteless – bean soup in the congressional formal dining room and quietly observed the waitress as she removed the dishes.

Small groups of people, mostly men, huddled next to each other over the white-mantled table cloths and plotted strategy of one kind or another. Many a confidence had been shared here. The high-ceilinged room crackled with the Capitol's exquisite power charge, electrifying any disclosures with a breathless sense of import.

Facing the younger man, Tip waggled his unlit cigar and began to speak. "Well, Paul…"

The waitress brought two cups of coffee.

120

"Will that be all, Mr. Speaker?"

O'Neill glanced up at the fine black features. "Yes. Fine, thank you, Beatrice. No dessert today."

They exchanged a smile. He'd known the server for years and they agreeably shared a commonality of purpose: they were part of running Congress. He'd helped her out-of-work husband get a decent job in the District. She always made sure he had the best table and best service. She nodded agreement and left them to it. Decades of waiting table to scores of congressmen and their guests had imbued her with the confidence of experience. They would not be bothered. And she would be tipped royally.

O'Neill's shaggy white hair topped a massive head. Thick black eyebrows perched above luminous brown eyes. The rotund face was pink and unlined, but his nose betrayed the telltale capillaries of the drinker. The congressman fixed his legendary gaze on Paul. This skillful practitioner of the political game had surely mastered each movement needed to communicate nuance. Add ineffable charm to an inborn ruthlessness and the natural gift of the Gaelic traditional storyteller. Tip was hard to resist.

"Well, Paul, you will understand what this matter means to me. Those American nuns just killed in El Salvador – on December 2 – beaten, raped and murdered - were friends of my aunt. She's been a Maryknoll nun for years, and if she weren't so old she'd have been there in El Salvador with those brave women. Easily her body could be one of those brutalized and thrown in the pit."

He paused and reverently said their names. "Ursuline Sister Dorothy Kazel. Maryknoll nuns Maura Clarke and Ita Ford. Lay Missioner Jean Donovan."

121

Tip's eyes reflected his intensity. "The congressional committee will only bring back part of the story. I want you to find out the reality, not the gloss. I know you can get along with the lords and the peasants equally well. And you can build a bridge with the ambassador there. Dick Warren. He's a fellow Irishman, one of the brotherhood…you should be able to trust him more than those people at State. He's a pro, smart and tough. Did a good job in Paraguay. But powerful enemies on the Hill and at State. And probably at the CIA. He's as honest and good-hearted as he is close-mouthed and diplomatic. A little puzzling too. That can be frightening, you know."

He wryly added, "A most unusual and powerful combination. You have those qualities, too, Paul. That's why you're my point man for this."

Paul acknowledged O'Neill's compliment with a slight grin. He had a small but well-merited reputation for honesty and analysis in a city known for flattery and subterfuge. With his dark red hair and green blue eyes, chiseled features and lanky, lean body announcing his Celtic ancestry, Fitzgerald fitted in well with half of America. Considering his fluency in German and Spanish and his experience in the military and Central America, he brought a breadth of scope to the table.

"Have you been to El Salvador before?"

"Not long ago, actually. Just for a day. I'm representing a big US coffee conglomerate there that feels threatened by a Brazilian entrepreneur for a genetically-engineered coffee bean. Trying to get into the country. My client is going the route of checking the US patents of the potential new guy. I had to go down and meet the bigwigs. Interesting."

O'Neill said, "Hmm." Then changed the subject drastically. "You played tennis in college as I recall. Varsity."

Fitzgerald marveled at the man's memory for small detail and replied, "Yes. Actually my friend James Whalen, who's now a Jesuit in El Salvador, and I were co-captains at Holy Cross. We always beat Boston College." This was a dig at O'Neill, a dedicated alum of the rival school.

"Okay. I got it. I mention it because the ambassador plays tennis with everyone in the capital at the San Salvador Country Club - the rightists, the leftists, the centrists. Be sure you get on his invite list." He mulled that over. "I'll just drop him a personal note."

He went on. "As you well know, grown men tend to share confidences more over games and food and drink than anywhere else...well, except...that's another story, though. Anyway, that's with women."

He patted his own substantial belly. "No tennis for me!" His hearty laugh boomed out. "It's bad enough having to sail with the Kennedys now and then. But at least I don't have to leap about on those damn' sailboats! Just keep my head down when the wind changes and watch the boom. A politician can do that." He smiled at his wit.

Then he shook his head. "Ye gods! Imagine! Tennis for grown men!"

Paul said, "Tell me a little more about the ambassador. 'Sounds like you know him well."

"Just a bit. When I met his wife in DC last year, she told me she'd overheard one of the ruling claque say he'd like to kill her husband...and this was at an introductory cocktail party at the embassy. What a welcome! She's rightfully unsettled! And I fear his principles are going to outweigh his effectiveness, one way or another. But you can use him to dig for the true story as long as he's alive and in place."

123

Now and then O'Neill called Paul for a special project requiring special skills. Surely this Salvadoran venture would be challenging. Conflictive. Even dangerous. First Fitzgerald had to set the scene of and study how the United States had become central in El Salvador's civil war. Communism was a real threat in global hotspots, not merely a Senator Joseph McCarthy dementia.

Paul mused How in God's name had four American women had gotten involved in Salvador's conflict to the point of being murdered?

As they stood to leave the dining room, Tip leaned over to tell the younger man, "I forgot to mention something that could be important. A young woman with Defense, on her way up to senior analyst for Central America and Cuba, might help too. Based in Washington. Cristina Franco is her name. I'll drop her a note."

Fitzgerald raised an eyebrow. "Cristina Franco? Good lord! I met her back way back when. She's a cousin of my buddy Whalen. Of course I'll talk to her."

CHAPTER FIFTEEN

"...ruega para nosotros pecadores ahora y en la hora de nuestra muerte. Amén.
-Ave María. (Pray for us sinners now and at the hour of our death. Amen.)

Four days later
San Salvador, El Salvador
Paul stepped off the plane to see machinegun-armed guards standing at the passengers' entry way. *Just like the Dominican Republic,* he thought. *Most of Africa. Much of the world.*

He loosened his tie. It was hot. He hoisted his duffel bag over his shoulder and joined the ranks in line, a mix of Americans and Salvadorans of all hues and dress. The immigration official stared at his face a moment, exercising his authority. Stamp! Stamp! Stamp! Paul smiled slightly, recalling a time at a Spanish police station reporting his billfold stolen. It took the same limitless number of noisy stamps to authorize any transaction in the Latin world, it seemed.

At the curbside he looked around. James wasn't here yet. Well, the only thing the guy had ever been on time for was a tennis match or Mass. Everything else had to be squeezed in among a dozen other activities.

About five minutes later, James pulled up in a derelict Suzuki Jinny. Its front bumper looked as though it had run through mudflats. "Fitz! Jump in! We're playing tennis with the ambassador in a couple of hours."

"Hey, James. Whatever you say. All is well?"

"Yep. But we'll see how the tennis goes. The ambassador's aide called to cancel, but then Warren changed his mind. Just for an hour. He's devastated."

Paul looked at James, who returned his steady gaze without expression. A decade after being assigned to this country, the priest still reflected that inner calm and quick heart so many aspire to and so few achieve. James possessed a remarkable focus on the moment at hand. He'd always had that special quality.

Whalen added, "And as Julian of Norwich said, all shall be well."

Paul leapt into the front seat, throwing the bag in the back, as Whalen revved the Suzuki into first and took off. He kept his eyes on the battered road ahead. A deep pothole could destroy the remnants of the vehicle.

Holding on to a battered handle, Paul spoke. "Okay, James. Let's cut to the chase. Tell me what you know about the American nuns."

James sped up the jeep. "Just a minute, Fitz. Let's get to your hotel first. I don't want to lose my concentration. Driving here is hellish." Keeping his eyes on the uneven road, he said, "I didn't invite you to stay at our house for a good reason. Wouldn't help you to be seen there. We've received so many death threats... I don't want you added to the list!"

Paul looked at the drab roadside buildings. The depressing scene reminded him of Avenida Barbosa in Puerto Rico. Much of Newark and Baltimore. Southeast Washington. The Bronx. Every big city in the world. Abandoned hulks of cars. Bicycle skeletons. Old stoves. Junked metal. Cast off tires. Shabby wood and flaking concrete. Neon signs missing letters. Pawn shops and auto repair. A stray wildflower. The detritus of commerce, complete with graffiti and a sense of hopelessness.

Paul shook his head at modern civilization's hallmark. "Thanks, James. Sounds good to me. I like life."

After fifteen minutes of bouncing and eating dust, they pulled up at the two-story simple building where James had made reservations. Fitzgerald checked in at the spartan front desk, dropped his bag, and they walked next door to settle down at the neighborhood bar.

James waved off the beer and took a bottle of water. "I've joined the club, Paul. No more booze, day by day. You know how it is."

They looked at each other silently, both recalling the bacchanalia of college days.

"Congratulations, James." Paul quaffed the cold Corona. Good, he thought. As long as you ran the railroad and didn't let the railroad run you. Thoreau was right.

James changed the subject. "It's probably bad enough that you're even seen with me at all, though no one important would hang around here I should think. On the other hand, there are spies and conspiracies everywhere in this poor country. Who can make sense of anything? God bless it!" He raised his bottle of water in salute.

He wiped the sweat from his forehead, took a gulp and went

on. "Well, as you know, almost a year ago Archbishop Romero was shot as he was giving Mass. Then there were random wholesale killings at his funeral, in the plaza. I was there. Remember my cousin Cristina Franco? You met her years ago in San Juan. Anyway, she was with me. You might want to talk to her in DC. She works with the US government now."

Paul replied, "Sure. Actually, Congressman O'Neill mentioned her too."

"Anyway, people are being dragged out of their homes and shot by the death squads. You can see them literally stacked on the side of the road sometimes. Six moderate-left government leaders were taken from the Jesuit school where I'd invited them to speak. Their mutilated bodies were found the next day. That was a month ago. I feel responsible."

James shook his head and heaved a heartfelt sigh. "Then the nuns were murdered. It's a reign of terror. I tagged along with the ambassador to the shallow grave where they'd been buried. It was awful to see the earth give up their bodies. They'd been beaten, raped, killed. I watched another nun – amazing she hadn't been killed – wipe the dirt from their faces and identify them. I didn't know them well. But I surely respected those brave women…dedicated to helping the defenseless in the midst of chaos."

Then he queried abruptly, "What else do you need to know?"

Paul pushed away from the table and stood up. "Good God, James, will it ever end?"

"Who knows, Paul? Remember when peace finally came to Ireland? I thought that was impossible. We can't ever give up, can we?"

James stood, too. Enough.

Paul returned to his question. "What else? Truly? Just talk to Ambassador Warren, and if I can, to the nun who identified them. Sister Mary Ann, I think, right? Anyone else you suggest? I was wondering about José Napoleón Duarte. I understand he's a Notre Dame graduate. He can't be ALL bad, right?" He smiled, recalling the rivalry between their small alma mater and the powerful Fighting Irish.

"Right," James responded laconically. "Duarte? Everyone on the extreme right and extreme left hates him, so he might be okay. I've only met him in passing, can't really say. It's hard to tell.. When elected mayor of San Salvador, he stressed adult education, tried to calm the troubled waters. Trying to find democratic ways to rebalance the wealth. Hmm, if that's possible…Maybe pie in the sky, don't you think? When was the last time you knew a rich man who wanted to give his gold away?"

Paul answered, "It's a hardball game. Who knows?"

The men left the bar as their conversation continued.

James went on. "Well, Duarte's gone through exile and torture, so I guess he's paid his dues in a way. Beating off D'Aubuisson and his bloody rightists and the oligarchy and the guerillas, all at the same time. He could be an authentic centrist. That means he doesn't have a chance of success, by the way… So, anyway, yeah, that would definitely be good for you to touch base. But the US seems to back D'Aubuisson's army bullies as well, so who knows what's really happening?"

Fitzgerald answered, "You know a lot about him without knowing him."

"Well, I live here, after all. He's a player. Of course, you probably

129

know that nothing works in this country. It's a tinder box, erupting in out-of-control fire. So many intrigues here you'll never know what's what. The killers are obviously not going to confess. Nor their bosses. Anyway, I already called the surviving nun for you, Sister Mary Ann. Set up lunch tomorrow at my house. She's packing her bags to go home after their funeral Mass. You can call the ambassador yourself for a formal meeting with him."

"I already have, from Washington, you dunce. What do you take me for? " He punched his old tennis partner in the arm and James grinned.

They'd reached Paul's hotel. "I'll see him tomorrow at ten in the morning for an official meeting." Fitzgerald stretched and yawned. "Well, let me lie down a while and read. Maybe a siesta. Good to see you, James. Sorry it's under these circumstances."

"For sure. I'll pick you up in an hour and a half. Tennis, remember?"

Fitzgerald found his room and collapsed on the bed.

But within two hours the friends were back in the Suzuki, on the way to the courts.

They walked down a fern-lined path to the red clay court. It had been neatly raked just before, pristine. The ambassador was there, whites on, waiting with his racket nervously bouncing a ball. "I was going to cancel this game, but sweating out stress is a good thing. Let's get to it. This is my aide and tennis partner, Tom Clote."

The men shook hands and began to volley, then to play almost immediately. Serving, running, grunting, grimacing, whacking, the four men played two hard-fought evenly-matched sets.

No small talk.

Then Warren drooped a towel over his neck. "Sorry, guys. I can't play any more. Too preoccupied to concentrate on the game. That's it for me."

He glanced at Paul. "See you tomorrow, Fitzgerald?"

"Yes, Ambassador. Until tomorrow."

They all shook hands and split up.

So much for confidences over a game! After picking up a sand-wich at the corner bar, Paul was ready for a shower and bed. The old friends departed, each carrying his own thoughts.

§

The next morning Fitzgerald was at the embassy fifteen min-utes early. The taxi driver had known exactly where to go.

Passing a series of locked doors and armed US Marines through what seemed a state of siege, Fitzgerald was ushered to War-ren's office. After shaking hands, Fitzgerald began. "I appreciate your seeing me on such short notice, Ambassador. I'm sorry to interrupt you at this time, but…"

"Of course, I know. Speaker O'Neill is persuasive. And I'm a public servant. It's my job." He gestured to the chair. "Sit. Fire away."

Fitzgerald sat. And fired. "He just wanted me to look things over. Maybe hear something the congressional committee might not hear because of protocol."

Warren looked at him somberly and frowned. "I'll tell you exactly what I'll tell them. It's what I tell everyone. This is not a diplomatic exercise. I'm sure someone in the Salvadoran government ordered the attack on the nuns...Low level soldiers wouldn't have dared. D'Aubuisson must be involved - he's a vicious thug who perfected his trade at our very own School of the Americas. The generals in the army are just as bad."

Warren shook his head in disgust. "It's a vicious cabal and we Americans are helping support it. Pure evil. The head of the junta is being forced out by his cronies – to placate us, I'm sure. The new one is Napoleón Duarte. Elected president several years ago but the rightists supposedly robbed him of his victory. I don't know whether to trust him or not, frankly, since I don't trust any of them. But I have to try to work with him."

Warren almost ground his teeth in anger. "It's absurd we give this country money without demanding reform. Our president finally cut off economic and military aid to protest the nuns' deaths. But...we'll see how long that lasts...I'm not too optimistic. But I'll just keep telling the truth. I can only tell Washington what I see and what I know. Remind Speaker O'Neill that the CIA doesn't share its secrets with me. Maybe he can have better luck at probing for the truth, with the power of the purse."

He stood up and brusquely said, "It's all I have to say...If you need to see me later for anything else, let me know."

Paul realized the diplomat was both a truth-teller and a professional: an extraordinary balancing act, an oxymoron in his field. "Thanks for your comments, Ambassador. I would like the chance to speak briefly to Duarte. Could you help in making sure I can see him before I go?"

"Sure, I'll set that up. I'm sure he'll respond quickly. I suspect he's backed by the CIA. So he probably sees me as a meal-ticket."

He picked up his phone and spoke quickly to his secretary. He glanced at Fitzgerald. "Wait just a minute. He'll take my call right away."

The two men sat there quietly, thinking. There was no need to fill empty air. The phone rang and the Ambassador picked it up. He looked at Fitzgerald. "Five o'clock today fine with you?"

"Yes, thank you."

"Done."

Ambassador Warren stood and escorted him to the door. "At another time, I'd invite you to my house for dinner. But I'm still suffering the effects of the nuns' death. Sister Dorothy and Jean Donovan had dinner at my house the night before they were killed. My wife and they got along very well. I admired them. They were valiant women."

He shook his head at the memory. "We all had a challenging conversation about their role and my role in El Salvador. I'm here to seek a stable, democratic government. They were here to help the poor. A different mindset, right? Naturally they were vocal opponents of the military and the oligarchy. I understand that. But I'm here to try to mold a diplomatic, realistic centrist way that will avoid violence and be firm in seeking civil rights. Use our monies for economic aid, under our supervision. No guns."

Warren fixed his eyes on Fitzgerald, who steadily returned the look. "The nuns' murder serves as a direct message that we have to be more outspoken against the tyrants. Mere smiles and empty threats on my part don't work, do they?"

He hesitated a moment and then, frustrated, slapped the desk with his hand. "Politics! Please tell Speaker O'Neill we have to have a good, consistent message coming from Washington. The CIA, as I said, doesn't share their plans with me. They seem tight with Duarte. I can but guess what may be going on."

He thought for a moment before adding, "And, frankly, I'm not sure of that Franco woman, where she fits in. I felt uncomfortable with her. God knows! But I'd welcome the opportunity to speak to Congress about the situation here. And I'll surely express my views to the new secretary of state and the president if I have the chance. I can guess the direction our new president and his crowd will go."

He added, "It won't be good."

§

Two hours later Fitzgerald was seated at the Jesuit residence with James and Sister Mary Ann. They sat on the little *terraza* off the kitchen, and the housekeeper was serving them goat fricassee with white rice and cool lemonade. The slight breeze blew the warm air over them, as the nun recounted her story. She was a tiny woman, dressed in a plain, clean dress. Her roughened skin and drab hair style reflected her lack of interest in feminine attractiveness. Vanity was definitely a back-burner. Courage and dedication were front and center.

The slender, unassuming woman must have been in her forties. About Paul's age, perhaps. But she had that timeless air of those who march to the beat of a much different drummer. Her voice was pitched high, nervous. "It's a miracle I survived, since I'd been working alone with the poor in Santa Ana. I was about an hour and a half from Sister Dorothy and Jean. They worried about me. Imagine!"

The nun could hardly get through it. "They were all so kind and so good. And happy! We all shared such good fellowship in

134

the midst of poverty. We all were dedicated to helping refugees, especially the women and children caught up in the fighting."

She stopped for a moment, unable to continue.

The housekeeper came out again and smiled at her.

"*Coma. Es Buena.* Eat! It's good." she said.

Sister Mary Ann obediently raised her fork and tried it. She was hungry. And it **was** good.

She said, "I haven't eaten for days."

Quickly, she ate her portion before going on. Then she related how her fellow missionaries had suddenly disappeared. The day after she was supposed to have seen them, December 3, she'd joined the search for her fellow religious. The next day, a farmer told his pastor he'd been forced to bury four white women he didn't know.

Dragging him along, the search party went out to an isolated spot in the hills and dug. They found the women, piled one on top of the other under the dirt. Sister Mary Ann knelt to wipe the dirt from Dorothy's battered face and wept. They all knelt in reverence.

She thought of that moment and now she wept again as she said, "I thank God for having known and worked with those wonderful women." Her little body shook with emotion.
James silently grasped her hand and all three sat for a moment without a word.

Paul couldn't speak.

§

Later, lying in his bed to read before going to his meeting with José Napoleón Duarte, Fitzgerald looked through the file he'd compiled. He wondered why the man's parents had bestowed the brilliant little emperor's name on their son. Did his father harbor grandiose dreams for his progeny?

As a young man, Duarte fought against the dictatorship and joined the opposition in exile in Guatemala. Then gone on to study at the University of Notre Dame. Back home helped found the centrist Christian Democratic Party and became mayor of San Salvador, stressing education and social justice. Losing in what was said to be a rigged presidential election, he tried for a coup. Was arrested. Tortured. Exiled.

Duarte had recently returned from exile and became El Salvador's foreign minister just three weeks before Monseñor Romero's murder. The Farabundo Martí National Liberation Front (FMLN), the leftist guerilla movement, was gearing up for full battle. D'Aubuisson's rightist ARENA party was trying to wrest control from Duarte's centrist supporters. Bodies piled up.

So much for that, Paul thought as he closed the file with a pop. Who knows where truth lies?

He took a cold shower to refresh himself and again donned his suit and tie. Immediately he felt sticky in the heat. At least the garb was tan-colored linen. But why doesn't everyone just give up and wear a *guayabera,* that loose cotton or linen overshirt brought over from the Philippines to the American tropics? It could look quite elegant, with pleats and pockets and starch. But he had to follow the ritual. Suit and tie, it was, the bureaucrat's uniform.

§

At five, Fitzgerald entered Duarte's office in the imposing Span-

136

ish colonial style building. Tiled floor, high ceilings. Huge desk piled with papers and books. Duarte was an olive-skinned and fit man, dressed to Paul's surprise with a *guayabera*. Lithe, athletic-looking. A firm, unpretentious air, very much in charge. An aura of leadership.

Duarte stood to greet him warmly. "I am pleased to meet an emissary from Mr. O'Neill. I know he's a promoter of social justice, as am I. I have hopes still, in the midst of bloodshed and poverty and hate, that we can find our way in El Salvador. It's always been a struggle here. I grew up with it. I hope the Americans can help us to make peace. Our society is in ruins. Please accept my *pésame* - how do you say it, my sympathy? - for the death of the nuns who were here to help our poor. We will find and punish the killers, *si dios quiere..* if God wills."

Paul thought to himself. *Si dios quiere...*God willing...for everything...so Arabic...those seven centuries of the Moors in Spain left that fatalistic imprint on the language and the people. And if God does not will it? What then?

Duarte was going on with his lecture to Fitzgerald, sure that some of it would be repeated in Washington. "And we have to make huge economic strides to change our system so the *campesinos* have food, education, health."

Duarte's clear grey eyes looked out from a clean-cut face. His manner was courteous and no-nonsense, his voice clear and harmonious.

If appearances could be counted on, he'd be a person to believe. But after many deceiving circumstances, Fitzgerald had learned that appearances could be just that. Just appearances. Even so, he'd make his report to O'Neill based on his own intellectual analysis and gut feeling. He liked this guy, in spite of the ambassador's hesitance. But he liked Warren too. Somehow he felt

137

that both were honest, though coming from different camps. It was interesting to hear Warren's reservations about Cristina Franco. He'd keep that in mind.

Winding up, Duarte said, "I've been told you are a friend of Father James Whalen. He's a good man. If you're his friend, I know you are trustworthy."

The two men regarded each other. Paul inclined his head. "Yes, he is a good man. And he has been my friend since college."

Duarte noticeably relaxed. "As you will see, Mr. Fitzgerald, intrigue and conspiracies are a way of life here. Trust is even more valuable here than elsewhere."

"I can understand that. And if you should ever have information for me to pass to Speaker O'Neill, you can always communicate with Father Whalen."

"Thank you."

The two men walked to the door and shook hands.

§

That night, after a brief good-bye to James, Paul boarded a military jet on his way home. Especially happy to live in the United States. Not El Salvador.

CHAPTER SIXTEEN

-Then leaf subsides to leaf,
So Eden sank to grief,
So dawn goes down to day
Nothing gold can stay.
-Robert Frost, "Nothing Gold Can Stay"

Elena
The next day
From the Dulles Airport to Alexandria, Virginia

Elena pulled her two bags off the Dulles International Airport luggage carousel. In taste she was a minimalist. With that in mind, she'd walked out of the charming cottage at Villa Pou, leaving everything but a boxful of books and CDs of her favorite music to be shipped, carrying only two suitcases of her favorite clothing and her old typewriter. At her invitation and *Abuelo*'s permission, her brother said he'd use the *casita* as a weekend getaway. But if she ever returned, it would be hers. That was understood. It was even in the old man's will, she'd been told.

She'd been in DC before when visiting her sister back in college days, when they'd both been struggling to find themselves and their way in the world. Books, boys, pot, studies, marches, demonstrations. Excitement and fear in the air.

Elena was a striking young woman, as blonde as her sister was dark-haired. She had the compact body and taut grace of a

139

gymnast. Blue eyes, classically chiseled and tanned face: all encased in a small lithe body. An ineffable joyous spirit emitted from her very being. It had returned, after several years of mourning Josh.

Used to the admiring gazes of others, she tended to dress in an understated way to tap it down. She was now in black sneakers, yoga pants and a black turtleneck sweater topped by a white leather jacket. She couldn't resist the red scarf. She loved the touch of color. As she walked through the huge baggage claim area, she thought, *now that I'm in another climate and work zone I'll have to go to Macy's for sweaters and warm clothes. Goodbye to a life of sandals and fresh simple dresses and shorts. Goodbye to lovely tropical air and soft breeze. Hello to frigid northern winters, grey skies, the cold city and challenging personalities - all with their own allure. To some. I'll adjust!*

At least DC and Virginia wouldn't stifle the spirit as the skyscrapers of Gotham had begun to, back in the day. She'd tossed everything from those years except a Saks black cashmere wool coat she'd picked up on sale. She'd also tossed that almost obsessive northern sense of getting things done immediately. The Hispanic Caribbean demanded a slower, more demonstrative time frame. Time to relish, calmly consider a situation, enjoy human relations. Now she'd have to change again. Elena hoped that a little bit of the slower southern states survived in northern Virginia. She didn't miss the near frenzy of New York City.

Shivering from cold, she waited for a taxi from Washington Flyer.

She spoke to the Ethiopian driver, "Hello. I'm going to an apartment in a place called Ridgetop Plaza in Alexandria. I think it's just off the Potomac, near Duke Street. Do you know where it is?"

140

The building had received lavish promotion when it had opened a year ago. She'd snagged one of the few one bedroom apartments, following Abuelo's advice: buy the cheapest property in the most expensive neighborhood. Its already high prices had skyrocketed just after Cristina had made her down payment. Its good environmental design had caught the media's eye. And lots of expensive advertising, of course.

The cabdriver nodded. "I know it." He turned up the mid-eastern music – the flutes and drums and sitars - on the radio and sped off.

Getting into a taxi in the United States is entering another world, she thought. How different from Puerto Rico. The drivers there were Spanish-speaking islanders – Puerto Rican or Dominican. They all wanted to talk politics or baseball.

Now she'd arrived in the polyglot capital of America. Suddenly the streetlights turned on, responding to the late afternoon dusk. The cab's windshield wiper busily flicked back and forth to eliminate the drizzle. Wet pavement gleamed and the city prepared for thirteen hours of darkness. The drear of urban winter.

The cab dropped her off in front of Cristina's building. She gave the man a generous tip, for she always had in mind the migrant's plight. She hurried into the gleaming foyer. Finding an upholstered straight-back chair, she sat and opened the book she'd read off and on throughout her life. Anthony de Mello's **Sadhana.** The counsel of this Indian never ceased to calm her, this exercise above all: close your eyes and recall a moment in which you felt great happiness, even joy. Seize it. Dwell upon it. Delve into it. Elena thought of her favorite scene: kayaking out of the mangroves near La Playa de Ponce. She'd kept the little poly-fibered vessel near a fisherman's shack that sheltered a couple of small fishing dinghies and her craft, all humble

141

vessels that braved a magnificent sea. In moments she was on the sun-splashed water, alone in the world. She aimed at the rising sun of the east, blazing through pink clouds. A brilliantly white egret emerged from nearest mangrove key, where shiny brown stick-like trunks bore the dark green leaves. A bright green iguana slipped from the squishy mud into the still water. They seemed to be the only living things on earth. A primitive and solitary escape, so close to a populated Caribbean island. Glorious! A celebration of life! Renewal!

She sat there in Alexandria, Virginia, content, waiting for her sister's arrival, at ease on the Caribbean Sea. Sitting in her kayak, moving with the waves.

After several minutes, refreshed, she returned to the here and now. She began to tick off the to-do list. Sor Isolina had called Doctor Moira Doran, her friend and head of Fairfax County Social Services, who by good fortune had a temporary spot open. They'd worked together in the gangland of the South Bronx when buildings were burning and drugs were flowing. Moran had great respect for Centro Sor Isolina in La Playa de Ponce, and done her doctoral thesis on the Centro as a model for community-based work.

Elena, armed with her MA in social work from Columbia University, years in Ponce and blessing of Isolina, was coming to the right place at the right time. She hoped. She had an appointment awaiting her, and, if all went well, perhaps the offer of a job. Even a temporary position would do for now. She had a couple of other leads, but this was highest on her list. Enough to be able to eat and have a roof overhead, though she knew this area of the United States was pricey.

If it didn't work out, she'd go to another state that had more jobs and a less expensive way of life. Maybe Texas or Florida, someplace with lots of Hispanics. After losing Josh to the Vietnam burnout, she'd been completely on her own. Her sensual appetite seemed to have burned out as surely as his plane. She planned to stay that way. Lonely sometimes, but...she'd survive. Do her best. Go forward. Seek the good. Find joy in music again. Maybe she could find a choral group here. She hadn't sung the **Messiah** since leaving New York City.

Restlessly, she looked at her watch. Puerto Rico didn't have daylight saving time, that strange concept of "saving daylight" which the Americans prized, and she thought so peculiar. But here she was, in the land of saving daylight. Odd. There were so many other things that should be saved. She reset her watch to comply with northern timekeeping.

The killing of the intruder in Villa Pou had shaken her balance. Thank God Cristina was here to lean on. Their close sister bond simply overlooked their disparate vision of how to achieve social justice in a cracked system. The heart ruled.

Cristina should be home any moment now.

Cristina
A few weeks later
San Salvador, El Salvador
President Duarte met her at the door of his office. They spoke in Spanish, of course.

"It's good to meet you, Miss Franco. I'm happy to see the government is using people who speak Spanish as a native language. And a Puerto Rican! One of my best friends at Notre Dame was a Puerto Rican, though we haven't kept in touch. He was a builder in Guaynabo." His handsome features lighted up.

143

She smiled at his attempt to charm her. Most men did this when meeting an attractive woman, she thought. It's how we're all made. "Good to meet you, President Duarte. Yes, we do get around.

There are about as many Puerto Ricans in the United States as there are on the island. Poverty is a great incentive for migration."

"Yes, of course." He looked embarrassed. "Poverty is a great incentive for social instability, too. My dream is to seek more opportunity for our landless peasants. And to seek peace. Not easy."

"No," she murmured.

LORETTA PHELPS DE CÓRDOVA

CHAPTER SEVENTEEN

"I want to cooperate with the United States to help bring reform to my country. Unfortunately, dictators and violence have been the norm for centuries. It's very hard to introduce a democratic way of governing. We need all the help we can get to change an imbedded mindset."

She nodded with a quiet smile. *Right. And only revolution works.*

Encouraged, he continued, talking about the need to give amnesty to the guerillas, to implement major reforms in landholdings, to build more schools and train teachers, to stop government corruption, to convert the oligarchy to a new vision.

If I were young and naïve, I might find him persuasive.

On and on he went. She made little comments here and there, while watching his articulate performance. She smelled the old building's hint of mold. *Probably here for at least a hundred years. It must addle their brains. Whether he's sincere or not, these things will never happen without revolution. Can't he grasp that?* She wondered.

At last the meeting was over.

§

Weeks following
Anacostia-Bolling, Washington, DC

Poring over her desktop computer in her little cubicle at the department, Cristina read the most secret details of US plans in Libya, what military and strategic action might be considered. She read pages and pages, recording the most pertinent information to her excellent memory. *People can find information about the newest weapons in the magazines, but policy is golden,* she thought. Her small space gave no indication of her top security clearance. Importance wasn't measured by square feet.

Cristina felt oddly under observance. Somehow, she sensed that that the courtly older gentleman several cubicles away was noticing her. He almost bowed when they met each other in the hallway. Her discomfort didn't rise from his overly cavalier attitude. She felt most uncomfortable and hoped her unease was but her imagination. Nerves were a part of this way of life, she knew. She'd have to deal with it.

In fact the gentleman, whose name was David, found her intense, secretive way to be well beyond the normal. After a lifetime dedicated to counter espionage, he'd found that his hunches often paid out. David watched how she leaned over her computer, as though hiding what she was reading. He knew she had maximum clearance and analyzed Central America and Cuba, apparently to the approval of her superiors. In fact, she was considered very much of a rising star. But, as did Billy Bottoms, he felt she was not trustworthy. Her stone face concealed more than it should, he considered. Though the tells he noted were far from evidence, they did make him especially alert. He would mention her again to Billy next week when they discussed whom they should be observing.

§

Her sister Elena had a new job. And she'd found a little place to

146

live in Falls Church, allowing Cristina the privacy that was key to her two-tiered work. Short weekend get-togethers, whether for lunch or walking, allowed the women to have sister time. Both of them worked exceptionally hard and prized solitary moments.

That evening in her apartment Cristina transcribed pages from her memory into her computer just provided by Sanpietri. Then she coded the material appropriately. Tomorrow she'd leave the chalk mark so they'd know to pick up the envelope the following day in a brush-by at a particular spot in the running path at Rock Creek Park. Simple, old-fashioned tradecraft. What Cuba couldn't afford in high technology espionage, it made up for with human intelligence and ingenuity.

§

The next day
The resident commissioner's office
Washington, DC

Cristina clutched her soft Segovia-suede coat about her, plunging forward in the cool winds off the Mall. The air had, unseasonably, just swept in from Quebec. Wrapping the soft cashmere pashmina about her frigid face, she glanced at the other cold souls who held fast in the currents, braving the Washington weather. Lining one side of the street at attention stood the cold Federal buildings, surreal and self-assured in their granite purity. Across the other side of the field sat the marble Capitol building, emblematic throughout the world.

All of these walkers, just as she, must surely have a purpose to be outdoors at this untimely moment of the day.

She squinted into the daylight breaking in the east, threatening to favor the frigid city with a ray of sun. Morning's frost sparkled on the frozen limp-grassed earth.

The young woman smiled at her momentary thoughts of the Caribbean breezes of her youth and mumbled to herself, "Miles to go before I sleep." Though only thirty-five, she felt very, very old sometimes.

Thinking random thoughts....someday under a *grosella* tree with a book of Neruda's poems in my lap. Gliding along the limpid turquoise surface of Boquerón Bay in my sister's kayak, inhaling the paradisical air of salt, sea, sun. Sitting in the patio of the Conservatory, as a student trio play and pay homage to Pablo Casals in the inner courtyard. Seeing poor children learn to love books and music and peace. Someday...Tranquility. Recalling what I will have achieved...Once my job is done.

Eventually she reached the Cannon Office Building. Putting her computer and coat on the security belt, she smiled at the armed guards as she entered the checkpoint, marveling yet once again at the cavalier approach to security in the nation's capital.

In moments she was striding down the long hallway, her well-polished high-heeled black leather boots clicking on the gleaming marble. She passed a dozen doors until the right one.

Giving a light knock, she opened the door and entered the green plush-carpeted office. Martín González smiled in welcome, warm grin parting a cherub's brown face, his black eyes reflecting simple joy. She thought perhaps he slept under the reception desk. Day or night he seemed to be here, always happy, neatly attired in tie and white shirt with a dark blazer, eager to help. It was the only job he'd ever had, through five resident commissioners of Puerto Rico here in Congress. His amiability and constancy and apparent lack of guile overrode partisan politics, so here he was. Getting rid of him would be like firing Martín de Porres, the sainted sixteenth century Peruvian almoner.

Then Jorge Parrachini came through the inner sanctum door

and she hugged him. Each time this happened, she once again flushed with pleasure. His strong, fit body, even with clothes on, delighted her. His warmth was emotional and physical. A treasure.

Now that her long-time lover was resident commissioner of Puerto Rico in Washington, she would be able to see him more than once a month. His blonde curly hair and bright blue eyes proclaimed the Irish in his Puerto Rican heritage and a tall lanky frame completed the picture. His fellow congressmen marveled at his Celtic good looks, a blend of County Kerry and Spanish Galicia and the Caribbean. So did the voters marvel at his charisma. And so did Cristina.

They kissed each other lightly and he briefly touched her beautiful black mane of hair, glossy and gleaming.

"So… why are you visiting me so early on such a rough spring day, *amor*? Aren't we meeting for dinner tonight?"

"I'm not sure. I might have to see my sister. Could I call you later?"

She smiled and her white straight teeth, thanks to thousands of dollars her father had reluctantly paid the orthodontist in Guaynabo, shone. Her vibrant Latin filmstar looks might tempt an onlooker to think she was merely another beauty. Until looking at those deep black eyes. Seeing the layers beneath.

"I just wanted to tell you face to face I'm meeting the president at the White House after lunchtime. I've been so nervous I couldn't mention it to you. No telling how long that might last. I have to give a rundown of the emerging leadership of the so-called terrorist group in Puerto Rico, ties to Cuba and suggest a few ways of dealing with it."

Cocking her head with a quizzical air, she added, "And how

it's mixed up with the status question…As you well know. Of course, any news you get from our governor and your take on the island at the moment is welcome. His latest assassination attempt must have sent chills up Bardini's spine! At any rate, I'll call you as soon as I'm free, let you know how it goes with the president."

She knew his job and he knew hers. To some extent…Inside, Cristina quivered with trepidation. She'd been eager to get away from her desk, from that old man a few cubicles from hers. David something. Always watching her. At least here in Jorge's office she could decompress while she prepared for her meeting with the president.

Jorge erupted with a laugh. "Really? Cristina! What a feat! You'll do well, don't worry! Depending on how you feel, we can run over to Café Milano or I can put on a couple of steaks at my apartment."

He paused and corrected himself. "Oops! Or salmon for you."

"Sounds good, Jorge… And if you don't have any visitors today, could I use this office to work this morning? If I'd stayed at the Department, constant interruptions… Nerves. You know how it is."

He raised his voice so Martín could hear in the other room

"Of course! Martín, please make sure no one bothers Doña Cristina this morning. She'll be working here for a while."

"*Sí, jefe.*" Martín's operatic tenor resounded, an impressive voice from a small man with a big heart.

Making herself at home at the conference table, Cristina sat in the big old wooden chair – a leftover from decades gone by - shed her coat and scarf and gloves, and took out her notebook.

150

Arranged it just so on the table, and, after turning on a little Ravel background, connected to the world. As gifted as she was in computer communications, she never ceased to marvel at this luminous sense of electronic connectedness. And yet at the sheer lack of understanding between humans, regardless of instant communication.

Now that she'd risen quickly and steadily to a dizzying place in the world of intelligence analysis, pressure had also increased exponentially. This would be the first time she'd give a report directly to the president of the United States.

She checked her notes, some very basics about her Island.

Puerto Rico. Christopher Columbus encountered it in 1493. Juan Ponce de León first governor. Taíno Indians exterminated as a culture in 50 years but mixed with Spanish gene pool. Black slavery until 1875. Present population mostly white and mixed blood.

United States took the Island in 1898 as result of Spanish American War. Puerto Ricans named citizens of the US in 1917. Limited self-government as commonwealth in 1952. An unincorporated territory subject to US Federal Government law. Permanent status still undecided.

Few jobs. High crime and drug trade. Bitter disputes about status issue. High degree of literacy. Spanish first language, English second. Many Dominicans seeking refuge, many educated Cubans.

Governor Pedro Bardini, a neurologist, has begun a universal health care program for the poor. Favors statehood for Puerto Rico.

§

She mulled over the summary points. Now the hard part, she thought. How to say much with few words. Most importantly, to be convincing.

There is no proof of terrorist activity on part of independence back-
ers. Connections with Cuba are few...the terrorist wing has disap-
peared from the scene. The independence sector relies on the world
forum to advance its cause, not violence. The recent assassination
attempt of the governor is almost surely a rogue act. Because of
anxiety caused by economic depression and status instability, the
US government should provide massive increased aid for education
and health for Puerto Rico and engage in no political activity.

She took a deep breath and stopped writing. That was enough.
She could answer any questions they might have. No more
notes. If they wanted specific data, she could quickly put together a fifteen-page report and be done with it. Her balancing
act in analysis was a constant challenge: How to convince her
superiors while downplaying the role of Marxists?

Then she simply shut off her brain and did some deep yoga
breathing. She and Elena had taken classes together and discovered it was the best way to prepare for any oral presentation.
In about two hours, she'd be at the White House. Now was the
time to relax.

§

A few hours later
The White House
As she was checked through the side door, Cristina smiled at
the aide who graciously received her. She glanced at the formi-
dable Marine standing tall at the entrance. She'd read enough
memoirs and spy novels to visualize this moment, and felt a
strange sense of déjà vu. After sitting the requisite half an hour
in a waiting area, she was shown through to an office featuring
a highly-glossed table for eight and a brightly-lit window overlooking the sere gardens of early spring.

Two men in US Navy high command uniforms sat there already – always more than punctual, she was certain. Surely admirals. The unobtrusive aide, dressed in sparkling whites, a twenty-something recent Annapolis graduate she assumed, helped take off her heavy coat, introduced her to the two large bemedalled men and pulled out a chair for her. The young man then stepped to the side of the room and waited. The officers looked almost like twins except for the body fat – both with big reddish faces, blue eyes, military haircuts, stern countenance. But one was fit, the the other very much overweight. They politely acknowledged her, without a smile. Their thoughts of Puerto Rico were doubtless negative…remnants of the Sabana Seca murders, closing of the Vieques base, Roosevelt Roads and more…

That fat one wouldn't survive basic training, she thought. *The other one looks tough.*

Then a well-dressed older woman with a big grey chignon and impressively large breasts straining at a simple black dress entered, nodded, and sat next to Cristina, after busily pulling out her own chair.

She looked directly at the younger woman and seriously said, "Hello, Miss Franco."

Cristina smiled and answered, with restrained self-confidence, "Hello, Miss Laporte, it's nice to see you again. We've met at debriefings for Intelligence Committees. I know you are special aide to the president for Latin American Affairs."

A vague look passed over Rita Laporte's face. She might have been practicing a smile. Her smoothly stretched face and large black eyes were inscrutable.

The dynamics changed immediately as the president appeared at the door, accompanied by a small bald man of distinctively Asian features. The little group stood and the president shook hands with all, radiating intelligence and geniality. The Asian, his self-deprecating air disguising a fearsome mind, was simply known as Dr. Lee. Cristina knew him to be the president's right hand since their college days. Lee introduced everyone.

The elected leader of the United States was rather chunky in body, tall in stature, his tanned handsome face cloaking an extraordinary brain which had been honed in thought at university and tested in battle in Congress. He had an amiability and wit about him that had served his political life well. Cristina knew he very much liked attractive women. She also knew that fact would serve her well.

The president sat at the head of the table, saying, "Well, let's begin, shall we?"

He spoke with a beautifully modulated voice and slight southern accent, a useful tool for a politician. It lulled the unsuspecting Ivy Leaguers and garnered votes from those outside the Northeast. "Mr. Lee, a little background…"

Lee spoke. "We all know what has happened recently in Puerto Rico, with the attempted assassination of Governor Rodrigo Bardini in his office at La Fortaleza. The president takes a special interest in this case, as he considers him a friend. We also know that the governor fended the killer off until security guards came to his aid… That he wishes to keep this secret while we help to find what was behind it all. And meanwhile we're keeping the attempted killer in a federal facility. The governor suspects that Fidel Castro's Cubans contributed to this, to retaliate for concerted efforts to control their movements with the *independentistas* in Puerto Rico, especially at the University of Puerto Rico…"

Inside, Cristina flinched. Outside, no reaction. She glanced at the hardfaced Navy officers. Nationalists known as *Macheteros* had claimed responsibility for the attack of the Navy bus in

Puerto Rico. Anything or anybody from the Island the authorities now considered suspect.

Lee continued, "We do know that Cubans recently organized the protesters at the courthouse against the US backing of El Salvador's government. That's common. They've always worked together with the *independentistas*."

The president spoke. "Now we have this aborted assassination of Governor Bardini. If he weren't a strong judo athlete, he'd be dead now." He inadvertently smiled at the prowess of Bardini, his buddy and tennis partner who had once been ranked as a top competitive athlete at Duke.

Cristina saw the two Navy men frown, saying nothing. They were fans neither of Puerto Rico nor of the governor.

The president pointedly addressed the others. "Cristina Franco is a distinguished analyst, a Puerto Rican who grew up on an Air Force base in Spain, then Puerto Rico. She's a product of Johns Hopkins and distinguished service in Central America. The governor and his staff think highly of her, as I do. Her take on the Island is to be much respected. The situation there is complex and always in flux."

The chief executive then addressed Cristina. "Could you just give us a very brief summary of Puerto Rico? We all know it, but just to refresh our memory."

He nodded at the young woman and said, "Please proceed, Ms. Franco."

Cristina answered with the brief rundown of her earlier preparation, adding, "The governor has been handling this just right. Political tensions always run high on the Island. It's up to the US to be calm, without bowing to the conspiracy crowd."

The president and Laporte nodded in agreement, while the emotionless Navy men looked on. They knew better than to comment. While the president might seem a figure of bonhomie, he would brook no argument. His way, his word.

"That pretty well sums up what I think too, Cristina. Thank you." He turned to the Navy officers. "You may go now. Thank you for being present."

He stood up and shook hands with each, ushering them out the door. Cristina imagined how chagrined they must feel to be shut out, in spite of their stolid reactions.

Then the president sat down again.

He tapped his fingers on the table and looked at her carefully before continuing to speak. "I'm concerned about Cuba's role in Puerto Rico and in this assassination attempt. I've received excellent reports about your skills and great experience in El Salvador as chief intelligence analyst. I want you to make an off-the-record visit to see Castro about several American prisoners he claims are CIA. Be very friendly. Appear to sympathize with him in regards to the United States. Mention in passing the attempt on Bardini's life. Observe Castro's reaction."

He interrupted himself. "That charlatan is a great actor. He knows what he wants the audience to perceive. That's all. At any rate, be aware. If you can get those Americans freed, more power to you. You can report directly to me and Miss Laporte. Call her on your return to set up an appointment with me. If this works out well, you can count on being my personal but unofficial emissary in Cuban and Central American matters, for various matters."

He stood up again and gave her his traditional bear-hug while seeing her out.

He added briskly. "Do this quickly. I have confidence in you." Miss Laporte handed her a card and said simply, "Call me later today. My office will make the arrangements."

Cristina left, walking down the hallowed walls, astonished with her meeting the most powerful man in the world. Looking out the sun-dappled windows, she saw the elm's bare branches allow wee green buds to appear. *Spring, at last.*

Now it has truly begun...

§

As Cristina left the White House, she shivered from thrill, expectation, and cold weather. She caught the subway and returned to her office. Back in the warmth of her cubicle/cocoon, Cristina switched on and off her agent/double-agent thought process, realizing this almost double personality was going to be more difficult that she'd imagined. She quickly read through her mail.

A get-together with some friends from the Latin American embassies, sponsoring a bandeon, cello and piano concert at the Argentine ambassador's home next week.

"Oh, good!" she thought. It was featuring the music of Astor Piazzola, followed by a small reception. That should be fun. The Argentines knew how to give a good party. She'd invite Jorge. They'd see Marta and her husband there.

Gala Theatre was hosting yet another re-run of the musical hit **Puerto Rico Fuá**! She'd already seen it. Satiric and entertaining. The other messages ran on. Her mother Lise was well, still helping Dominican refugees in San Juan and going off to the mountains, to San Agustín del Coquí, to help the children there when she could. Now that she was retired from paid work

157

at the family restaurant, she never stopped. She wanted her children to join her for her birthday in September. Without fail!

Her brother Manuel, a bankruptcy judge in Puerto Rico overseeing the Island's scary flight of capital amid trails of widespread fraud, sent his *cariños*. Her cousin James the Jesuit, still a history professor at la Universidad Centroamericana in San Salvador, sent her a cryptic note saying, "It goes on." A note from Dr. Sanpietri asked her to meet him in a couple of days at his office at SAIS about an important academic matter. And her favorite wine store in DC was featuring a tasting of Italian wines and special sale. No response from the guarded message sent grudgingly to her father. She was trying to reach out. She didn't understand why she bothered.

Well, she rather expected that. As kind and nurturing as was her mother, harsh and hostile was her father. Why should she expect that to change? She'd never hear from him. And if she did, what then? Though she no longer believed in prayer, long ago she'd prayed for him, that his mean spirit – his jaundiced autocratic bullying Freud-stoked psychiatrist heart - would show love and respect for his children. She marveled that patients would see him for mental problems, considering his own deepset chill, his cold heart. Of course, he had good professional manners and a good education. That patina glossed over the deeper reality. Recalling those days, long ago, when she'd been gentle and pure of heart, filled with hope, her mother's pet, her siblings' champion...No. She put aside memories. Switched mind to her work.

CHAPTER EIGHTEEN

...Show your mettle, but wisely...
-Number 54. Baltasar Gracián, **The Pocket Oracle**

Cristina and Fidel
Two days later
Havana, Cuba

As Cristina stepped off the little private turbo jet, accompanied by another employee of the agency, she paused and breathed in deeply the wonderful, thick Cuban humidity. Others in DC had complained about the oppressive tropical air, but she loved it. She liked steam baths better than saunas.

She and Mr. Smith - he never used any other name - alighted on Cuban soil and wrinkled their eyes at the brilliant sunlight. Cristina fished in her purse for sunglasses, found and adjusted them, and walked down the stairs to the tarmac towards a two-story unpainted cement building. Mr. Smith followed. He was short and rotund, with reddish skin and receding grey hair, a paunch, a dark suit, light blue shirt and striped tie. His face displayed no emotion, as bland and unmemorable as possible. He, she thought, was the perfect spy. Smiley lives. She suspected he was her minder as he was always prying into her work. The DIA trusted no one within its own ranks. One of her CIA friends had spoken slightingly of the DoD arm of intelligence. One hand hardly knows what the other is doing, he'd said. Amazing, even so, that Smith had been assigned this trip. It seemed rather obvi-

159

ous. She thought he must have engineered his invitation.

A giant mural of Castro, bushy-bearded and booted, standing amidst sugar cane with the iconic cigar in his hand, greeted her. The words of "¡Viva Cuba Libre! ¡Viva Fidel!" painted in thick black letters, took up the rest of the wall. It was all beginning to peel and mold. The moist tropics do that to walls. To overly energetic people as well. Emerging from a glass door set in the side, a short dark-haired man in a *guayabera* shirt open at the neck, approached with a hesitant smile.

"Señorita Franco?"

"Sí, y Señor Smith. Usted?"

"Soy Guillermo González. Bienvenidos a Cuba."

"Muy amable. May we speak English since Mr. Smith doesn't understand Spanish?"

"*Por cierto.* For the moment that's fine. But with others, we should speak in Spanish, and you can translate for him. All right? I will accompany you throughout your stay."

"Thank you. What do we do first? I'd like to see the Americans who are held in prison as soon as possible."

"Yes, yes. But first to your hotel to freshen up. Then to the prison to see the spies. Afterwards to a conference room where we can talk. Tonight, after dinner, you may meet Fidel."

Cristina smiled at Mr. González. Word choice was always so revealing. "May." In other words, it will happen. You will be permitted to see him. Or perhaps not.

They checked into *Habana Libre*, once a Hilton. Outdated but clean, it was often used for official visitors. Gleaming marble floors, high ceilings and architecture reminiscent of the early fifties made Cristina think of the last days of Las Vegas-styled and Mafia-dominated Havana, and always the remnants of four centuries of Spanish colonialism in the Americas.

Her room was equally clean and dated, no dust to affect her asthma. She was sure it was also for sound. With a sense of humor, as she hung up a light jacket in the closet, she burst into song. The first thing that came into her mind, the traditional children's ditty. "*La cucaracha, la cucaracha, ya no puede caminar. Porque le falta, porque le falta, una patita pa' caminar.*" (The cockroach can't walk because it lacks a leg.) She laughed at the thoughts that would be going through a listener's head...A cockroach? Uggh! This woman is a puzzle! She assumed, trusted, that only the highest echelon would be aware of her true loyalties. Everyone else would surely think her another US government employee, a mid-high level bureaucrat running errands.

She drank a glass of bottled water, left the room and headed for the lobby. Smith was sure to be there already.

Yes, he was. Standing stiffly next to González.

González smiled slightly and shook her hand, then led her towards the porte cochere, where a well-polished old three-rowed Ford station wagon awaited. Smith followed them, odd man out. González helped her up the steps into the relic and slipped in next to her, in the second row, gestured to Smith to take the seat behind, and barked orders to the driver.

As they wheeled through the narrow streets, Cristina feasted her eyes on the three and four and five storey shabby buildings, once the glory of Old Havana. Many of the few cars seemed to be old and well-tended. Now and then a new Toyota. A random highly glossed Buick, more than a decade old. People in the street

161

dressed poorly, lots of flipflops and scanty tops and shorts. It must have been lovely once, since a musty charm still pervaded the scene. The people walking the streets exuded that kind of buoyancy that Latins – especially those of the Caribbean - seem to have in their DNA. She compared the scene with the grim faces she'd seen walking the streets of Moscow. A world of difference between two Marxist visions. She'd take the Latin one.

A forty-minute drive and they arrived at their destination. Rusty grill work adorned the nasty-looking façade. This was doubtless always a prison, Cristina thought. Probably dating back to Spanish times more than a hundred years ago, before what the Americans called the Spanish-American War. The Cubans had fought long and hard for their freedom from tyranny.

Within moments they were inside a foul-smelling room. It smelled of rat and cat urine. The three Americans in question were brought in. Dirty and dressed in shabby blue overalls and t-shirts, the prisoners were stood in the corner, their wrists in manacles. Two guards bearing machine guns stood at the door.

"Well, speak," González told them. "These people have come from your president to see you. Our Leader has allowed it."

The smallest of the three, squinting, probably having lost his glasses, apparently the group's head man, spoke. He shuffled his feet. His round pale face looked bruised. "We are happy to see you. We were arrested on false charges. We're all associated with the Jewish Federation for Freedom in New York, but we're here as tourists to see the wonderful island of Cuba. Of course, we are interested in seeing and hearing about freedom of religion for our brothers, and asked around so we could go to a service. Some snarky individual claimed we were spies for the United States or Israel. Preposterous! Mr. González has been very helpful with us, and told us to expect you. Please get us out!"

162

Cristina said, knowing her lines well, "I know your group is religious rather than political. We know you are not spies. We'll do what we can. Keep up your hopes. And behave yourselves so there are no complaints." This is what she'd been instructed to say, though she considered the words foolish, useless.

§

That night Cristina and Smith were taken to Castro's small palace, formerly an elegant mansion for a wealthy *habanera* family. It was rumored he had close to a hundred personal resting places. In keeping with the general environment of Havana, this one was scruffy rather than well-maintained. They walked through a garden with a working fountain, bubbling among the abundant ferns and *trinitaria,* a descendant of the brilliant flowering plant the Marquis of Bouganville had discovered in Brazil in his botanical expedition and circumnavigation of the globe a couple of centuries before. Cristina loved the flower, its vivid colors of the three-in-one accounting for its name in Spanish. A rustic stone bench sat there. Fidel must like gardens. Or a caretaker liked them enough to pay attention to the vegetation in the midst of peeling painted walls. The arched walkways around the patio were pleasing too. Agreeable form and color existed amid decay.

They were ushered into a large room on the first floor and left standing together with González. A man dressed in black pants and white shirt approached them. He could have been a flamenco dancer. He pranced so well in his slightly heeled boots; his longish black hair gleamed with oil on his well-shaped head.

"Coffee?"

They all accepted the brew, the pride of Cuba, together with *azúcar moreno*, brown sugar.

163

Minutes went by as they drank their coffee, gave back the little white porcelain cups to the waiter. Silence. Cristina had heard of this pattern. Meetings with Fidel were always at night, at some unannounced place. Coffee was served. The visitors were made to wait at least an hour, standing around in an empty room. With her back to the door, Cristina was looking at Smith, deciding whether or not to engage in conversation. Then the door opened, and she felt, heard a rustling as several people entered. The hair on the back of her neck prickled as she slowly turned around.

There he was. Fidel. Tall, dressed as usual in combat fatigues and boots, bushy and unkempt beard, piercing and mesmerizing black eyes under thick eyebrows. Two armed subalterns accompanied him.

"*Señorita Franco? Un placer.*" His eyes actually sparkled.

"*Un placer, Señor Castro.*" She knew he refused to speak English though he understood it well enough. She also knew Smith spoke Spanish though he pretended otherwise. *The games people play,* she thought. Of course, Fidel knew her true identity.

She said they represented the president in asking him to free the three Americans who were simple tourists. All knew that in fact the prisoners had come on a clandestine mission. But Fidel and Cristina also assumed that the Cubans wanted to give her a feather in her cap, to impress the president and her agency with her effectiveness.

He didn't respond to her request. Instead, "¿Usted le agrada mi país?" (Do you like my country?)

"*Por cierto. Es tan bello como mi isla, Puerto Rico. Una joya tropical,*" she answered truthfully. (Surely. It's as beautiful as my island, Puerto Rico. A tropical jewel.)

164

He smiled slightly. "*Bien. Hay algo que quiere llevar de Cuba…
aparte de los espías? Cigarros?*" (Fine. Is there something you'd
like to take from Cuba, apart from the spies? Cigars?)

She smiled in return. "*Café, gracias. Es exquisito. Cigarros, no.
No fumo.*" (Coffee, thank you. It's exquisite. Cigars, no. I don't
smoke.)

Suddenly he turned around and marched out the door, as
abruptly as he'd entered. The air felt as though it was being
sucked from the room.

What has happened? she thought.

Smith, Cristina, and González were escorted out. That evening
a ten pound package of coffee, packed in brown wrapping paper, was delivered to her room. A box of cigars as well. *Cohiba.*
She'd give them to the president.

The next morning, after a breakfast of fresh grapefruit juice,
pan *criollo* with *guayaba* jam   and *café con leche*, they departed
the hotel. Awaiting them at their plane were the three American prisoners, still smelly and dirty. But no longer manacled.
They grinned through the grime and boarded the plane, discreetly sitting in their stench towards the back.

She'd accomplished her task. Mr. Smith and she had exchanged
perhaps a dozen words. Better that way.

CHAPTER NINETEEN

-A dash of boldness in everything is an important element of good sense.
Number 182. Baltasar Gracián, **The Pocket Oracle**

Elena and Cristina
Five weeks later
Falls Church, Virginia

Cristina sat on the small sofa bed, a glass of her favorite chilled *cava* in hand, watching her sister sauté a skillet of vegetables, leftover wild rice, and small chunks of breast of chicken. Elena knew how to decorate a small area and cook a tasty, simple meal without fuss. They'd both picked up these gifts from their mother, who'd had to relocate a dozen times as Ernesto, her officer husband - their father - had been transferred from one base and one country to another. The female secret to survival had been focus.

Taking a sip of the *cava*, Cristina asked, "So how's your job, *hermanita*? Are they keeping you busy and out of trouble? Do you enjoy it?"

Elena glanced appreciatively at her older sister. "Yep. A lot. Being right-hand for the director, Moira Moran, Sor Isolina's contact at the Fairfax Public Schools. Not too much money, of course. But who would enter social work to be rich anyway? There's a budget crunch, of course. Always. And of course it's temporary, but it's a beginning."

As do so many Latins, Elena used her hands to communicate. Tie her hands and she'd be mute. She put down the skillet to gesture around the room. "This little apartment in a pretty rundown part of town is all I can afford. The good thing is the big windows that let in the sunlight! That's what I already miss from Puerto Rico. The sun. I'm trying to get acclimated… Get to know the people we serve…lots of people struggling to survive. There's a public library around the corner. And a good parish church with a Spanish-language group. Korean, too. All that's the way it should be."

She smiled at her sister and went on. "I bought a beat-up Volkswagen, runs okay. I'm travelling throughout the system to see how we can keep costs down while doing a better job. Easy, right? There are some great professionals here, good to work with."

She lifted a spoonful of chopped leaks to test in the palm of her hand. A bit more fresh parsley. A touch of turmeric. Ahh. Perfect. She continued, "There are so many immigrants and special needs students, something like 60 languages spoken – more Hispanics and Asians than any others. Everything under the sun, autism, depression, bipolar, you name it. Of course, I work with families. Housing, Jobs. Mental health. History… I'll have to ask you some questions about El Salvador. Many refugees from there, fleeing violence."

Cristina grimaced and responded, "Another day, another day…"

§

An extreme sadness welled in Cristina's heart, as a scene just two weeks ago in that violence-ridden country leapt to her mind. On occasion, she'd dress in the simple style of a poor Salvadoran woman: plain blouse, plain nylon skirt to the knee, sandals, hair pulled back in a bun, no makeup. Then she'd ven-

167

ture out on the streets alone, seeing and hearing what was really happening. This was part of why Cristina was so much ahead of the rest in her work: her sense of observation was acute and deep and first-hand. Not only in the capital but in the towns as well, especially the more troubled areas where military, rebels, and gangs fought endlessly for power. Once bloodshed began it seemed never to end.

To see the reality up close, she'd assume the stance of the down-trodden around the world. Stooped over, fearful, expression-less. In Washington known for her self-confident manner, here she was an extraordinarily different person. That day in San Andrés, she'd walked slowly down the dusty street holding a basket with two breadfruit, ostensibly going about her daily tasks. The bullet-pitted walls of adobe buildings showed streaks that could have been blood. Galvanized roofs were ajar, some of them just lying on the side of an empty house. Windows were gutted. At this moment held by government forces, the town was quiet. Just miles away were Mayan ruins. This area had seen conflict for centuries. And now the hot quiet afternoon sun beat down and few people stirred. She saw three mangy curs trotting slowly together. Being able to feast on roadside cadavers filled their stomachs. They were likely better fed than some humans.

Then three men and a barefoot little boy appeared on the road ahead. Instinctively she darted into a shadowed doorway and waited for them to pass. She tried to make no sound. Even breathing. All three dark-tanned men wore military fatigues, but one of them also sported a Pancho Villa-style bullet sash and a large gun in its holster. His long greasy black hair was held in place by a red sash, and his big mouth opened to show missing teeth. He was repeatedly shoving the smaller man who held the hand of the young boy.

"I told you. Give me your money, scum!"

168

The father cringed and put his son behind him. "I told you, *Señor*. I'm sorry. I have no money, no food. I work for the militia but haven't been paid. I'm taking my son to my mother's house to see if she was able to get rice from the truck. He hasn't eaten all day."

The man spat in disgust and turned to the other man. "And you. I'm sure you have a dollar at least.

Give it to me!"

The tall, thin, white-haired man was just as arrogant as the gunslinger, unwisely responded, "*Pendejo!* Leave us alone. Go with the dogs and rob the corpses. I have nothing either."

The armed man's eyes bulged in anger. He swept his hand to the pistol and pointed it at the man's forehead. "Die, stupid one."

He pulled the trigger. Brain matter spattered on the trembling little boy, as the father tried to cover his eyes from the scene. Once again, the killer scowled. He spat. He scratched his crotch in a nasty way, turned around and saw Cristina hovering in the doorway. She lowered her eyes in submission. He leered. Then again, he scratched his crotch and stalked away. His bloodlust seemed to be sated. For the moment.

Thank God! she thought, shaking.

The father bent over to his son to embrace him. "He's with the angels, son. He was a good man."

He stared at the body, weeping. "My dear friend. Benito." He wiped his eyes and shook his head.

The *campesino* addressed the boy. "I'll take you away from here.

169

Be strong, Rafael. I'll take you to the United States. We'll make a new life."He pulled his friend's body out of the middle of the road and crossed the man's arms. He knelt next to him and said to the boy, "We'll pray together and then go to *Abuela's* to eat something."

In the doorway Cristina watched. The breath had left her body and she waited a while. She would run to the center of town to catch the local bus and return to the hotel.

She thought, *I can't help the United States to keep this war going. Even President Eisenhower warned about the military-industrial complex… It's insane! Hundreds of millions of armaments thrown here…and for what?*

§

Now in her sister's apartment, Cristina, remembered the scene in a fugue state, her eyes unfocused.

She'd remained silent as Elena went on to serve her plate.

Elena looked at Cristina in a peculiar fashion, prudently quiet. She placed the breast of chicken and wild rice and leeks on the two lovely pottery plates she'd acquired from the international mart. Then garnished them with a bit of romaine lettuce topped with extra virgin olive oil, Spanish of course. Balsamic vinegar. A little kosher salt. She served the plates on the small round wooden table she'd picked up at the flea market. It was covered by the white table cloth she'd bought at a Macy's linen sale. A cup of inexpensive but decent sangiovese from Trader Joe's.

"Voilá! A feast! Let us sit."

The sisters pulled up the two ladder-back chairs that Elena always seemed to find wherever she was. They sat on the rush

170

seats while Elena made the sign of the cross. Cristina enjoyed seeing her sister keep a tradition, though it was not one for herself. Then they began to eat, adding a little ground pepper here, a little of their mother's rich homemade mango chutney there, silently enjoying the first few morsels.

Elena spoke. "And Cristina? Are you happy? You look tired. Worried. Is your work all right? Are you thinking of marrying Jorge and that distresses you?"

"*Ay*, little sister. My job is always stressful, so that's just the way it is. But I love it anyway. I like to think I'm helping change things for the better – just as you do. In a different way. And as far as Jorge is concerned..." She stopped a moment and thought. "I do love him, in a way. We've been lovers for many years, as you know and have never approved." She gave a mischievous grin. "We're monogamous, I think. I am, anyway. But he understands I don't want marriage."

She smiled at her younger sister, whom she'd always tried to protect from her father's violence. "Usually, Elena, you intelligently keep such questions to yourself. I'll never marry Jorge or anyone else. Don't want to lose my independence. Ever! After seeing our parents' miserable marriage, and how Mother suffered until finally divorcing – Ernesto the Sneak – how all those dreadful years she'd kept with him for the good of the children...well... That lesson didn't go unheeded. And remember the great love story of Abelard and Heloise? I'm not the first to prize my independence! I notice you haven't remarried either. Only our brother in the family has a spouse, that Bardini girl. Amazingly, they claim to be happy. Well, that's good for them..."

Elena was silenced.

Cristina continued after a nibble at a lettuce leaf. "So it's better that we don't discuss this topic, right?"

Her sister replied. "*Pues*, of course. It was indiscreet of me. But I love you so much, Cristina. You've always been such a supportive sister. I hate to see you so unsettled." Elena twisted the gold ring on her left hand. "Some day I may marry again. But only for deep, deep love. The months Josh and I had together can last me a life time. Even though I still have nightmares about his plunging to earth over Viet Nam....I suppose I miss having a good man in my life...I do get lonely at times."

Mischeviously, she went on, "But Confucius say, better no man than poor man! Is Jorge poor or excellent?"

Cristina smiled back and took a large sip of the Catalán bubbly. "Nope. Forget it, little sister! You can't sell me on the idea of marriage! But I do appreciate the effort, dear. Why don't you tell me some of the cases you've encountered? Why don't you tell me about the Salvadorans, especially? I'd like to learn what they've encountered here, since I've worked with them in their own country."

Elena replied, "Well...it's a fascinating microcosm. It's the most prevalent Latino group in the Fairfax area. They work so hard. I love them. You know more than I do about the civil war of course."

She sighed with frustration. "But the gangs! The refugees to Los Angeles, including guerillas, formed a gang called Marasalvatrucha 13. Weird name. *Mara* means gang, of course, *salva* is save and *trucha* is trout. I wonder who thought that up! It's known here as MS 13. It started in LA, spread back home to El Salvador. Honduras and Guatemala, the US. Northern Virginia. Even Canada. International. About 70,000 members, the FBI thinks. Very big. Robbery. Rape. Drugs. Child and adult prostitution. Human trafficking. Central America has become a cauldron of crime. Mexico doesn't help."

She pursed her lips at the thought. "Now, even in Fairfax, the jewel of the crown in public schools, girls are enticed with offers of jobs by well-dressed people, not the blowsiness we associate with prostitution. And of course the refugees. The teenage sex trade is huge and growing with social media....I want to find out if they're linked to anything in Puerto Rico. And after Ponce, I do know something about gangs. The Zetas are in our island, and they're international."

Cristina said, "Frightening."

The sisters quietly ate their food, each lost in her own thoughts.

CHAPTER TWENTY

-Understand what the pulse of what different jobs entail...some need courage and others need subtlety. Intolerable jobs are the ones that require counted hours and certain materials; the ones with variety are more pleasant, they refresh the spirit.
Number 104. Baltasar Gracián, **The Pocket Oracle**

Elena
Months later
Fairfax, Virginia
Finishing her meeting just on time, Elena walked out of the Fairfax County Mental Health Clinic near Poplar Tree, again marveling at the services offered. She'd been observing the team for a high school boy recently released from the Oak Park residential facility for emotionally disturbed adolescents. Earlier, she'd seen the mother, yet another person fleeing El Salvador's violence and poverty. The woman now worked two jobs in Virginia and had not enough time to spend with her troubled son. At least they could eat and not fear killers in the street. She most likely would not be raped again. The Fairfax streets were far safer than San Salvador's.

Today Elena had joined the boy and his mother with another social worker, a psychologist, a therapist, a counselor, an interpreter and a representative of Oak Park. The youth had heard voices telling him to kill his stepfather. After a months's intensive treatment, he'd been released to return to South Lake

High School, still under the vigilance of the Special Education Department and now going to weekly therapy.

As Elena descended the steps of the unobtrusive, unmarked building, she thought about the boy. He seemed calm and lucid. For the moment.

What dreadful tales she'd heard. They made her own experience in Ponce pale in comparison. She looked at her watch. Yes, she should make it if she went five miles over the speed limit on Route 66. *Pedal to the metal.* She laughed at the expression.

Alexandria, Virginia

Elena pulled into the parking lot at the marina in Alexandria with time to spare. She parked her six year old Volkswagen and looked around. No one else here. After removing her skirt and sweater, she pulled on her stretch pants, heavy nylon top and rubber slippers, and took her paddle and life vest from the back seat. Then walked rapidly fifty feet over to the dry dock where her kayak awaited. It was on the second shelf of the small boat and canoe rack, just right for sliding easily onto the dolly. Wheeling the forty-pound vessel to the ramp jutting three feet into the water, she eased it off and returned the dolly to its site.

Aah, wonderful! She sat in the molded seat, scooting the kayak into the Potomac River. Used to kayaking in the south coast of Puerto Rico, she'd been ecstatic to find this soul-satisfying pastime was so readily available here.

Paddling against the current, she headed upriver so she'd be floating down on return. Very little traffic on the water at this time. A couple of crewed sculls and a few Laser sailboats seeking wind. Not much at the moment.

As she rhythmically dipped the paddle in the water, pulled it out, dipped again, she glowed at her surroundings. In the midst

175

of about ten million people, here she was. Alone.

Meanwhile she mulled over her brother Manuel's phone call last night. After checking out what was involved, she'd sent out her reworked resumé at six o'clock this morning, just before heading off for work. Manuel's best friend, Santiago Vázquez, had been an FBI special agent in Miami for years. Now Santiago was coming to Washington to head up the effort to ferret out Cuban spies, especially those working within the Federal government intelligence agencies. There were a couple of positions open in his new office and he wanted her to apply for the mid-level Spanish language analyst position. He knew she had all the entry qualifications and that she'd be an outstanding addition to his team. It had benefits and she would have access to an eventually permanent job. Why not? She mused. Her present social worker position afforded neither permanence nor much possibility for advancement.

Elena picked up the pace as the water beneath became more placid. The kayak slithered over the surface, fast as though lunging for the prize.

It will be well.

§

The FBI offices
Washington, DC
Two years after Elena's hire

Elena hunkered over the messages on her audiophones and computer. From her position in Santiago's office, she was translating hours of wiretapped conversations of known Cuban spies working out of Miami that the FBI had already uncovered. It turned out, to her surprise and Santiago's expectations, that she had a natural talent for this work far beyond mere competence. It was her special ability to focus and to detect nuance, using her natural intellectual gifts. The Fidel-allied Cuban network

176

called "Las Águilas" had penetrated Cuban exile groups and now was trying to burrow into US military sites in Florida, Virginia, and Texas. Elena was translating, reading, and hearing much of their talk and offering excellent observations.

She said to her immediate supervisor, "I hear so much information dealing with the Middle East and Russia. Even Yemen. Libya. Why is Cuba so interested in receiving confidential information that mentions them? I could understand a bit, but why so much?"

Eloise Bartlett, a longtime analyst for the Bureau, answered rather tartly, annoyed that someone who appeared so bright should ask such an obvious question. "To sell or trade. Cuba is probably one of the best conduits of information about the United States intelligence reports and they make major money for it. They sell to the highest bidder. All enemies of the United States. Is that not obvious?"

Elena ignored the putdown. She'd been subjected to worse in her career. "I'm beginning to see a pattern in these two. Look." Ms. Bartlett peered over her shoulder, where Elena had entered her two translations side by side. She mentioned, "It seems to be from the agent called *PALOMA,* and copied to…*AVE.* Their obvious code names."

"Hmm. Just keep on. Follow it."

§

Billy Bottoms
The DIA headquarters at Anacostia-Bolling Joint Base
Washington, DC
At the same time
In the Defense Intelligence offices, a portly white-haired fellow by the odd name of Billy Bottoms was talking to his boss. Billy had been around a long time, but his commitment and energy

never seemed to flag. In spite of his unremarkable appearance, Billy possessed a sharp mind.

"I'm telling you again I'm sure something is fishy about Cristina Franco. She just doesn't seem right to me. Let me repeat to you one incident that bothers me."

He nervously cracked the fingers of his large hands. His boss listened. One should always pay attention to Billy's ruminations, he'd discovered.

"I keep thinking about that incident at the Pentagon. There they all are, a top-secret meeting. Everyone had been told not to bring a cell phone. David was there too. He's the one who reported this to me. Yet Franco not only brought a cell phone with her, she got up to answer a call, took several minutes, then came back in to say she'd have to leave early. Please! They were in the middle of talking about how to handle Cuba in a particular situation and complaining about the huge number of double agents working for Cuba in the US Federal Intelligence Agencies. Please! No one answers a call and then comes back and announces she has to leave early. Come on! If anything is a trigger, that is! What arrogance! Her double life is doubling back on her!"

Peter Lassiter shook his head. "Come on, Billy. If arrogance were a crime, how many people do you know who'd be in jail? Come on! She's passed the lie detector test not once, but twice! She's just become full of herself with her continual upswings in career. Not unusual. I don't think she's so splendid, so competent, but she's leaving us in the dust behind."

Bottoms insisted, "David is on to her also. He's just cubicles away from her. And you know his reputation. Outstanding."

Lassiter grumbled. We've already gone over her finances. We

178

checked out her trips to the Dominican Republic. Cheap and warm, why not? She's frugal in her spending and her savings account matches her salary. She bought that expensive apartment when it was a bargain. She even got that merit award from the CIA director a year ago. We checked her out thoroughly several years ago when someone else was complaining about her. Finished her Masters thesis at Johns Hopkins and now a volunteer advisor to her old professor there. You really can't do too much better in this business!"

Billy insisted. "She lives like a monk, Pete. She never goes out for lunch, has practically no social life, except for some Latin American embassy receptions. She just studies and runs. The only people she sees are a professor, her sister and a boyfriend who's always travelling between here and Puerto Rico. She works late almost every day. I'm telling you; I know. I just know it. When I try to talk to her drinking coffee in the cafeteria, she just freezes up. She'll only talk to the higher-ups. And you know Cuba doesn't pay its spies. It uses people who are ideologically committed. Remember last year, when we caught six of our own spies in Cuba who turned out to be double agents? They're fanatics, not money-grubbers."

Billy continued in trying to convince his boss. "She has access to everything and has pushed people to share information with her. She's gotten a big award for outstanding service and now is poised to go even higher in the government. I tell you, she's scary! We've run through all the employees who have access to the leaks about the Muslim terrorists' plans that we've set as a trap, and she appears on every list. She knows everything. So she's a Johns Hopkins product...Bullshit! You know that Cuba targets the wonks at the top universities."

He paused before going on. "And I'm not a bigot, Pete. You know that."

Peter said nothing for a moment, thinking just the opposite. That quality did not obviate Bottom's real capabilities.

"My instinct is often right, Peter. You know that."

Lassiter nodded, "Just go on, Billy. Your clarification has been noted."

"Besides, she's a University of Puerto Rico graduate. That place is a hotbed of homegrown Marxists. They love Castro. I've been reading up on it…She probably goes way back. And her cousin is a Jesuit in El Salvador. You know those people can't be trusted."

Peter grimaced. His brother in law, a graduate of Loyola University in Baltimore, certainly didn't seem corrupted by the Jesuit association! But he gave in to the obstinate fellow in front of him. "Okay, okay, Billy. Go ahead and keep checking her if you feel so strongly about it. Make sure you keep your head down. You could be burned yourself. I don't agree with your take but … Go easy. You can go ahead on this since you've been right more than you've been wrong."

Peter considered for a moment. Extremists and terrorists were taking increasing advantage of the Marxists' hatred of America. As the United States became more and more mired in the Middle East, Asian and Latin American political and military machinations, things were surely getting worse. North Korea. Iran. Libya. Syria. Burma. All scary.

Well, this is what we do, he thought. Try to put the dots together. He said, "Go ahead and shadow her lightly awhile. Get one of your hotshots to cull through what's coming to and from Havana and see if you can trace a connection. Tedious work, but maybe it will give you something to hang your hat on." He yawned. He really didn't like this part of his job. It was so simple. And so complex.

180

"And dig into her friends in Puerto Rico, the group she ran around with before coming to the States. Might as well dig deeper."

Billy grinned in appreciation. "Thanks, boss. For now, I only have my old friend David keeping his eye on her. He has a great sixth sense, but one is not enough. I need a bigger cadre of good helpers. Two or three more to start with. We'll be low-key. Just persistent. You know me."

"Do I ever! Who do you have in mind?"

"Shea Wyman, outstanding in computers and very organized. And Jimmy Collins. He has a good cop's mind, an innate sense about ferreting out the bad guys. I can trust his judgment. Of course, I'll tap Smith now and then since he went to Cuba with her way back when. He may be no bolt of lightning but he's reasonably alert. Discreet. I'll send him to San Juan to look around."

"You have it. Get back to me as soon as you think you have something. Remember. Go easy."

"Thank you, sir."

Bottoms always uses the term of respect when he gets what he wanted, mused Lassiter. *What a bulldog!*

CHAPTER TWENTY-ONE

-Think ahead. Some people act before thinking, and then look for excuses.
Number 151. Baltasar Gracián, **The Pocket Oracle**

Cristina and Jorge Parrachini
A resort outside Washington
Middleburg, Virginia

Cristina and Jorge swam back and forth in the indoor heated pool. They both loved warm water, spoiled by the year ´round temperature of the Caribbean. After their exercise they lay next to each other on a big chaise longue to drink a caffe frappe. The resort was well laid out, a favored getaway for the Washington crowd.

"This was a great idea, even if only for the day," she said, toweling her long hair. "Thanks so much, Jorge. I really needed this respite. I've been working too hard, but you know how that is."

"I know how it is with you, *mi amor*. I've finally learned how to relax a little. The regular ten-hour days are not bad for people our age, but that's not all there is to life, is it? Eighteen hours is not an okay workday. Simply not acceptable anymore."

"Sure, sure. You're going to Puerto Rico again next week, right? Every other week, like clockwork."

"If I don't attend my constituents, I don't win elections. Simple. Anyway, that's been my job for awhile."

"Well, you've won once already.. What will you do next time, run again?"

"Supposedly. But if I can convince the governor to name me to the Puerto Rico Supreme Court, he can have a new running mate. Since I was sort of foisted on him, he'd probably be happy with that. And are you going to ever move back to Puerto Rico? Not interested in living on the island again, are you?"

Cristina closed her eyes and shook her head. "Well, Jorge, let's talk about it later, all right? Who knows? I'm not sure."

He smiled. He'd known this for years, just as he knew she'd never consider marriage. Several times she'd said so, as recently as a month ago. And it was definitely time for him to make his life without her. Now he must tell her it would be sooner rather than later. In fact, at this moment. Though they'd never discussed it, she'd assumed he had women friends in Puerto Rico. She'd never asked and frankly didn't much care, as long as they were together here.

Jorge thought of last week and how to break the news to her. There was no easy way.

§

The week before
Piñones Beach, Carolina, Puerto Rico
Jorge Parrachini and Maria Teresa Pascual gazed at the roaring sea in front of the deck where they'd been eating fried fish and *tostones*. He loved those deliciously crunchy fried green plantains with lots of salt. He looked at her once again, admiring the woman's lovely cinnamon skin, luminous eyes and perfectly shaped figure. In a

183

word, she was a knockout. Most amazingly, she wasn't awestruck with her own beauty. And her brains and buoyant personality matched the figure. Even better, she was honest and forthright. She might be the one, he'd thought for a while. Last night, he'd run his hands over that same beautiful body.

Each time with her was so special, he thought. I've never felt so excited and so loving at the same time. This was a first. Jorge hadn't realized this was possible, surely not in his relationship with Cristina. He loved Cristina in a way. But this was different.

As they sat in silence he thought about Maria Teresa's world and how they'd met.

After putting herself through college, Maria Teresa had become an invaluable administrator in her brother's office when he was mayor of the town of Loiza. Members of the Pascual family, famous in their area for being gifted musicians, dancers and entrepreneurs, the Pascuals also had political clout in Puerto Rico's northern coastal strip.

Then Governor Bardini had sought her out for his office at La Fortaleza in Old San Juan, where she'd met Jorge Parrachini a couple of years ago. The governor had to be in constant communication with him as he would be the only voice for Puerto Rico in Congress, as a non-voting member representing the US territory. They were of the same party and would try, at least for public consumption, to be on the same page. Each would have to win on his own merits and each would be bolstering the other. That's when it had begun between Jorge and Maria Teresa. Slowly.

Bit by bit, encounter by encounter. And finally, six months ago Jorge and Maria Teresa had ended in bed together. Anyway, Cristina wouldn't mind, he thought. She's so cool and analytical. I love her in a different way. We have another sort of relationship.

184

He looked at the deep dark blue waters stretching in their immensity to the horizon, where the lighter blue marked the sky. The rest of the earth beyond. Close by him the white crests rolled in, huge waves breaking on the golden sand, rumbling and plashing on the ear. It would be a great surfing spot if the surfer were adept. And very brave. He dreamt of his youth riding the waves. That fabulous sense of riding the waves, being at one with an inexorable natural force. Like lava flowing down a volcano. Like...Master of the universe. Not to be stopped, ever. Tropical wind blowing in his face, caressing. Eternal. I never thought it would end, he mused. So idyllic...Thank you, God, for youth...

Maria Teresa's voice broke the dream.

"Jorge, I have important news for you."

"Yes?" He looked away from the mesmerizing waves just a few yards in front of them.

"I found out for sure this morning. I'm pregnant."

His mouth fell open and eyes widened. "I...Congratulations, Maria Teresa. When can we get married? That is, will you marry me?"

She'd expected this reaction and had been mulling over her response. "Soon. I want the child to know he was wanted by his father. But we don't have to live together...we can divorce afterwards if you prefer ..."

"I prefer that we marry and stay married. Truly married. And rear a family."

"Then it's settled."

Silence a moment.

"Obviously you'll have to give up Cristina and any other woman. You'll be all mine, or not mine at all. And I, the same, of course for you. Fidelity. Trust. Is that what you wish?"

"Yes, yes, I do, Maria Teresa. I suppose that I was hoping this might occur…"

"Well, I, too, obviously. I've already spoken to the priest in my parish. Week after next, during your next trip he'll marry us at the rectory. We can go do our required blood work and papers today. Is that all right?"

Jorge laughed. She was always organized, very much ahead of the game.

She continued, sweetly. Her tone was always agreeable, never harsh or demanding. But firm. He liked women who were decisive. "And as you said earlier, you can continue your conversation with the governor about a judgeship for when you near the end of your term. He's already mentioned something about it to me. Favorably, of course. You should have time to tell Cristina and make it official in the next few days, when you're back in Washington. Formal," she said firmly.

"We'll be happy. We suit each other," he replied.

They grasped each other's hand, then kissed, passionately. Then they began to talk at the same time. What it would be like to be spouses and parents. Where they'd live…Dreams for the future.

§

Back at the resort
Middleburg, Virginia
Jorge told Cristina it was over.

She stared at him a moment, then said, "Well, it had to happen. Let's go back to Washington now. It's over and there's no reason to draw it out, is there..."

She forced herself to smile slightly and stood up to go. She could hardly breathe.

Not exactly heartache. Depression maybe. Anger? This part of her life was over. So abruptly that she hadn't had time to plan. The bastard.

How had she ever thought that she loved him? True, there were many parts of her secret life she couldn't share with him. So be it. But she'd thought their physical intimacy and their ease with each other, their intellectual and cultural interests, would be enough for him. As it had for her. She'd accepted that as the best she could do in the scenario of what people called "love".

She spoke in a low voice. "Let me change. I'll be ready to leave in about half an hour. Fine?"

Jorge was relieved, though he hadn't expected a scene from this self-controlled woman. She handled everything with finesse. "Sounds good. Meet you in the lobby."

They sped back to the city, both of them seeming cool and collected. Jorge turned on the classical music station WETA and they listened to Handel the whole trip. Wonderful music through a great sound system filled the car. Within, Cristina boiled with hurt and anger.

§

Later
Alexandria, Virginia
At their monthly supper, this time at Cristina's apartment, Ele-

na nursed a glass of Malbec. Each time Elena drank the Argentine wine, she thought of tango music. And how Josh and she had taken a few tango classes, when he'd come home for three weeks leave, before returning to war. And to his jet plummeting to earth in southeast Asia. Thinking of the *milonga* brought bittersweet memories. They'd never had a chance to go to Buenos Aires together to practice that romantic, sensuous dance…

Her sister was still recovering from Jorge's decision. It was a good time for them to be together. The balm of sisterhood flowed.

Elena's voice spoke up. "Cristina, I won't talk about my job, just as I know you can't talk about yours. But I know you used to be a Castro fanatic, so you'd be interested. I was reading the other day in **The Economist** about Fidel's killing three of his former comrades, who'd been with him from the very beginning in the Sierra Maestra. Everyone knows he killed a lot at the start of taking power from Batista, with supposed traitors…but now? What's the message? If you hang around him long enough, it's to the *paredón*?

"Hmm…"

"Oh, come on, *hermana*. I'm sure you have an opinion. Through your college days you were always preaching the gospel according to Fidel. And now you work for the other side, the Department of Defense. I'm sure you've changed your thinking, but even so…"

Cristina answered, "Well, I'm surprised to hear this, I have to admit. What issue did that appear in? I want to read it myself, though even you know that magazine is right-wing and capitalistic to the core. Every word is tainted with greed. Color it green."

"Well, I'd call it centrist right. Certainly it's capitalistic. But many good ideas. I read **The New York Review of Books** even though I don't agree with some of the writers. And please remember how you used to tell me to read all sides of the equation, as long as the sources are serious."

Cristina smiled at her sister's correction. "Yes, dear. Of course. I was very bossy when we were growing up, wasn't I?"

"You certainly were! But I always looked up to you. Admired you. I still look up to you. Your being in the DIA makes me proud I joined the FBI, too."

Cristina swirled her *cava* in her champagne glass and watched it go around and around. "You're kind to say so, Elena. You're a loving sister. You have always been very special for me."

She changed the subject slightly. "Did you read the recent comments of Gabriel García Marques? He adores Fidel, you know. Did you see that big picture of him with Fidel, both in their bathing suits in Cuba? **El País** in Madrid always features Gabo, as the fans call him."

"Yes, I know. Gabo also adores certain Central American dictators. He takes rides on their planes. In fact he adores celebrities who pay attention to him. Being a good writer doesn't mean having good political judgment."

"*Pues, hermanita.* That's true." Cristina sighed.

"Would you mind if I clean up the kitchen now? I have to leave tomorrow early for work." She stood.

Enough of this conversation. It disturbed her. She already felt desolate with Jorge's news that he was leaving her. And Fidel's loyalty? Surely he could be trusted!

189

The sisters hugged at the door as Elena left.

In fact Cristina had to go to Cuba in the morning. She'd stop at La Romana, her supposed destination for a short break from work. Then don a wig, change clothes, use her false passport and take a plane to Havana for conversations with her handler there.

But tonight she'd scan the article and surely mention it to her contact. The news had shaken her. And she was nervous about that fellow David always hovering around her as well. And his friend Billy Bottoms. She knew Bottoms' reputation as a dogged counter intelligence officer who played the buffoon. She knew he was no fool. And now he was always hanging out with Smith, trying to approach her. She was nervous. Though not admitting it to herself, Cristina sought reassurance. She'd started taking Lexapro on a regular basis, pleading stress about her romantic life to her cardiologist.

She turned on her laptop and read the article that bolstered Elena's comments about the executions. Of course, much of the press owed their access to the Miami rightists. Finding truth in the media was a self-deceptive exercise. How could she make good judgments?

Cristina's usual sangfroid had been slipping the last few days.

Before falling asleep, she thought of Teresa de Avila's observation: Faith without doubt is meaningless. Testing was part of it. Cristina added to herself: sure! In her case, faith in Marxism and Fidel demanded constance. There was no room for doubt.

CHAPTER TWENTY-TWO

-Strictly speaking...when once a country opines of another, it's probable that the opinion will be largely incongruous.
José Ortega y Gasset, **The Revolt of the Masses**, p. 400, E. Tecnos, 3d edition, 2013, Spain

The following day
Havana, Cuba

The emerald green island, all shades and hues, shone between the deep blue ocean below. Above the rich royal blue of a tropical sky at sunset. She felt the warmth awaiting her. It almost took her breath away. Why such a reaction? she thought. Maybe those months once upon a time in Spain on her father's military base, where winter's grey skies oversaw chilled earth and a mean-hearted father dominated the home. His voice in English, harsh to her ear instead of her mother's sweet-flowing Spanish and melodic Bavarian. Perhaps this beautiful island of Cuba, so close and yet so far from the United States, had become her talisman for warmth and understanding. It reminded her, of course, of her true homeland, Puerto Rico.

§

Diego Castello, her Cuban handler for the last few months, greeted her as she deplaned. She walked down the stairs onto the tarmac... No sophisticated air-conditioned skywalks for

Havana! Diego was a good-looking man, a fit five ten, thick black hair, piercing grey eyes, tanned skin, aristocratic nose, a relaxed air. He grinned at her disguise and they kissed each other de rigueur on the cheek.

"I know you, *PALOMA*. That wig doesn't fool me! But good try. If you want to work on disguises, we need to give you a couple more sessions when we meet again at La Romana."

She blushed. "Well, I just thought it would be a good idea. I used one of the passports your people gave me that had me with a wig, after all. Just trying it out."

"I don't know whose idea that was. To give you a passport like that! It was before I came on board. If you're going to use disguises, it should be highly professional. Otherwise, it just looks suspicious. Really strange! Well, you're here. That's good. Welcome."

"Thanks. By the way, it's good to see you in Cuba instead of Rock Creek Park on the jogging path, trying to look as though we don't know each other. Or in La Romana, cramming trade-craft. But speaking of tradecraft, now we're in Cuba I can call you by your real name, Diego. Your codename Zorro sounds so very, very stagey. Don't you think?"

He chuckled. "I suppose. Well, it's good to see you too, Cristina."

He let the comment sit a moment before going on. "We're going to a safe house we're using now for our most valued informants. Very nice, on Guardalavaca Beach. No telling who's coming to our country these days, we have so many tourists in Cuba – especially from Europe, Russia, Canada, some from Latin America and Asia and even the United States - that we must be extra careful in dealing with our special friends. Like you. You'll have space to walk around, several acres around the house. Back in the old days it belonged to one of the wealthy sugarcane oligarchs. "

He picked up her bag and led her to an ancient black Mercedes in mint condition, driven by a stone-faced thin black man that Diego used as his factotum.
"You've seen Leandro before," he said as they got in the car.

Leandro and Cristina nodded at each other in recognition.

Sitting in silence, they drove through the streets. No traffic jams to worry about. Few new cars. A few virtual antiques, repainted and outfitted. The buildings as decrepit as usual. A couple of nice looking, tight-pants girls in high heels cuddled next to a couple of older, prosperous-looking sunburned men in flowered shirts, a throwback to earlier days. Yet more of the same, she saw. She knew much of the tourism was sex-orient-ed. Poor people sell their bodies to eat and to buy a few extras not generally available. She knew Fidel complained about it, but the trade had become lucrative for the establishment as well as for the poor. That whole subculture flourished. Cristina couldn't help recalling Winston Churchill's comment that so-cialism allowed everyone to be poor together. Economic incen-tive for the individual was irrelevant to the *fidelistas.*

My existence seems so surreal. Sometimes I wonder where I am.

§

Evening had fallen. A big white colonial house loomed ahead at the end of a long graveled drive. The stucco showed signs of age but it was still elegant. She was shown into a large room with a canopied bed and an old-fashioned armoire, sitting re-gally in the ample space. A huge white mosquito net draped over the bed. A small upholstered chair and simple wooden desk stood in the corner. She stepped outside to a little balco-ny overlooking a stand of lime trees in blossom, white flowers

193

exuding a delicious scent. The fragrance floated up to Cristina. Nature's gift.

Then she entered the old-fashioned bathroom with thirties-era porcelain. Very neat and clean, Ivory soap and fluffy towels on the little bench. She quickly took a handheld shower, changed into a pair of white jeans, sandals and a bright magenta cotton pullover. Looked in the bathroom mirror: the little wrinkles around her large eyes, the somber expression, stress-lines. I've changed, she thought. It's not just age. I'll have to take better care of myself, not only exercise, nutritious food and sparse alcohol…maybe start yoga. Perhaps…a new lover. Someone who knows who I am.

She joined Diego in the patio, who sat awaiting her in the shade of a flamboyant tree. Fallen red petals had laid a carpet over the grass, illuminated by spotlights. Light and shade, dark night beyond, subdued colors in this garden. Beautiful. Two wicker chairs and a little table awaited them. He offered her a glass of water and a plate of farmer's cheese with sugared *guayaba* shells and crusts of *pan criollo*. "Would you like a cup of delicious Cuban coffee?" he said.

"Of course! Always! Thank you."

"Sugar, right?"

"Yes, please. Two."

Diego nodded to Leandro who was standing nearby.

He quickly returned with the demitasse cup on a little tray. She sipped the delicious *espresso*. The scent, the taste, the breeze… She inhaled all with great gusto. A moment of contentment.

They sat quietly a moment and Diego spoke. "I know your re-

194

lationship with Jorge Quintana-Kelly is over. I know that your agency is aggressively seeking out sources for leaks and that you are one of the people on the list. I also know your sister is now working for the FBI. And that your mother wants you and your sister to celebrate her birthday in San Juan. These conflicts must be causing you anxiety. Yes?"

"True. All my own problems. I'll take care of it…"

She took a deep breath and went on. "And now it seems that Fidel has ordered the execution of three men considered his stalwarts. Is this how the revolution progresses? Is this what I'm working for? The reward for loyalty?"

She marveled at how they seemed to know so much about her. They owned her, an unsettling thought.

Diego said, "There was proof that the trio was betraying the cause, selling our secrets to the United States. It had been going on for a whole year. Very damaging for Cuba. Treason is punishable by death, you know. It's not trivial. That's always been the way."

"Could you show me any proof? I have to admit I've been very upset by what I read."

"If I could arrange a personal meeting with Fidel? He can tell you himself. Would that help?"

She swallowed a sip of water, surprised with her own audacity. "Perhaps."

§

Later that evening, Diego said, "It's been arranged. Rest for awhile, read some of the material I've given you. Take a nap.

195

I'll fetch you around midnight. We'll see the leader tonight."

Of course. Stalin-style, she thought unhappily.

Later on, Cristina was taken to a different place from the one she'd gone to three years back to meet *el Jefe*, just an hour's ride from the safehouse, also in the country. This was a simple bungalow.

Now for the waiting interlude. Diego and she sat on a little porch, slowly rocking in two country-style mahogany rockers from the old days. The tiny noise of the rockers on tile was steady, clickety-clic, clickety-clic. The humid night air, being near the sea, smelled of salt and seaweed. Fireflies, poetically called *cucubanos*, flashed in the dark night. It was so quiet, other than the rockers, she thought she detected the sound of waves crashing on the shore nearby. Were it not for this meeting, she would have called the scene idyllic.

An hour later, to her surprise, an attendant came out to bring another rocking chair. Moments afterwards, Fidel emerged from the doorway. Dressed of course in fatigues and boots. But the venue was certainly different from the usual.

Diego and she stood as he approached.

"Good evening, Cristina. Or I should say *Paloma*. It's a pleasure to see you again." He smiled and put out his hand to shake. She responded.

He nodded at Diego. "*Saludos, compañero.*"

He gripped Diego's hand in greeting and pulled him close in a typical Latin bearhug.

Then he stepped back, took out a cigar from his shirt pocket, cut off the end. A guard sprang from the corner of the porch to light it. After puffing to get the fire going, Fidel held it in between his fingers and considered it before speaking. Not only one of the world's great orators who could hold thousands spellbound for hours, he also had a way about him. He stood comfortably. His expressive voice resonated though he didn't raise his voice as he addressed her. "How are you? I wanted to congratulate you personally for the work you're doing for Cuba. I consider you one of our most important patriots working in the United States."

Fidel's gaze was steady and radiated sincerity. In fact Fidel usually believed what he said at the moment, even if later in the day he might add or subtract something to the former truth. "You know we are in an economic stranglehold because of the Yankees. Life is a struggle. Yet people don't starve. We provide education for all our youth, not just a privileged few."

Then he gestured towards the chairs. "Let's sit."

Diego looked surprised, and Cristina assumed this was highly unusual, a sign of intimacy afforded very few.

The three sat in the rockers. Fidel continued speaking. "Our math literacy rate is better than that of the US and the Americas. In the New World only Canada beats us. Our doctors are considered among the world's best primary physicians. In times of emergency we send doctors and teachers to Venezuela, to Africa, where they are welcomed with open arms. Our athletes are Olympians. World-acclaimed writers seek us out." He stopped to stare at his cigar before going on. "We are a people of intelligence, passion, hard work. And not capitalists, for sure! Wall Street doesn't dictate to us. Armament companies and bankers don't give me millions in kickbacks as campaign funds. I listen to the people."

He took a few puffs and waited for her to speak.

She stuttered. "I know this."

197

Then she took a deep breath.

It was one thing to have a commitment to an ideal. And quite another to be conversing with the world's longest living world leader, who had unlimited power in his country. Who had long been the epitome of her ideal of Hispanic culture and social justice.

Cristina spoke. "It's why I work for Cuba. I've seen bullies in my lifetime and I know the United States government qualifies. I realize the work you do...And ever since high school I've understood the horrible chasm between the haves and the have-nots in the world. Ever since then I've wanted to do something to remedy it. My life's work. I saw you on television in the earliest days of the revolution. You inspired me then and you still do. What you've done with Cuba is so important. And you've given me this opportunity to be part of it. I can't tell you how vital this is to my life."

"And yet?" he queried. With his huge frame, he bent down a little to her.

She dared say. "News is circulating on the internet that three revolutionary heroes were executed last week. Of course, I find that disturbing."

"Ay, *Paloma.* I'm happy you are concerned. When I discovered those three were *gusanos* (worms), spies for the Yankees and traitors, you can imagine how I felt. They'd been with me since the early days. I risked my life for each of them. Many times. Traitors have one end. Death with dishonor."

He began to slowly rock in the chair. ""Of course the *gusanos* in Miami are always sending out anti-Cuba news. Lies. Sabotage. They'll do anything to take over our country, to enrich themselves with stolen goods."

Caught up in the *commandante*'s charisma Cristina smiled and acquiesced. Relief. Surely it was the way he said.

Fidel abruptly stood up. "Well, my dear. I must leave. It's been good to talk you. Again, I admire your dedication, your courage. Know that you are truly appreciated. The information you give us is of the highest quality. It allows us to go forward, to achieve victory in a savage world. Know this. Treasure your knowledge, your actions. Some day you'll come here to live and grow old in peace. But before that – whenever you visit Cuba, I want to see you. Understood, Diego?"

Diego answered, "*Si, jefe. Con gusto.*"

His aura outsized the porch. Castro held out his arms to hug her. Then he gave a slight bow and left. Just as in their meeting before, it seemed to her that the air was being sucked out of the area when he left.

Diego, enthralled with the exchange, gave her a little bow as well. "It's time for us to go, too, *Paloma*. Congratulations. This has been a memorable evening for me."

Soon enough they were back at the safe house. Cristina lay in her bed, the ceiling fan droning, the sound of frogs and insects singing in chorus, the gentle breeze wafting the mosquito net. She found it hard to sleep, still thinking over her encounter with Fidel and her own life. Her need to be solitary yet not so alone.

She heard knocking at the door. Moving aside the netting, she got up to open it. "Yes?"

Diego was there. Dressed in brown shorts and a white t-shirt and holding two wine glasses and an open bottle of *cava*. "Would you like company? Walk? Or…"

"Yes. Come in."

CHAPTER TWENTY THREE

-Don't be mistaken about people...
Number 157. Baltasar Gracián, **The Pocket Oracle**

Returning from Havana to Dulles
Cristina recalls her sixth visit to El Salvador
in December 1981
The Mozote Massacre
Flying from Havana to La Romana, then on to Dulles, Cristina had ample time to consider what had led up to her meeting with Fidel. She recalled the time in El Salvador when she'd heard about Mozote in gruesome detail. It was such acts that confirmed her faith in her cause. And Castro.

It had been unusually cold in Washington, and the warm respite to El Salvador had been welcome. Cristina greeted the sinewy young man who slouched into the tiny office assigned her for his bi-monthly trips from Central America. She eyed him appraisingly. Tanned and fit and dressed in a disheveled khaki-colored suit, he didn't belong here, but in the jungle.

"Hello, Raymond. It's good to see you again. Sit down, please. Would you like a glass of water? Coffee?"

She indicated the visitor's chair in front of her small desk. "Let me know what you have for me. It's Mozote, isn't it?"
He grimaced, his tight face straining to control itself. "Well,

200

yes, water and black coffee, please. No sugar. And of course it's Mozote. I'm going to tell you exactly what I saw."

She filled a glass of water from the dispenser, and heated up the coffee in the old electric coffee pot that rested on a rickety little table. Serving him at her desk, she watched him drink. She'd learned to be patient.

A litter of papers organized by colored file tags cluttered the desktop. Setting them in order, she pulled a yellow tablet and pencil to the front. Meanwhile her shoe tapped on the tape recorder switch on the floor that responded to the light touch. The recording would go to her boss in Washington. The mini-recorder between her breasts would provide the recording for her real handlers.

"I want to take notes for myself, as you know," looking at him with that serious, intense way she had. She knew her fellow analysts at the Agency didn't especially care for her, thinking her a cold if polite and smart machine. They feared her frigid manner, her ambition and ferocious work ethic. She knew they sought a way to bring her down, fueled by office politics that could masquerade as patriotism. If they only knew the passion that raged within, opposing all they believed in. Even so, she could relate to some of those in the field. She admired their bravery, her enemy or not.

"How've you been? You look distraught. Not your usual stoic self."

Raymond nodded his head in agreement, his tired dark eyes reflecting a wounded spirit. "This is the worst assignment I've ever had. You'll see."

He sipped the warmed-over, stale coffee and frowned. "First I have to tell you that I know well the rebels have assassinated various government figures here. No doubt about it. They are far from being angels. They have learned the ruthless way of communists everywhere. We can't trust any of them. The rebels are their good students and have become adept at the trade of guerilla warfare. They're ably taught by Nicaragua's Sandinistas and Castro's Cubans. Just as cruel. When I was undercover in Castro's Cuba, I saw innocent men shot down at the *paredones*. No excuse for that. But I never saw children executed until now. There were babies, for God's sake! And I saw it done by the rightists, the government military, the ones we support. I helped train one of their leaders."

He stopped a moment and closed his eyes. "*Hijo de la gran puta! Mierda!*"

This experienced warrior opened his eyes quickly and continued. "It makes me question why we are here in the first place. To return to the village of El Mozote. I went with an advance of the Atlacatl Battalian to the village just to check it out two days before the army was to go through, making sure the village wouldn't cause any problems. We alerted the big man in town, Marcos Díaz, that the military was coming, to stay calm. Mozote wasn't the target, I'd been told. Díaz, who had been a good leader in the past, gathered the villagers to warn them the troops would be passing through in a counterinsurgency operation. He said not to leave, since if they fled they'd be mistaken for guerrillas by the military. Peasants from nearby villages flooded Mozote then, to be out of harm's way. The town was normally about 300 but it had more than doubled in size within days. A safe haven."

He took a deep breath and paused. Cristina waited in silence.

Then he went on. "By the way, El Mozote was mostly Evangelical Protestant, so they weren't associated with the *Monseñor* or the Jesuits. You know the government and military consider the Catholic radicals to be rabble rousers, even terrorists. And

202

the village of Mozote did supply food to the guerillas, to the communists. All the villages had to. Or be burned out. Even so the village wasn't known as fertile ground for recruits. It had a reputation for neutrality within what has been an increasingly rebel-held territory..."

Cristina tapped her pencil on her desk. *Please get through with this,* she thought. *I can see it all in my head. I've already heard what happened.*

The soldier shook his head. "I saw this with my own eyes. It was dark, early morning. Mist was beginning to rise from the woods. An eerie feeling. The Atacatle battalion roared into town on open trucks, followed by marching troops. They pounded on the doors of the thirty or so mud brick homes, each one packed with people. Forced everyone to come out and lie down in the plaza. After about an hour they let them go back home. People were sure the worst was over. But then, just as dawn was breaking, they forced everyone back to the plaza."

Raymond stopped speaking for a moment, as he saw the scene in his mind. He took a sip of water before going on.

"The women and children were put into a single home, and the soldiers took the men and started beating them. At noon, the soldiers took the women and young girls out to the hill next to the village. Raping and killing them. I kept talking to the army leader, telling him to stop the savagery. I had taught this monster at a class at the *Escuela de las Américas* in Panama. Then they took the older women and children into the church where soldiers waited to shoot them. Some soldiers hesitated to kill children, but their officers insisted. If they hadn't obeyed they'd be killed themselves. After murdering all the villagers but one who escaped, they burned down the houses and left the ruins. Those innocent children..."

He shook his head and closed his eyes, visualizing the scene again. It was one that would haunt him all his life. "The soldiers went on to the next village to keep on slaughtering, but I had to leave. I knew military. That's my job with the Department of Defense special operations, in cooperation with the CIA as need be. That's it."

Eyes burning as he finished, this strong man brushed his cheek.. "Only you. I'm not allowed to report to anyone else but you."

Horrible. Horrible. And how embarrassing for him, thought Cristina. *Strong men don't weep. Even over such tragedy.*

The two sat in silence.

Cristina felt anger roiling within. How could people be so vicious and her own government be so crass, so evil as to support these killers? Her face remained stolid, a mask she'd mastered.

"Thank you, Raymond," she said crisply. "You have to go back, you know. And keep reporting to me every three months. Just do your best. You always do, I know."

He looked at her uncertainly. *She's as bad as the ambassador now,* he thought. *Just as cold, lacking understanding. Stupid.* A previous ambassador, Robert White, had been a polished professional with the Foreign Service with an outstanding name as a man of integrity and knowledge. Coming to El Salvador with full lifetime experience, he'd mounted a thunderous dissent against what he'd called the "primitive anti-communism" of the US government in Latin America. He'd spoken clearly to press and Congress about El Salvador's repugnant and immoral regime, and received death threats in kind. Summarily dismissed from the ambassadorship, he quit the State Department.. The new ambassador, properly compliant, was certainly not going to rock the boat. Raymond pushed back the chair, scraping the

204

floor. He nodded to Cristina, gave her an ironic smile and left the room.

She understood Raymond's disillusionment. The repetition of violence was numbing. And who in the USA really cared about all those foreign names and places? Better a dream of ideals than a nightmare of reality. Once again, she considered her own options.

Yet... She wondered if yet another pending congressional committee's findings would dissuade the US Congress from funding the Salvadoran military. Not likely...Lobbyists and huge amounts of cash flowed from armament contractors. Always had. Always will. Abraham Lincoln had problems with corrupt legislators and lobbyists during the Civil War. Men died then because of shoddy boots and misfiring rifles.

She thought, *Fear of communism in Latin America is a given in American politics.. The powers that be don't know how to act.. They think it's about money. Power. Ambition. Arms. Defend and arm the oligarchs, the masses will follow, and all will be well. If they only knew the truth. That we, the true believers, will never give up.*

She had watched Raymond leave the room, regretting that she couldn't show empathy. But to keep her reputation as a hard-line follower of the official line demanded it. Her double life perturbed her at times like this. Unsure of who she was. Unsure of what she truly believed. Unsure of her own loyalties.

CHAPTER TWENTY-FOUR

-The beings I love are creatures. They were born by chance. My meeting with them was also by chance. They will die. What they think, do and say is limited and is a mixture of good and evil. I have to know this with all my soul and not love them the less... We want everything which has a value to be eternal.
"Chance". Simone Weil, **Gravity and Grace**, Paris 1947

Elena; Paul
Falls Church, Virginia
Washington, DC

Elena Franco had fitted into her job at the FBI as though she'd been groomed for it. A perfect fit. A glove. She'd enjoyed her social work career, but this was interesting on so many other levels. She did miss working with people, helping resolve their problems. But she also loved this: working with language and therefore culture, looking and patterns, trying to resolve problems in a very different way. She was re-reading Benjamin Lee Whorf about language, the extraordinary way mindsets create and are affected by the possibilities of word choice in a language. Not the now-old adage about Eskimos' having more than a dozen words for snow: good for building, storm, travel and so on. But even concepts differ. One Southwestern Indian tribe, Whorf claims, intrinsically understands the principles of physics better than Indo-European speakers simply because a noun for a phenomenon carries within it the action. Such a lightning. It doesn't merely strike, as the European mind would visualize. It simply IS.

The constant workshops she'd been sent to opened a new world. A whole different mindset from intense personal interactive social work, for sure. But life was full of possibilities and choices. It forced her eyes open even more to the world around her.

Jogging early in the morning before going out to catch the Metro, she padded by the *bodegas* and meat markets that were still covered with grill work. They'd open at 9 o'clock. She'd gotten used to the down at the heels neighborhood where she lived, had decided to stay here though she was making a better salary. She just saved the money for travel and gave a healthy chunk to charity. She considered it a reality check: not a slum, not yet anyway, it reminded her of Santurce back home, minus blue skies and warm air. The buildings, the graffiti, the sidewalks all needed cleaning. A nearby park allowed trees to grow in the densely-populated area. Just a few people were out: a couple of joggers like herself, frisky school children walking to the early bus with their mother, a smelly vagrant shuffling along with his cart. She smiled at each as she passed them by. From her studies in New York City and work in La Playa de Ponce, she'd early on decided she would recognize passersby as human beings, fellow souls, not cogs in a machine. It was too easy to fall into the habit of self-regarding greymind. Wherever she might be, Elena would always seek the light.

As she passed the street person, he looked up from pushing his cart to respond to her smile. His rheumy eyes blinked at the unaccustomed attention. Then he winked at her. Startled and inexplicably pleased, she smiled again and went on. *Así es la vida!*

Back in her apartment, Elena showered and dressed in her regular outfit for work. Today was a striped navy and white knee length linen dress that showed off her figure without ostentation, a white cardigan, comfortable and stylish low heel pumps and leather purse. She'd bought five good-looking coordinates at Ann Taylor Loft for each season and tended to wear them over and over, just replenishing as needed. Her wardrobe had definitely gone a little upscale since she'd left her job as a social worker. They were good quality and lasted. Either that, or the styles will change so drastically she'd have to buy new clothes. Fine with her.

At 8 AM she trotted down the right side of the escalator to the depths of East Falls Church Metro station. As usual the morning workers clogged the area, and she had to dodge an elbow. Within half an hour was at her building, flashed her badge at the entrance and was going up to her cubicle at the FBI building. Her cell phone rang, the sound a temple chimes effect, and she looked at the number. She didn't recognize it.

"Elena Franco?" a well-modulated man's voice spoke.

"Who's calling her, please?" She couldn't place the accent.

"Hello. Elena. This is Paul Fitzgerald. Your cousin James gave me your number. We're friends since college days. Holy Cross. In fact we were room-mates for awhile. He went off to join the Jesuits and I went off to law school, practice here in DC. Anyway, I just saw James in San Salvador. I'm a lawyer, have a couple clients there. Actually, your sister gave me your number years ago, and I lost it, didn't call her back to retrieve it. James asked me to call you and see if we could get together ... maybe a sandwich at lunch time?"

"I see. What's your name? Paul Fitzgerald, you say?" She thought she vaguely remembered the name. She'd call James to make sure. Or ask Cristina.

"Yes. Fitzgerald. I visited him in Puerto Rico once, just after

208

college and we went to the beach with you and your sister. Many moons ago! I even met your mother once."

Now she vaguely remembered meeting him at the beach and later her mother Lise's saying that James and his good-looking room-mate at college had come by their apartment to see the girls. Her mother, a Salzburg native, had been so delighted to speak German with James's friend. There wasn't much of an opportunity to speak German in Puerto Rico.

"Do you speak German, Paul?" she asked. Just to make sure he was the person she thought.

He chuckled. "Yes, a bit rusty now. I studied it in high school and was able to go as an exchange student to Austria before going to college. Salzburg, your mother's hometown. Just for a year, but I studied hard and learned it. Anyway, your mother and I had a great conversation in German, mine with a bit of an accent of course."

He sounded definitely on the up and up she said. "Well, I have lots of work to do still and won't be free until about seven or eight. But...How about a light dinner then? Are you in down-town DC?"

"Nearby," he replied.

"Well, I'm in Arlington now. I can be in DC in minutes...We could meet someplace if you'd like, at eight if that would be good for you."

She thought, I've been working so hard, not gone out at all except to concerts by myself. An occasional glass of wine or supper with a co-worker or my monthly dinners with Cristina. Now and then an exhibit at the National Art Museum. Why not? He sounded interesting. And she'd love to hear a first-hand report about James.

He continued. "Old Ebbitt's Grill? I can make reservations for 8:30 if you need more time." "Sure, Paul. That sounds good."

He responded "Fine. I'll wait for you at the bar, just next to the entrance." She liked the salads and soups there. Oysters, too. So be it. It would be fun to see someone from way back when. And hear how her favorite cousin was doing in that wartorn country of El Salvador She knew Cristina had seen him when she'd been there for work. That evening Elena walked through the doors at Old Ebbitt's, right on time. Noisy and crowded as usual, yet welcoming with its well-oiled dark wood and agreeable ambiance, the marble-topped bar spanning a good forty feet. Towards the door sat a fiftyish, fit man with a shock of dark red hair, brilliant blue eyes and a smile on his handsome face. He looked like a pure Celt she thought. *My lord, the Irish areeverywhere!* He bounded to his feet and walked towards her with an athletic step.

"Elena?"

"Paul?"

They laughed and nodded in unison as they greeted each other with a social kiss. "Well, good to see you again, Elena. We have a table over there." He gestured and led her to it. Within moments they were talking about the past, renewing acquaintance, mentioning James and Paul's visit to Puerto Rico years before.

"That was a great time!" he said. "We were all on fire then, weren't we? I remember Cristina talking about a big march she'd just taken part in, in front of the University of Puerto Rico on Ponce de León. I was so impressed with a street being named after him. Cristina was a big socialist at the time, I think. And now she's with the US government…"

He paused and raised an eyebrow.

210

Elena smiled and said, "That's true. It was very important for her."

"I recall meeting your mother on another trip with James, her filling me in about the colonial status of Puerto Rico. She gave us a glass of *coquito* and a little plate of *turrones*.. Same thing my mother's Cuban families do at Christmas, serve that Spanish almond and honey candy and the coconut drink. Christmas food in January, Three Kings and all. Amazing how one's memory comes back to such small incidents."

Elena closed her eyes for a brief moment, and her own childhood memories ran before her. "Yes. It's lovely. My sister was a leader. I've always looked up to her, my brilliant, intense older sibling. And she was always kind and generous to me. It surprised us all that she wanted to work for the Federal government later on. But College is the time to be a rebel, isn't it? I didn't like the greedy capitalistic system either, but I went more the Catholic Worker route at first...I wasn't that austere in character though, in the long run, I have discovered I can live simply. Actually, I enjoy it. Even so, I was never pulled into the same group as Cristina. I always figured there were more pacific ways to save the world! Thank God we live in the US, as decadent as it can be! We can choose our own path. And at least we have a vote and are open to change. As Cristina's guru Gracián says, 'never lose your self-respect...integrity is all.' The world around us has to be taken with a grain of salt, doesn't it?

"True, true," Paul replied. "We have corruption, of course. Always. Up and down, isn't it? I've been reading biographies of the founding fathers. Become a fan of sorts of John Quincy Adams, old prune face. But did he ever have smarts and integrity! Always against slavery. Did you know the only way Jefferson beat him for president was because the votes from the South included three fifths of a vote for every slave? And of course, who would in fact vote in place of the slave? And then

Jefferson didn't even free his slaves in his will. Equality? Great leader? Hypocrite! Our adoration for him is absurd!"

Elena replied, "Those were my thoughts when I went to visit Monticello, Jefferson's beautiful old home. I left there unhappy...."

Then she asked abruptly, "Have you been married?"

"Yes. A long time ago. My work got in the way. We were both in law school then, and our careers came first. I know you're a widow, James told me."

"Yes." She was glad to get that out of the way.

He shook his head and returned to the subject. "Today mirrors those days of Jefferson in one way or another, doesn't it? Families change. Our rights are always in dispute. Politicians haven't gotten any better. The problem with immigration, for example. If we were to impose heavy fines on employers for hiring undocumented workers, don't you think that job market would dry up? People come here to work and to have an education! It's better than staying home in Central America and risking death to change the system. El Salvador is horrendous. Just thirteen families or so control the whole country. It doesn't occur to them that democracy and laws just might be a way to avoid the awful violence of their leftover feudal system. Honduras is even worse, Guatemala not far behind. Ironically, the most left-leaning Nicaragua is probably the least violent. Now."

He paused and then said, "Of course, my mother's homeland, Cuba... Cuba was not better under Batista for the poor... there were the haves and have-nots and the vestiges of slavery...but racial lines were not as fixed as in the United States. Twentieth century progress had erupted more there than most places in the Caribbean and Latin America...electricity, cars, inventions, colleges, music…some upward economic mobility…Now, it's a different world. Middle class wiped out. I was able to go there just a year ago, and…My mother's family had left long before, during World War II, when her father worked for the War Department in Washington as an economist. She grew up in the States. A Virginian. Met my father in DC when she went to a women's college here. Trinity. I became good friends with my Cuban cousins when they visited us…"

He stopped, embarrassed. "You don't need to hear all that. I'm sure you've had your fill of Cuban refugee stories. Lots in San Juan. So many of my friends and relatives fled to Puerto Rico. And Miami of course."

Smiling, she said, "On the contrary. I love to hear the stories. Tell me about your cousin and why they left when they did. What happened to prompt it?"

"My cousin was a boy, only twelve. His father favored Fidel at first. Batista had been a thug, remember. Fidel seemed promising at first. Remember, Cuba had a definite class and racial strata – rich whites, middle class *mulatos* – that Spanish word has fallen from favor, hasn't it? and, poor dark blacks. Race and money usually went hand in hand, but there was also crossing over economic and racial lines. The family was middle-class, always a little pinched for food and clothes. It was hard to make a living. My uncle was an electrician, light brown of skin, very hard working, happy, a good father. His own father was from Asturias, Spain, his mom from the island. She was the reader. My maternal grandparents. When Tío got a chance to get a job in Miami through one of his old bosses, he jumped at it. The very same month Fidel entered Havana, imagine! We were all excited about the fall of Batista but the offer of a sure job was too much to turn down for my uncle. So his family left before Cuba really changed. My cousin got the chance to go to a good public school in the States, learn English, even go to Madrid

213

for a semester…and got a scholarship to college."

He stopped to drink a sip of water. How much should he share with Elena? Obviously not the part of his job that entailed keeping his eye on her sister while he still probed the unresolved story behind the American nuns' killers. But the rest…why not?

"My father was Boston Irish. And I grew up in Virginia. He was just fanatical about being Irish as my mother was about being Cuban, but they were also fanatical Americans. So – my ancestors were all immigrants to this country Of course, anyone who isn't American Indian is immigrant.."

The waiter interrupted their banter with the menus. "Good evening, madam and sir. I'm Fong, your server this evening. Oysters of the day from Prince Edward Island? Beer? Wine? Our specialty of the day is rockfish from our very own Atlantic Coast off Norfolk, Virginia. Comes with tamarind sauce, served with roasted little potatoes and herbs, and marinated beets. Delicious."

They looked up at the young man and thought a moment, didn't bother opening the menus.

Paul said, "Let's order right away. What would you like, Elena?"

"Good, I'm starving! How about a sauvignon blanc and rock-fish?"

"Sounds good. I'll have the rockfish and a dark Guinness, Fong. And a dozen oysters, that you can help me polish off, I hope, Elena."

Within minutes they were served the drinks and oysters and fresh bread.

214

He slathered hot horseradish over it before slurping one of the oysters with gusto. "This is delicious! Will you have a few?"

It was done. Bread was broken.

The couple fell into a rhythmic patter of speech and eating. Elena hadn't felt so comfortable with a date for a very long time. Paul had naturally changed since she'd first met him at the beach years ago. His brilliant blue eyes still reflected his love of life and intense interest in the moment. But now little crow-feet wrinkles around the orbs showed some thought had gone on in the brain, sun on the face. And some wrinkles around the mouth. Laugh lines. That was good. He was still good-looking, but his flaming red hair had dimmed darker, with a little white at the temples. He hadn't lost any of it. That was good. Still lean, strong looking, hadn't acquired the paunch that so many deskbound men did. That was good. And best of all, he had a way about him of unpresuming self-confidence, attention to detail but a casual, real politeness. His way of expression was clear and thoughtful. He had gravitas. She liked him.

He looked at her eyes. They understood.

He said, "After all this time not seeing each other, I feel as though we've just been interrupted in a recent conversation."

Laughing at his reaction, she answered, "I feel the same way. But go on," she urged. "I love to hear stories." Elena was a listener. An analyzer.

"So…back to Cuba…as you know, Miami has become the capital of Latin America. It was the Cubans who started the trend not all that long ago."

He hesitated. "I don't know why I'm talking so much about this. I never talk about it with anyone." He was embarrassed at his spilling out these stories. But Elena inspired him to share his life…somehow…

"Go on," she encouraged. "I'd like to hear more. Everyone has a story. And yours and mine dovetail somewhat,"

"Well, the elite had access to good schools and college, good jobs, travel, all that. Some were phenomenally wealthy – you know the Cubans in Puerto Rico always talk about their family's great fortunes…well often enough it was true. '*Oye, hermano, como en Cuba mi familia era tan rica que…* (Listen, brother. Since in Cuba my family was so rich that…) and so on. And it was a cockeyed system…the grandfather would have huge cattle farms and sugarcane, and then buy houses so his heirs could live on the rentals and belong to the yacht club…"

"The private and Catholic schools were good I hear. Excellent education for those who could afford it. Many maids and gardeners, lots of illiteracy. But a burgeoning urban middle class, too. In the eighteenth and nineteenth centuries, there were vast sugar cane and cattle farms, worked by the blacks. In the late eighteen hundreds, Spain encouraged a lot of immigration to Cuba, since it was turning into a black colony – like Jamaica under the English. And my family…we just didn't think about the very poor. My mom's great grandfather was from poor tenant farmers in Andalusia, so to be poor working class in Cuba was a step up. He was able to study accounting and did well, was able to get a decent job with one of the fruit companies."

His face lit up. "Truth of the matter is Cuba must have been a great place to be a child! It was buoyant! The beautiful beach, the incredible music, the crackling personalities. The beautiful sun never failed… exciting. Probably like Puerto Rico, where you grew up."

Elena nodded. "Puerto Rico was great. But I've never been

to Cuba. I hear mostly about Central America in Fairfax. My friend has simply lost hope. She says she'll never go back there. It makes one wonder...

"Well, Castro has changed Cuba. Totally. The absurdly rich and very white no longer control the island. The chargers – rich and poor – and of course the *marielitos* and some others down the ladder - went to the States by plane or raft. The ones who were left spied on each other and the anti-*fidelistas* went to jail. Most are trying to figure out how to escape without risking their lives at sea. But everyone did learn to read and write. Could be vaccinated. Now the surgeons make the same income as the shoeshine boy. No one can aspire to more, so why work hard? No initiative to do better...it breaks my heart. But they survive. And still make music."

"Last year I walked through Havana, visited the little apartment where my mother's family used to live. The island is a virtual ruin now. Everyone's poor ...unless you're one of Castro's inner circle or a top athlete. Everyone receives health care, lives long...The young run away when they can. It's an aging population. Hopeless. Hungry. Equal."

He shook his head. "There's no easy answer, is there, Elena?"

She responded. "Hmm."

"And no more *joie de vivre*. We Cubans, all classes, were famous for that. And our music...where's the music? There's some." He laughed at himself, as he just remembered hearing some great guitar music there. So music kept on playing. And it was "we Cubans", "we Irish", and "we Americans", depending on the context. Fine.

They both sat in silence, mulling over his comments.

He repeated, "The music... remember Celia Cruz? My mother

217

walked in the funeral procession for her in Miami. I think every refugee in Florida showed up…and the notables and artists and politicians…. what a paean of praise! That black verve, great voice and *carisma* of that woman, great heart in exile."

She answered, "She was something else, wasn't she? I saw the funeral Mass on a big screen television. Waiting for someone to attend me about four hours at the Social Security office in San Juan. Everyone in the waiting room was watching it, weeping. Me too. The power of music and personal triumph can be overwhelming."

"Our cultures… Paul, listening to you makes me think. How people react varies so much! The other day at the doctor's office, I got into a chat with a couple of Salvadoran migrants. The man was saying 'The gangs control my country now. You can't live there with your family since you know they'll target your sons…to either become a gangster or die. No choice. When the military was in power, the streets were safe.' The man looked at me for a response when he finished his passionate cry. I could answer nothing. Nothing at all, except, 'I'm sorry.'" Elena shook her head. "You know, when people open like that to me, I can't help visualizing it all. See myself in their place…It dislodges my certainty about the way things are…It was hard for me to be a social worker. I don't have the answers…maybe just a few, now and then."

He smiled. "I understand. It's so easy to think just one way. Then, suddenly other ideas just seem to rush in from the side, and make you question yourself."

Both ate quietly for a while, considering their thoughts in silence.

Then a text message appeared on Paul's phone.

"Excuse me a second, please."

He quickly read and message and his face fell. "It's James. Six of his fellow Jesuits and their housekeeper and her daughter were gunned down at their residence in San Salvador. An old priest hid under a bed and survived. James is the one who first found them. He wants to talk to me about it."

Appetite gone, minds shaken, they lay down their forks and silently dabbed their mouths with the large linen napkins. The starched cloth irritated Elena. Here they were in the land of luxury, and there…

Paul paid the bill and they left quietly.

"Let me get a cab for you, Elena. I'll call you later, all right?" She nodded her assent and they parted.

CHAPTER TWENTY-FIVE

*-No one moves away from another without
moving away from charity.*
No. 668. Blaise Pascal, **Thoughts**

Washington, DC

Cristina heard the news the next morning. She'd turned off the cell and computer all night for quiet. At mid-morning the next day in the office, she remembered to activate the phone and saw the message. Headlines. "Six Jesuit priests, their housekeeper and her daughter, murdered at the Jesuit residence in San Salvador university."

"James!" she thought. She thought of her first time in El Salvador. Of meeting those dedicated, brilliant men who'd been like his brothers. I envy them, she thought. They've died nobly. Heroes. I want to die a hero.

Then she felt as though her breath was being taken from her. Years ago she'd suffered from asthma, and now a similar lack of air racked her lungs. Slowly, she practiced the yoga breathing that helped control spasms. Slowly, she felt a sense of order returning. But so many things seemed to be declining around her. Jorge Parrachini was now a married man. The professor - AVE - had returned to Spain. Diego was still her handler from Cuba, but he'd been responding less and less frequently. She had thought they were becoming mates on many levels. But nothing for three weeks. Was he angry with her? Or had their physical intimacy caused him to reconsider their relationship? She was due for another lie detector test soon at the DIA. Could she pass it again?

The machine measured blood pressure, pulse, respiration, skin conductivity...called psychophysiological detection of deception examination, it was obviously not foolproof. She'd outfoxed it three times already. But the depression she'd been suffering lately could impact how she'd react to questioning.

She'd read that only Americans put such trust in the PDD test, the lie detector, supposedly because truth was such a vital part of the American culture, that the threat of lying made them anxious. All the US intelligence agencies checked and rechecked their agents, fairly confident of the lie detector's efficacy. Supposedly Asians and Arabs could deflect the judgment of the PPD, because they were so used to dissimulating. Did the Americans not know that Arabs and Asians considered it rude to be so blunt as are the Westerners? The Westerners considered those people devious, accomplished at lying, because they avoided offending the other person, even if their comments were not straight...The Spanish had surely inherited a bit of the Arabic mindset which had ruled Iberia for seven centuries. Each culture has its own way of being. And of truth-telling.

I, Cristina Franco, have Andalusian blood in my veins, ergo Arabic, she thought. And more. Westerners, Easterners, whatever...I treasure the brotherhood of man, not imperialism. Not sophism. Not capitalism. But Marxism. That is the ultimate truth. And I have been able to, will continue to, fool the lie detector. Running extra hard for three hours before to relax me. Then all their stupid questions...and my being friendly and clever with the questioner. Have you had sex with an animal?

221

Well, with a man, that animal only… What prior research have you done about polygraphs? *Whatever I could find; I am a researcher by trade.* Have you taken drugs? *I did go to college, so of course. Cocaine and marijuana.* Are you loyal to your country? *I am loyal.* And so on and on.

Returning to the day world, she began to work. At lunchtime she opened her small cold packet of food. As usual she'd brought yogurt and a salad to eat at her desk. Looking around her, she again noticed the thin, tall white-haired man whose desk was in the corner. He was watching her. Was she becoming paranoid or had he always stared at her? She shook her head, gulped down her lunch. And went to the ladies' room.

She vomited. Her head split with a sudden pain. Migraine. And again the asthma threatened.

I'll go home now, she thought. I can't handle this. I need to rest. I need to lie down. Music will help.

Excusing herself, she hurriedly left the building and walked to the Metro station. Was someone following her? She wasn't sure. Perhaps.

CHAPTER TWENTY-SIX

-Don't be mistaken about people.
Number 157. Baltasar Gracián, **The Pocket Oracle**

The Counter Intelligence group, Department of Defense, DIA
Anacostia-Bollings Joint Base, Washington, DC
"I'm growing old looking at this woman! What's it been…almost twenty years we've been re-checking her! I can't believe it!" Shea Wyman shook her head in disbelief. She showed them three white hairs and plucked them from her scalp. "Look!

She handed over the copies of Cristina Franco's travel reports for the last five years to Billy Bottoms and Jimmy Collins. A pattern had emerged from the past years: every several months to El Salvador, an understandable part of her job, and every five months to La Romana, ostensibly for a short vacation. Three times to Nicaragua and three to Honduras. Four times to Cuba on orders from the President. Twice yearly to San Juan to see her mother. Once to London and then to Prague. Five times to Madrid and then disappeared. Many times to New York City. Twice to Miami."

Bottoms glanced at the paper and said, "Good. You know I've always had a gut feeling about her. The bosses love her. But I'll never give up! Every year I want another run through. She may

223

be powerful, but we have a job to do. Continue on her trail. I want to see everything she downloads on her government computer and all her credit card uses for the past three years. We're seeing more and more of our confidential information regarding the Near East seeing the light of day in reports we access from Iraq, Iran, Pakistan and Afghanistan. That damned woman has access to everything, as you know. And I'm really worried about the Arab terrorists. They'll do anything."

He took a deep breath. "The terrorist threats grow daily. Of course, hundreds of others have top security clearance, so we must be careful and vigilant in identifying the real source of leakage. Castro has been bragging to his inner circle about a Latin woman at the top of the intelligence chain in the U.S., who has been theirs for years. He keeps talking about his 'little bird'."

Shea interrupted, "And, believe it or not, Franco's sister Elena who works for the FBI has unearthed a network of Cubans in Miami who are being fed some of our info regarding our agents in Central America. She talks about someone with the tradename *PALOMA*. Is that a coincidence?"

Bottoms said, "We want to know the whole story…where they got their information in the first place. We may get them to talk. I hope so."

He turned to Collins. "Jimmy, I want you to put together a team to tail Cristina Franco. Even at her work. Get very sharp people to be able to work next to her and stay on her all the time at the Department. And another couple who can be glued to her out of work. Let's hope she goes off to La Romana or El Salvador in the next few weeks. If so, follow her. I want details. Everything."

He addressed Shea again, the young pretty geek with long wavy brown hair, glowing brown eyes, quirky smile and quick wit.

In an automated wheelchair she sped around the floor faster than others could walk and her brain moved at an even quicker pace. She'd sailed through computers and mathematics at a community college and state university in Virginia before going to Georgetown and then being recruited for her incredibly high scores on standardized tests. She was a natural for intelligence analysis. She'd never walked. But her brain had worked to the fullest since childhood. Bottoms recognized that special quality and put it to good use.

"Wyman, I want you to put everything together on your computer and look for patterns. Give me an update weekly, more if you spot something that springs to the fore. You're a great analyst and we want to use you to the max. Even though Elena Franco works for the FBI, you can keep tabs on what she's doing over there through our inter-agency collaboration. She has a clean slate herself but we don't want to overlook any possibility. And you must be very, very careful since Cristina has become the key officer for reporting on Cuba for all the intelligence agencies. I stress **all.** If, in fact, she's clean or if in fact she's guilty, she could double back on us and all of us could be ruined. You do understand this. We can't make any mistakes. Be prudent and aggressive."

He raised his left eyebrow. "Hard, isn't it? But that's what makes this fun!"

Wyman and Jimmy chortled their agreement.

Bottoms rubbed his hands in something approaching glee at the approaching danger. "Jimmy, I want you to check out that Spanish professor at SAIS, Sanpietri. He might have gone off to Spain, but follow up completely. And also find out if Cristina has any friends dating back when. Especially during college. Don't forget the old ex-boyfriend, Jorge Parrachini. And her other Puerto Rican connections. Her cousin in El Salvador and connections there. Her neighborhood in Alexandria. Her sister. Her mother and brother in Puerto Rico… ”

Bottoms cracked his knuckles, as he did when under tension. “I strongly suspect there are many moles at top levels in our government. But only solid evidence will ferret them out. We just have to be smarter that they are. And more devious.”

Jimmy exclaimed, “Boss! I’m going to need a least a couple dozen people to do all this.”

Bottoms said, “I’ve signed authorizations. Get all the help you need. And Wyman, if you need any back-up, just tell me.”

He reconsidered. “Forget it. I’ll get someone for you now. You should have someone to bounce ideas off of and run through leads. Could you suggest anyone you’d like to work with?”

The girl said mischievously, “Well, there’s a handsome black guy a few cubicles over who seems pretty clever…”

Bottoms shook his head and snarled. “Well, that’s fine and dandy. We’ll just get Uncle Sam to play cupid. Get serious, girl!”

Not intimidated by Bottoms, for she knew his playful posturing for what it was, Shea grinned. “Well, one thing doesn’t negate the other. The handsome black guy does know what he’s doing, and he has a good manner to work with. Very cooperative as well as highly intelligent. He’ll do.”

“All right, all right. I’ll ink him in. What’s his name?”

“Jacques Maritain,” Jimmy said.

“Please! Give me a break! The reincarnation of a Thomist theologian in our midst?”

"He can't help his name. His parents are from Saint Lucia, he told me, and they admired the thinker."

Bottoms rolled his eyes. "Let's get on with this, then. I'll see you both tomorrow at this time, and you can tell me what you've organized."

Shea wheeled away with something of a flair. She was pleased with her assignment, while Jimmy Collins just sat there a moment thinking. This was a great challenge. And he did love challenge.

CHAPTER TWENTY-SEVEN

-Know how to leave things to one side...
Number 33, Baltasar Gracian, **The Pocket Oracle**

A month later
Washington, DC

Elena was listening into a conversation regarding the agent called *PALOMA*. Fidel had bragged more than once to the CIA's most trusted counter-agent in Cuba that he had a very high-ranking agent in the very top of US intelligence, who fed him the most complete information possible about the U.S. military. Elena had learned the name of the U.S. counter-agent in Cuba: Laura Martín, sister of Arturo Martín who'd died in the Bay of Pigs debacle. Fidel loved having beautiful women nearby and Laura qualified. And, as with many men, he couldn't resist speaking about his successes to other females he lusted after.

Careless of Fidel. Elena smiled.

On a trip allowed to Barcelona, Laura had e-mailed the encrypted information to Humberto, her contact in Miami, who'd sent it to Elena. In turn, she'd shared the information with Shea at DIA. They were both excited about this mysterious *PALOMA*, referred to by Fidel. She - for apparently it was a woman - seemed a fount of information regarding military bases, strategic planning, agents in Latin America, and increasingly, details about

Iraq, Pakistan and Afghanistan. Lately Yemen. And Castro, in turn, sold the valuable information both to Russia and selected countries in the Middle East. Thousands of people had access to top security level, but only dozens in the multiple agencies dealing with intelligence had top security access to information regarding all those areas. This mole didn't dig into the earth. On the contrary. That euphemism in the spy world for an embedded traitorous agent didn't apply. She was a *paloma*, flying high.

"We suspect someone at our own agency," Shea wrote her back. "Thanks to you, we know her code name is *PALOMA*. We're checking fewer than a dozen people who seem to have similar access. A counter intelligence man in Miami has sent us a couple of messages that are helping as well. We assume it's a woman because of the codename. That narrows down the search far more."

It's too bad I can't talk to Cristina about this, Elena thought. *She's so knowledgeable about so much and so highly-positioned I'll bet she'd have some excellent ideas. Well, it can't be. She can't tell me about her work, not I about mine. A shame. I'll just have to keep muddling through, do my best.*

§

Cristina's migraines were getting worse. She called Dr. Muller, whom she'd begun seeing a few months ago. Of course, no truth to the psychologist. It would be naïve to think her employers would not have access to her sessions. But she could vent a little. And get prescription drugs to counter her anxiety. She could plead asthma and sinus.

She told the doctors receptionist. "I'm feeling bad and am on the way home. I'll stop by the pharmacy on the way ...you have the information. Please e-mail me a time for an appointment. Soon."

By the time she'd taken the medication and lain down in her

bed, she was feeling a little better. Drowsy. She turned on her favorite music...Victoria de los Angeles singing Manuel de Falla. The lyricism lifted her heart.

My passion to change society gives life meaning, she thought. *Not whacking away at my computer, tied to a desk. But...I have no real friends. And my cause? My connections with Cuba seem faulty. Why? Is all I've worked for useless? Marta's gone to Argentina. Or so she says. No openness with my own family, though I love them. Acedia haunts me. I understand that dread of the noonday sun the desert fathers wrote about... What will become of me?*

Cristina dreamt of her parents. Her childhood.

§

Her mother Lise. Orderly, self-disciplined, loving. If anything, too orderly. She could use a little looseness. A native of Austria, she'd moved to Puerto Rico with her parents while in high school. The family started up a restaurant that quickly became an establishment in the island, the Viennese Chalet. Then Lise, the only child, had gone off to study accounting in Baltimore, where she met the talented young Puerto Rican medical student, who would become her husband. Within a year they'd wed. She dropped from college to have babies. Happily, at first, though her parents didn't agree with such an early marriage and dropping her studies. Even so, it seemed a good match, and a few years later, when her husband Emilio was sent to Nuremberg as a psychiatrist with the Army, it seemed especially good for Lise. She'd be able to speak German again.

But as Emilio learned more and more about the mind, he learned less and less about himself. As he advanced in the military which had paid medical school, his own brain became confused in a mix of dominating behavior, aggression, cynicism. Rage. While Lise bore three lovely, healthy children and

230

began working part-time with Turkish refugees in Germany, Emilio became another person. Then they'd moved to Spain, which they all thought would make things better because of the language, Emilio's native tongue.

Lise tried to combat his tyrannical behavior, the free use of the belt, the shouting, the snarling. The putdowns. The children found refuge in their mother's love and their studies. But Lise realized his behavior was increasing in violence and she finally broke. It was that horrible last day when she'd been in the laundry room folding towels. She heard loud voices coming from the living room, and closed her eyes. Emilio enraged again. God help us! *Mein Gott*!

She left the laundry for the living room.

He was raving. "No, Cristina! Look at me in the eye when you speak. You will obey me! You will read the books I tell you to, nothing else! You will listen to the music I tell you, nothing else. You will go where I say, nowhere else!" He whipped out the belt and this time struck her across the face with such force that blood welled up. It would leave a little scar. With his other hand, he grabbed her arm and brought her next to him. He was big, strong.

"Leave me alone, Father! Just leave me alone! Keep your hands off me!" She was all of twelve years old, but already she had developed character and courage, stoicism . This grabbing had happened before, out of her mother's presence. Cristina had never told her, wanting to be strong on her own. She simply would not let her father terrorize and threaten her. But she was frightened of his power. And of his sexuality. She'd felt his penis against her, moving in his trousers, without knowing for sure what that hard thing was.

Lise came into the living room just at that moment. One look was enough.

"Emilio, leave immediately or I call the police. Immediately!"

He looked at her, his eyes wild, tearing up. He stuttered, "No! You leave now! You leave! This is MY house. I pay for it, not you. I'm the master here."

"Emilio, you have one minute to get out before I call the MP. Now."

He looked at her and rushed out the door, slamming it so hard the frame shook.

Lise took Cristina in her arms, saying, "I am so sorry, Cristina. We should have left before this. But that's it. Your father is out of his mind. We'll go to San Juan. We'll be happy."

She gently washed her daughter's face and began to weep. They both wept.

§

It took Lise just a week to pack up the children and their belongings. Talked to the military command and did the paperwork to file for divorce. The children were not unhappy to leave their father.

Back in Puerto Rico, the embattled mother enrolled her children at the competitive university public school, thanks to their excellent grades and a relative in the school's administration. Everything in Puerto Rico happened with *pala*, connections. Everything. Lise began working in the family business office of the Viennese Chalet, where her numbers acumen was welcome. Emilio had been torn out of the fabric of their lives, never to return except in nightmares. Life began again.

§

Cristina returned to the moment and sighed. "I'll call Mother tonight. I must see her." She fell asleep atop the bed.

232

CHAPTER TWENTY- EIGHT

Size up fortune...

Number 36. Baltasar Gracián, **The Pocket Oracle**

The following week
San Juan, Puerto Rico

The American Airlines plane cruised over the vibrant green vegetation and blue water, landing at the Luis Muñoz Marín Airport in Isla Verde. Cristina weaved her carry-on bag down the narrow aisle. It was good to get out of the crowded plane. It was going to be another sunny, lovely day in Puerto Rico.

She walked through the throng out to the brilliant light and wonderfully humid air. Even in bad economic times, the airport was crowded. Islands depend on air travel. People of all hues and sizes hustled to the sidewalk.

"Cristina!" a voice called behind her.

She turned to see Rafael Medina reaching out his arms for a hug. "I haven't seen you since college days. But you don't change, dear." He embraced her with a hug, his big frame enveloping her. She barely recognized him. No huge moustache. An elegant suit. No jeans and sandals.

233

"What happened? Where is the bohemian? Is that really you, old friend?"

The burly fellow smiled. He'd always been a livewire and fun, even in his student militant days, marching with banners, shaking his fists, yelling anti-*yanqui* slogans, plotting revolution.

His pleasing bass voice answered. "Well, my dear, I learned I had to make a living. That meant work! No more Pell Grants! I put myself through law school by teaching Spanish at a private school and now I'm a corporate lawyer with a big firm. And I like it! The research. The negotiating and all. The plotting! We did extra training in that, didn't we? Remember when we threatened the university administration and rocked the car of the dean? But times do change a person. I have a lovely wife, Irene Hevia, our claque's treasurer, remember? Two children, another on the way. Your old friend is now an establishment person and enjoying it. Scared of what my own children will do! Afraid they'll learn how I was back in the day. Amazing, isn't it?"

She shook her head in disbelief. "For sure, for sure."

"Well, I heard you're working for the federal government now in Washington, DC. And doing well. Is that so? That's another turnaround!" He gave a big belly laugh, his amusement kind and infectious.

Cristina couldn't help smiling. Then she swallowed, paused a moment. "Yes, Rafael, that is so. And now I've just taken a little break to see my mother. How about you?"

Rafael grinned with that still irrepressible air. "Back from New York, scrambling and trying to outwit Wall Street hotshots. Can I give you a ride? My wife is picking me up."

"No, Rafa. But thanks. I don't want to intrude. It's wonderful to see you and know you're happy. You were one of my favorite people, back in the day. Great memories! Give my best to Irene."

A cab stopped in front of her, and she stepped off the curb. Rafa rushed to open the door.

"*Adios,* amigo. See you one of these days…"

She blew him a kiss and waved goodbye.

He waved good-bye and said what he'd always said, *"Ciao, nena!"*

Her past discarded, in moments she was on her way to her mother's apartment in Miramar. The taxi slowed in the traffic in front of the dilapidated public housing, called Lloréns Torres after the poet. A few palm trees waved in the breeze. The project, inspired by social engineers decades ago, had addressed the problem of substandard housing: now people had indoor plumbing and electricity and didn't have to wade through muddy water to get home. But criminality was worse than ever, fueled by gangs, drugs, human trafficking. Cristina had visited the project years ago with a college friend who lived there, struggling to escape through education.

As always, the sides of the buildings facing the highway were painted white. Fresh murals showing beach and mountains adorned the facades. Each election year, this side of the building was painted for the public and politicians. The other sides, grey and dingy for life, marked with obscenities and graffiti, reflected reality. So that hasn't changed, Cristina thought. *"La misma cosa, la misma mierda."* Same thing, same shit.

Soon enough the taxi accelerated in the traffic and passed that monument to unfulfilled hope.

They soon approached Miramar, a tree-lined in-town neighborhood harboring expensive tall condominiums and more
economical seventy-year old smaller buildings. A few buildings still boarded-up from the last hurricane. Four miles and a
world away from Lloréns Torres. Her mother still lived in the
first floor of a three-story apartment building she'd moved into
with her children way back when they'd arrived from Spain.
Big rooms and tall ceilings from the 'thirties gave her space,
a little garden at the back, a good walking area. Daytime was
great. At dusk the evil ones began to emerge.

Down the hill one arrived at the Condado Lagoon, an idyllic
spot nearby the ocean, lined with trimmed mangroves on one
side, modern condominiums on the other. Beneath one bridge
you could kayak towards the ocean and beneath the other pass
the marina into the San Juan Bay. Considering the island's
population density, Cristina always marveled at the quietude
of so many pocket parks and beachfronts and mountains that
were uncrowded throughout the work week.

My island is such a mix of contrasts, she thought. Lovely people, scoundrels, beautiful scenery, slums, brilliant scholars, awful public schools, the wealthy, the poor, McDonald's, french
fries, *mofongo*, wonderful garlicky food…Smiles, hugs, emotions, song, laughter. Rage, anger, nasty gossip. The endless
chismes. Song, she thought again. And San Juan, contrary to
Washington, has sea and sun. Always.

Her mother Lise's ground floor entrance abutted a thick hibiscus
shrub and little yard separating the front door from the sidewalk.
Café de la india, a fragrant jasmine-like bush bloomed at the entrance, its aroma filling the air. Black iron grill-work guarded the
tinted glass windows that hung within the old-fashioned wooden
shutters. Rose stucco walls and creamy white window overhangs
reflected the building's tropical feel. Cristina once again approv-
ingly noted the neatness, the understated grace of the whole, and

236

of course, the security. Would Lise have wanted anything else? Her Austrian and Benedictine heritage would claim no other. Simplicity and order. Grace.

Cristina rang the bell twice, knowing her mother was becoming hard of hearing. She waited a moment for the look through the peep hole. The door opened, and she was folded into her mother's arms. Lise had become a little plump with age. Good mother-daughter squeezing material.

"*Mi amor!* How I've missed seeing you! Thank God you were able to get away from work for a few days!"

Cristina glowed at the unreserved welcome. It refreshed her spirit to realize again that she was so loved. Balm for the soul.

The two women went to the small kitchen for the usual *café con leche* and took the cups out to the little back patio to sit in the wooden rocking chairs. A favorite in the early nineteen hundreds, they'd belonged to Cristina's paternal grandparents. It was the only remnant of a deteriorated marriage. Mother and daughter rocked slowly back and forth. Mesmerizing. Comforting.

Silence. In the background they could hear the low steady lull of traffic. It sounded like distant cicadas. They sipped the coffee and savored the moment.

Lise spoke in English, a touch of her soft Bavarian accent still present, tinged with an undercurrent of Spanish. "Well, dear. I hope your health is all right. You look a little wan to me, maybe underweight. Do you feel tired? Is that why you came home so suddenly?"

"Yes, I suppose so. And of course just to see you, since I missed the last family celebration."

"Please make sure you get time off for Christmas! I know you

237

never miss it, but buy your tickets soon, before the prices soar." Like mothers around the world, she had to instruct the child, regardless of age.

"I will, Mother. For sure." Cristina took another sip of her coffee and felt the tension begin to ease.

She closed her eyes.

"Do you see Elena often? It's lovely that you live in the same city."

Her mother always repeated this refrain.

"Yes, Mother. We get together monthly. Always."

"It makes me happy to know my only daughters are close."

"And you, Mother, how are you these days?"

"For awhile I was going up to the mountains with my friend Donna, to help out at San Agustín del Coquí with the troubled children. But that drive has gotten too long for us. Do you remember it?"

Cristina nodded. She'd gone with her once, up the mountain roads to a remote rural barrio where land was still cheap and the children could walk to the village school, casting off thoughts of abuse at home while they opened their hearts and minds at the hospice. The nuns were smart and dedicated, but only three of them were left. What would happen when they died? But then nothing remained the same, did it?

Her mother continued. "So now I go to that halfway house in Old San Juan for single mothers and their babies. In front of La Perla, looking out at the sea. I can just hop on the bus, no worry about driving. With my pension and social security…and your help in refinancing this apartment… fine. I don't miss work and I don't need much. The parish church is around the corner, sometimes with a priest who understands people, though the bishop banished that wonderful young monsignor…. A few friends and cousins. Your brother drops by every week. The sun shines and the air is soft. There it is… And of course, I talk to my two girls every week or so. I am blessed."

Again, Cristina nodded. It was true. Her mother was blessed with a radiant sense of love.

Three days passed quickly, and she was on the plane again for DC. This respite had momentarily calmed her. And now…

CHAPTER TWENTY-NINE

-Practice self-restraint.

Number 207. Baltasar Gracián, **The Pocket Oracle.**

Alexandria, Virginia

The plane landed at dusk at Reagan National Airport. Once again Cristina looked at the Washington Monument, always a moving sight to the returning traveler.

At her apartment building, she entered the elevator and almost forgot to key in her floor, lost in thought about her experiences in El Salvador. The killings. Wondered about AVE's leaving his plum appointment at Johns Hopkins to return to his homeland. Jorge's leaving her for the other woman. Now, worst of all, Diego's not responding to her messages to Cuba. Her own panicky thoughts which she thought she was hiding successfully, for the most part, from others. She must control herself.

She found her key and the elevator landed at her floor. She opened the door to her apartment.

Immediately, she detected something was off. The view of the Potomac was immutable, of course. Thank God some things don't change!

240

But the paintings had been moved. Someone had exchanged their places. How clever. That impressive seriegraph by Mirna Baéz, the blacks and reds and dark aquamarine capturing the doves of Old San Juan, now hung next to the entrance instead of in the hallway. And Sureda's huge acuarela of one of his famous street scenes of Old San Juan, the browns and blues and reds and greens so perfect, now hung next on a different wall in the kitchen. It had moved from the living room, to be replaced by a tiny photograph of her family. How obvious! She grimaced at the nasty message: we are watching you.

She checked her desktop computer. Next to it, she'd carelessly left a stack of the disks with her highest security summaries that she'd prepared to code and send to her handler, just before leaving for Puerto Rico. Shaking her head, she thought how very stupid she'd been. The disks were now spread all over the furniture.

"Even so, I'm on the right path," she told herself. "*No pasarán.*" She quoted to herself *La Pasionaria's* famous phrase from the Spanish Civil War, even though the communists lost that one. They shall not pass. I will stand firm, whatever happens. But she realized her subconscious mind was plotting her downfall. Just so. How odd...

She rang Elena. "Mother sends her love. All is well. I'll get back to you soon. I'm too tired to talk now, dear," she dictated to her sister's message machine.

Cristina scrubbed the make-up from her face. She stared at herself in the mirror: her usual cool and unblemished face seemed to be cracking with worry. She was looking anxious. After a hot shower she toweled herself vigorously and slathered body oil all over, before putting on a long t-shirt to sleep in. She lay down. Then got up abruptly to put on music to help her sleep. Something calming. She picked up her old CDs. It would have to be chant, when all was said and done. Or maybe Hildegarde von Bingen. No. A Mexican Baroque Mass. That should do it.

Funny that a God-denier would seek out that sort of music.

She lowered the thermostat and crawled under the down-covered quilt. Closed her eyes. Got up to take a heavy dose of her prescribed Lexapro to calm herself and an Ambien to sleep.

I know they've discovered me. And I am being isolated. Can I be strong? Do I truly care about all this? What lies ahead? How will I respond? What is my life worth?

That night she tossed between one strange dream and another. On a whim she'd picked up one of Tolkien's books, couldn't remember the name. Now some of those weird creatures were taking on a life of their own in her half-dream state. Frightening. Should she gulp down all her pills? Should she walk on the bridge spanning the Potomac, look at the moving river beneath and hurl herself over the side? She visualized those scenes. Tempting. Terrrifying. But life was still precious. And she was strong…

At dawn, she dressed in mourning, all black. Elegant. She knew what awaited her. She would dress the part. She looked around, put her volume of Baltasar Gracián in her black leather bag. Checked for her cosmetics and medicine. She decided to stuff in a paperback of Cervantes's **Don Quijote**. After all, she thought, he did write part of it in prison. And I can read it again and again. At the last moment, she plucked her grandmother's rosary from the night table and tossed it in the bag. A talisman.

Coming out of her building, she could feel eyes at her back. She pretended not to notice.

Walking down the street to the Metro station, she made a sudden decision. She wouldn't go just yet to her office. Instead, Cristina made a detour and took the subway to Dupont Circle Station. Walking the three blocks to Saint Matthew's Cathedral, she knew the followers traced her path. She could feel it.

Going up the old cement steps to the church, etched on a generation's memory with JFK's funeral Mass, she paused. She fished out what few dollars she had and gave them to the ill-kempt beggar who perched there. Their eyes met and smiled at each other. He reminded her of the misery of El Salvador. Opening the heavy wooden door, she entered the cool dark high-ceilinged traditional church, walked slowly down the long aisle to approach the main altar. Surprised, she saw the dim light on at an old-style confessional at the side. Haven't seen that for awhile, she thought. We must be approaching an Hispanic feast day. Well. Why not? It's been years since

I…

She veered towards the confessional. Pulling aside the dusty velvet curtain, she entered the little cubicle and knelt. Somehow, the quiet, dark space reassured her, reawakening memories of childhood. Good and bad.

"Bless me, Father, for I have sinned. It's been many, many years since my last confession. I have sinned in that time and I ask God's pardon." She wasn't going to list them. Too many.

They spoke in Spanish. He sounded Central American, she mused. Maybe El Salvador. What a world!

"What kinds of sins, my dear? The worst are against hope and charity, you know."

"Yes. Well. Hope and charity mostly. Faith, perhaps," she blundered. She'd forgotten that this could be a real workout.

"Don't worry too much about faith. That's God's gift to us, and perhaps we don't accept it graciously," he counseled. "And hope? Work on that. Of course, charity."

Silence.

"Remember, charity above all."

"Do you have the will to try to sin no more?" asked the priest. He didn't bother asking her to enumerate her offences. He'd heard them all before, and his voice sounded old and quavery. Probably the only one they could find with the endurance and interest to follow the old tradition of hearing confessions, she thought.

"I do," she replied. "I have the will."

"And do you truly repent?"

"I do." *Yes. Of so much.*

She thought of Gracián's emphasis on the four cardinal virtues: prudence, temperance, justice, courage. She had kept those in mind throughout her adolescence and adult life, as she'd kept his book as a sort of personal code. Of course she had stumbled. It had been a journey of contradictions, light and dark. But she would keep on trying.

She repeated, "I do."

"Then say a Hail Mary and an Our Father. Go in faith, hope and charity and help the poor. Sin no more." He gave the blessing.

She knelt there a moment, said the prayers, took a deep breath and stood up. She felt stronger to face what surely would come.

She emerged and bowed at the altar, walked back down the aisle, her heels clicking on the old ceramic tile. Cristina opened the creaking door and saw the agents awaiting her on the sidewalk.

I suppose they got tired of my wandering. They wouldn't know for sure I'd be going back to the office. Who knows? Maybe I'd have gone back to throw myself off the Key Bridge. Or hurled myself in front of a car. Or...

She descended the steps.

She held out her wrists. Billy Bottoms hadn't been able to resist making the arrest himself. A U.S. Marshal put on her manacles and Billy read the Miranda warning.

The beggar on the steps watched perfunctorily, uninterested in this theatre of well-dressed people. At least the woman had smiled and given him enough for a bottle of rum and a hamburger today. Maybe for tomorrow too.

THE END

Note: *Though drawing on historical incidents and characters in Washington (DC), Puerto Rico, Cuba and El Salvador,* **The Franco Sisters** *is fiction and any resemblance to actual events, persons and places, living or dead, is entirely coincidental. Of course, I was inspired by several true stories. People from all these places have contributed their tales to the writer and are much appreciated.*

For years CIA operatives considered Cuban intelligence agents to be outstanding students of the Russian espionage school and several were discovered to serve in high level US government positions for a number of years. Despite global diplomacy, intelligence gathering remains an important tool of all states at the highest level.

El Salvador's homicide rate as of 2018 was one of the highest in the world, and its gangs (the Marasalvatruchas *originated in California) spread throughout Central America, the United States and Canada. Cuba continues poor, complex and evolving. Puerto Rico, for more than a hundred years a territory of the United States and now having the highest educational level in the Caribbean, struggles under crushing public debt, underpaid wages, the usual corruption, an aging infrastructure, an unresolved political status and still, the devastating results of Hurricane Maria in 2017, and the same drug problems as the mainland U.S. The Hispanic presence in the mainland United States is expected to soon be the majority ethnic group. There are already twice the number of Puerto Ricans in the mainland as in the island. And in spite of all this, there is a vibrant, well-educated, bilingual middle class and the earnest poor.*

The Jesuit presence is known to many XXI century people through Pope Francis, a priest of that order founded by Ignatius of Loyola around 1548. Many of Spanish Jesuit Baltasar Gracián's thoughts start up chapters of **The Franco Sisters** *to focus on the characters' paradoxes and are from his bestseller,* **Oráculo Manual y Arte de Prudencia - The Pocket Oracle and the Art of Prudence,** *1647. It is still published. Óscar Romero, whose murder in described in the novel, was bishop in El Salvador. And the Jesuits still work in Puerto Rico.*

ACKNOWLEDGEMENTS

Many thanks to friends/readers who helped this novel on its way: Carmen Teresa Ruiz de Fischler, Leamir Candamo Pou de Córdova, Frank Kelly, David and Polly Herpy, Shea Megale, Ruth and Robert Fahl, Marina Rivón, Mario Ramos, Teresita Bolivar, Donna Sabater Kathy Jones, Betty Kaplan, and Jay Chevako. Thank you to Anne and Ron Chevako for their continuing support

Besides reading dozens of books and articles regarding stories on which this novel draws, I was able to speak with many Central American migrants in Virginia, where I was working as an interpreter, and throughout my life with many Cubans who have left their homeland. And, of course, the tale continues...

BOOKS BY THE AUTHOR

Other historical books:

THE CHRONICLES OF MARÍA TERESA DE VILLALOBOS
(Osage Group, 2018)

EL COMISIONADO RESIDENTE DE PUERTO RICO: SU INICIO Y EL PRIMER PERIODO DE FELIX CORDOVA DAVILA
(Asamblea Legislativa de Puerto Rico/ Oficina del Historiador Oficial de Puerto Rico, 1999)

PONCE, REBIRTH OF A VALUABLE HERITAGE
(Publishing Resources Inc., 1991)

INTO THE DESERT
(Puerto Rico National Guard, 1992)

FIVE CENTURIES IN PUERTO RICO: PORTRAITS AND ERAS
(Interamerican University Press, 1988 and two more printings by Publishing Resources, Inc.)

www.ingramcontent.com/pod-product-compliance
Lightning Source LLC
Chambersburg PA
CBHW030408020726
47493CB00003B/986